Goddess Of The Dawn: A Romance

Margaret Davies Sullivan

Doris

GODDESS OF THE DAWN

A Romance

BY

MARGARET DAVIES SULLIVAN

ILLUSTRATIONS BY
GEORGE BRIDGMAN

G. W. DILLINGHAM COMPANY
PUBLISHERS   NEW YORK

1919

40

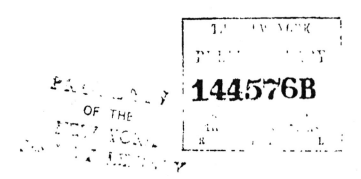
COPYRIGHT, 1914, BY

G. W. DILLINGHAM COMPANY

-Goddess of the Dawn

F

ILLUSTRATIONS

Goddess of the Dawn

CHAPTER I

BEAUTIFUL old sky—how blue you are!"

The sun had not yet risen, but a full red glow across the East heralded its coming, while elsewhere the vault stretched deeply turquoise, as it spreads only in the South at dawn.

Doris, just blossoming into womanhood, had crept softly downstairs, not arousing even Mammy Rose, her nurse since birth, who still insisted upon careful supervision of her ventures into dampness. The rose-garden was always damp when she best loved it—as dawn came.

Having safely gained it, she breathed freely in relief; then, forgetful of all else, began to marvel at the early morning's glories, to which she never could become indifferent.

A few steps along a graveled path, and she was submerged in trellised roses, swaying high above her head on either side. She paused, reveling in their beauty made mysterious by the half-light of dawn, and luxuriously drew into her lungs the dew-wet, scented air. Its stimulation thrilled her. Intently she listened for a signal from her little friend, the wild canary.

Dressed in a sheer, white morning-gown, delicately revealing her neck and arms; her face of that type which, among our Southerners, sometimes suggests the best of the high Spanish; with large soft luminous eyes; a wonderful complexion—neither light nor dark; quantities of light golden hair and perfect teeth, continually displayed in involuntary smiles born of the unquenched joy of merely being young and full of health, she made an almost startlingly delightful picture, as with roving eyes and tilted head, she searched for the tiny songster in the swaying sprays of bloom about her.

When she visited the garden thus early in the morning he was usually there and ready to burst into song as if he had been waiting for her coming; but to-day she could neither hear his voice nor see the quick flash of his golden wings darting in and out among the branches of the highest rose-bushes.

She knew of no intruder in the garden, and therefore did not guess that her generally melodious little friend had been frightened into watchful, silent lingering in the forest trees beyond. That he was not waiting for her, was a genuine disappointment.

Guarding her steps upon the gravel with great care, so that no pebble crunching against its fellows would disturb the lightest sleeper in the nearby house, she went with an expectant, searching stealth into the very center of the wakening wonderland of bloom.

"Where can my wild-canary be?" she pondered, as she peered and listened.

Then the intruder of whose existence she was ignorant, but who had frightened the canary, caught sight of her, and stood an instant, spell-bound.

After a quick, worried reconnaissance, noiseless as possible, he found a curving path which took him (much to his relief) out of the danger of discovery into the tangled, semi-tropical, Louisiana woodland, which abruptly reared a forest wall upon the garden's southern side. Relieved because he had escaped without her notice, he breathed easier, although his face was still flushed vividly after he had found his covert.

He was her senior by five years and yet she terrified him—exactly as the glimpsing of a golden princess might terrify a pauper prince. It was a pleasant terror, yet, withal, a note of tragedy was in it; a sense of being shut out by circumstances from the most delightful privilege in all the world. That neither she, nor those who loved her, held against him the misfortune which oppressed him through no fault of his own, gave him no sense of freedom.

Doris was greatly disappointed by the absence of the wild canary. He surely had been in the garden. Before she had left the house, she had heard him twittering, as he always did, what she was pleased to think an invitation to her to come out and share with him his dawn. She liked to think that he believed the dawn exclusively his own, and that he looked upon her as a guest while she enjoyed it in his company. Peering up into the branches of the shrubbery, she searched closely for him.

While thus engaged, she approached the very thicket wherein the young man, tense of face, excited, stood shrinkingly, dreading, yet desiring to be found. They might have clasped hands through the greenery.

Had not the songster, perhaps reassured by her appearance, begun suddenly to trill his little heart out, thus making known his presence on the tip of a superb Marechal Niel's swaying, topmost branch, in quite another section of the garden, she might have searched that selfsame thicket, but she turned and hurried joyously toward the bird.

Smiling with relief, the youth, gazing through a leafy loophole, followed her with his eyes. Her pleasant thoughts were fully occupied by her surroundings. If the remembrance that her mornings in this wonderful rose-garden were now numbered, obtruded upon the moment's happiness of living where the Southern sunshine was so glorious, the fragrance of the dew-dampened roses so intoxicating and the glory of the dawn-awakened flowers, so marvelous, it in no wise drove her to such gloomy reveries as those with which the news that she was going north to college had affected most of the rural neighborhood's young men and not a few resident in the nearby city of New Orleans.

As he saw her turn, responding to the song-salute, the hidden watcher in the copse considered none of the surrounding charms. His artistic soul was throbbing in response to the bewitching beauty of the girl, as, now, her attention was diverted from the bird by the appearance of the sun's red rim, aureoled by a glory which bejeweled and inflamed with color the wide horizon above the forest to the east.

"The Goddess of the Garden!" rose involuntarily to his lips. His soul suddenly had deified her.

Then, in one illuminative flash, a statuette took form within his mind. He watched her as an artist sometimes does a vision which arouses him to high appreciation, and then something more—a sense of helplessness, a terrible conviction that his art is insufficient and is ineffectual.

But as he gazed he thrilled with the conviction of new

power. True inspiration seized him. Confronted by the opportunity, his art sprang into unprecedented competence. His eyes, which had been partly closed to make the lights and shadows on her definite, now opened wide, expressing the sudden hunger of a soul which sees within its reach the great thing for which it has longed unknowingly.

A radiance diffused itself about the girl, almost as visible to him as if it had been real and not that wonderlight encompassing, to all of us, the ones we love, encompassing peculiarly to artists those things which they are certain they can truly portray.

Its magic worked until he did not see the girl at all, but only the inspired, inspiring effigy of her, which he now knew that he would truly mold in clay and later carve in lasting stone.

Other inspirations had been his; other sudden visions of completed work which he might do had come to him, but never anything so vivid as this. Without warning, in an instant's flash, he not only had discovered that he loved her, but that his art could and would be equal to great tasks. He had hoped that this might be so, but had not known; now he was certain of his victory.

Despair gave way to dreams. With that tremendous art athrob within his soul, might he not conquer every obstacle? Poverty? A stain upon his name, which was no fault of his? Could they be barriers so high that that winged art, with pulsing pinions, might not help him to surmount them?

He madly fancied that this great achievement was a certainty—dreamed as he stood among the leaves and gazed at her. With the twin marvels of his love and his ambition helping his determined spirit, could the drawings, which he was that day to finish and the next day submit, for the carved figures to adorn the new bank building in New Orleans, fail to be worthy of approval? The spirit of his youth was tautened like a coiled steel spring.

All doubt had left his mind. Struggles of such ardor as possessed him must inevitably triumph. His should be a royal road to fame and glory! And when he had reached the goal, then—then he might stretch out his arms toward even this angelic being!

Fear always had obsessed him that from another's past, a grim hand would extend to snatch from him whatever he might gain through work and through ability. For the moment this fear left him.

The wild canary burst into new, excited floods of song; the dawn came with a rush; the sun thrust its whole brilliant disk above the rim of trees.

Spellbound, the girl stood listening.

How he sang! He seemed to realize that she had been waiting for him, and to be determined to repay her for this honor she had done him. Perched upon a swaying, gorgeous spray of blooming rose-bush just in front of her, he cocked his wise, black beads of eyes at her, nodded, and excelled the most extraordinary efforts of his whole past life.

It was as if he felt beholden, like a theater's orchestra, to provide befitting music for the entrance of the star before an audience of which the princess of the royal blood was one. He heralded the entrance of the sun, the greatest star of all, before the princess of this blossoming domain.

But Stoddard Thornton did not raise his eyes. To him, the sun was a mere lantern swung to cast but an imperfect radiance upon the girl.

Her eyes were fixed upon the bird. Having finished with his overture, he raised his wings a bit, in preparation, puffed out his little chest, and nodded as if he wished to say to her: "That was for the sun, but wait! Now you'll hear what I am capable of doing in *your* honor—as a tribute to a princess."

As she gazed, enchanted, he darted from the bush, circled toward her to assure her that it was not fear of her which started him away, but a desire to let her hear his song to the best purpose, and then flew up and up, lark-like, in circles, stringing his melody behind him in extraordinary beads of sound, bursting, every moment, into new vocal marvels. The continually softening notes of liquid happiness descended in a melodious shower.

She watched until his tiny form was lost in the gilt sun-dust sparkling in the semi-tropic atmosphere, and then stood, spellbound, her eyes fixed on the sunrise.

The untried but ambitious sculptor, who was now also the unavowed, determined lover, gazed with devouring eyes, his fingers working nervously as they yearned for clay to fashion, with quick appreciative touches, into a model of the wonderful creation which had taken form within his brain.

Presently the marvel of the sight before him grew, as the perfect morning moved from the delicate rainbow-realm of dawn into the golden, if less glorious zone of the real day.   The girl's emotions swept her close to ecstasy.

"Oh, you wonder-sky!" the watching sculptor heard her softly cry, addressing the blue dome and the gilt sun. "How I shall miss you!"

It was as if the North, to which she was to journey, would not have a sky, a sun, or glories of whatever kind.

Yet, although her voice thrilled with regret, there was no actual sadness in it.   When has the soul of youth been really sad as it stood upon the threshold of the world!

She slowly raised her arms and stretched them toward the glories of the East, on her face the rapt expression of a devotee, in each line of her lithe attitude the flowing grace of one swept by an ecstasy of appreciation. In another age, he thought, she would have been a sun-worshiper, no doubt.

And the bird sang, and the flowers bloomed and breathed their fragrance through the garden as the censer's incense floods a temple, and the sun rose   .   .   . rose   .   .   .

There was now no sound save the bird's song again approaching, and the silvery tinkling of the crystal fountain in the center of the garden.

With the passing of the magic moment of the actual dawn, she relaxed, dropped her outstretched arms, turned, and again stood listening.   She was not a goddess now, but only loveliest of girls.

Presently she laughed, chirping as if to tempt the bird out of the gem-blue sky to perch once more within the garden.

The sculptor sighed. She had not become less beautiful, but she was human, now, and for a moment she had been far more than that—to him. Gently he parted the thick shrubbery, and found his way by curving paths to the wide lawn before the low, rambling, shingled residence of its owner, Colonel Orlando Marquis, his friend since boyhood, the father of the Goddess, and, for a week, his host.

"Miss Dawiss, chil'! Miss Dawiss!" he heard Mammy call. "Lawsy massah, honey, w'at yo' doin' out so eahly in de mo'nin? Yo'll ketch yo' de'f o' col'."

Stoddard went immediately to his room, and hurrying lest some detail of his vision fade, first sketched, and then began deftly to model, with gray sculptor's clay, which he took from his trunk. By breakfast-time, a little figure, which he knew was quite the best that he had ever done, the fruit of rushing, actual inspiration, was upon his table by the window.

He sat back and wiped his brow as might a man whose labor has been physically arduous. He was exhausted; he was happy; he was indefinitely somnolent. His eyes half closed and smiling, he gazed at his creation with glowing satisfaction. Upon the pedestal he cut "The Goddess of the Garden." Never had true artistic frenzy so possessed him; he had seen nothing but the growth of his idea in the clay as it formed beneath his fingers, heard nothing but the song of his own consciousness of power, felt nothing but that thrilling ecstasy of love which had arisen in his heart.

.   .   .   .

The tap-tap of the maid Desdemona's knuckles on his door, as she announced the breakfast hour, aroused him from abstraction far more complete than ordinary slumber.

"Pow'ful sleepuh, Mistah Tho'nton," she told Mammy Rose, when she had gone downstairs. "Mos' had to break de doah down wakin' him."

"Desdemona Snowball," Mammy Rose reproved, with a stern glance, "why you done tell so many lies? Ain't I seen him come in from a walk a couple houahs ago?"

"Mus' a' bin a sleep-walk," Desdemona answered. "Skeered me, de way I had to hammuh dat dere do'."

"Dere yo' go," said Mammy, "pastin' new lies on in front ob old ones fo' to hide de holes trufe pokes in what yo' says!"

But later, when Mammy Rose, herself, saw Stoddard at the breakfast-table, as in white robed dignity she stood at the sideboard, serving, while Desdemona played the part of waitress, she began to think the girl might after all have been quite accurate in her description. She, herself observed the rapt look in his eyes, as, taking not the slightest thought of the old black woman, he studied Doris's face whenever opportunity afforded.

"Twa'nt sleep dat stunned 'im," she assured herself, however. "He's in a trance. Miss Dawiss, she's plum hypertized 'im, like she does 'em all."

And her heart went out to him, for her kind old eyes saw that his clothes were not of costly cloth nor perfect cut; when he had come, the day before, she had observed commiseratingly his meager luggage. Thornton's eyes showed no intention of attempting to impose his poverty on Doris—they showed only longing. Mammy Rose did not know about the exultation and resolve which for a time had been in them. It now was gone.

She liked him very much, and sorrowed for him as she looked at him. "Seems like de good Lawd makes mistakes, sometimes, in pickin' out de backs to wear de robes o' poverty," she mused. "Now dere's a few, right in his neighbo'hood, dat might be stren'thened if dey had to dress deirselfs a little shabby fo' a while, but all dat poverty 'll do to him is jes' to hampuh him." She paused in thought. "But he could be a buhden-bearer for a million yeahs an' nevuh git discou'aged."

Mammy Rose was his partisan from the first moment of this sage decision. Later, when she went to tidy up his room (because the unusual work of preparation for departure absorbed Desdemona's and the other servants' time) she was surprised to see him cover, hurriedly, with a wet cloth, an object on a table by the window. She knew naught of sculptors and their craft and ways; she was much puzzled.

"Looked jes' like a image," she told Desdemona, later. "Dat's what Ah thought, fust off, but Ah ain't gwine believe no sech a thing. He ain't no wuhshiper of images. But he ast me fo' a box, an' when Ah got one fo' him, he jes' waited 'fore he used it till Ah went away. When Ah went back what he had kivvered up was sho'ly in it. So I ain't quite suah. Looked like a image, still——"

She gave up the problem in despair.

Before Stoddard started for New Orleans the following day, he shyly went to Mrs. Marquis with the statuette. It showed a charming, girlish figure, sweet, demure and pensive.

"May I have this cast in plaster for you?"

Mrs. Marquis looked at it with real amazement and outspoken delight. "Why—it is Doris!"

"As I saw her, for a moment, yesterday morning in the rose-garden," he acquiesced.

"It is wonderfully like her."

"You are pleased with it?"

"It is absolutely perfect," she declared, examining it with care. "What is this which you have lettered on the little pedestal? 'Goddess of the Garden.' Charming!"

"It seemed very fitting."

"I don't know how to thank you, Stoddard."

"I beg you not to try. I shall not attempt to thank you for your delightful hospitality, Mrs. Marquis."

"But the 'Goddess of the Garden'! Oh, it is lovely!"

"Not half worthy of the original. Among the flowers, as the sun rose, she was wonderful."

Returning to his room, to make ready for the little journey of big import, to the city, he packed the model very carefully with dampened cloths in a board box, which he held solicitously as he departed.

CHAPTER II

It was late the following afternoon when Stoddard Thornton returned to the charming home among the roses. In New Orleans he had been unable to get a judgment on his drawings for the Bank. The directors would not meet until the following week, and that depressed him.

When he reached the veranda and returned the varied greetings which were offered, including Colonel Marquis's own welcome, interspersed, as they all were, by enthusiastic praises of the pure white, dainty figure he brought to Mrs. Marquis, he knew that he had hoped too high the day before. Even if all went well with him, the fair original of his statuette would still remain beyond his reach.

The conversation, of which his part was somewhat strained and weary, was interrupted by the soft thud of horses' hoofs upon the graveled drive.

"Here's Aunt Virginia!" Doris cried, delighted.

"The mere fact of darkness doesn't make her ride slowly," exclaimed the Colonel. "I'm sometimes afraid——"

"Oh, Bobbie's so sure footed, and Jack is with her," Mrs. Marquis commented.

"So he is. I had been wondering where my son was."

The horses certainly were racing. The Colonel hur-

17

ried down the steps to await the arrival of the speeding riders. His wife joined him.

Julian, the coachman, his white teeth gleaming in the gloom, had run from the stable at the first sound of the horses. He felt no worry. He knew how much Virginia Marston gloried in high speed, and as for Jack—well, he was incorrigible.

Disdaining the gallant Colonel's hand, the fair equestrienne dismounted, in a gale of laughter, which belied his fears and justified the coachman's confidence. She kissed Mrs. Marquis gaily, and was evidently in the highest spirits as she ran up the porch steps, avoiding as best she could a lumbering hound puppy, which, with half a dozen other scampering, delighted dogs, had rushed eagerly to welcome them.

Jack was a handsome youth, almost eighteen, joyous with the college-boy's vacation-spirit, and inordinately proud of the big "C" upon his sweater, which he wore continually although the southern days were warm, and the garment had been knitted for cool hours upon the Harlem.

"Great Scott! These dogs remind me of a freshman rush," he cried. He pushed the larger of them from him, but tenderly picked up a pup, whose spraddling legs made its position in the capering pack a little perilous. "They must want their supper. Come on, dogs!" Laughing, he went with them to the kennels.

"Where's my beautiful Doris?" Virginia demanded merrily, and then, when she saw her niece, caught her in her arms and whirled her in a dozen waltz-turns.

"Virginia," chided her sister, smiling: "you are really cyclonic."

"Yes, am I not? Life is so—vivid!"

She now saw Stoddard, and greeted him with gay apologies which left him smiling quizzically.

"Father has the most wonderful and solemn young man in the world at home this evening," she began, explainingly. "I absolutely could not breathe the atmosphere. Gravity has no attraction for me." Again she rippled into laughter, then beckoning to her sister, exclaimed: "Oh, I have so much to tell you!" She moved toward the door invitingly. "You will pardon me for being rude, won't you? I really must have a talk with her. Secrets are very impolite I know, but this one is most important," she said, with a merrily apologetic glance at the remaining members of the party.

"But who is the solemn visitor?" the Colonel demanded, detaining her for a moment.

"Oh, the son of an old law partner, Judge John Chapman, of dignified and wondrous memory." Then to Doris: "Careful, Doris! You know how much your grandfather thinks of him! I've been accusing him of wishing to be a match-maker!"

"Virginia!" said Mrs. Marquis laughing.

"I'll admit irresponsibility for anything I say to-night. Come inside, dearest: I must talk to you."

It shocked Mrs. Marquis's sense of hospitality, as well as other of her manifold proprieties, to be thus called upon to leave her guest for the discussion of things secret; but, perforce, she yielded to her ebullient sister's urgings, and turned indoors with her.

"Doris, you also may come," Virginia called across her shoulder, as an afterthought.

Doris, whose keen curiosity had been aroused, went gleefully, but her mother made real protest in a whisper.

"It's scarcely hospitable, or——"

"My darling sister," Virginia insisted, "there are moments when—there is news—there are—oh, this is not an ordinary secret I'm to tell you!"

With one arm caught in Doris's and the other about her sister's waist, she urged them on.

"How radiant you are!" said Mrs. Marquis, smiling at her when the three were in a room alone.

"I am so happy!"

"And you've come to tell us why?"

"Indeed I have, honey."

"As if I did not know!"

"How *could* you know?"

Mrs. Marquis seemed amused. "How could I *help* but know?"

"I am——"

"——in love."

"Well——"

"Virginia, what did he say to you, last night? We all saw you there beneath the palms in the conservatory. He is handsome."

"Who is handsome?" Virginia, cheeks aflame, now battled against the revelations she had come purposely to make.

"Retlew Baron," said her sister.

"Oh, Aunt Virginia!" Doris interjected. "Retlew Baron! He's a dear!"

"But," said Mrs. Marquis, "you've not answered me. What did he say?"

"My dear, my dear, he poured out his whole soul to me!"

"I am so glad you are happy, dear," said Mrs. Marquis. "Mr. Baron is a fascinating man. You will be a wonderfully handsome couple. And did you admit to—to him——?"

Virginia was in an enchanting mood of sunshine. "Frances, he told me he loved me!" she cried, springing to her feet with a charming vividness of joy. She made a joke of her intensity, waving her hands, becoming stagey in her fun. "I swear it by the nine gods of my ancestors!"

"And—you?" queried Mrs. Marquis, smiling infectiously.

"I did not tell him, but he knows, he knows. . . . Yes, at last I've found my real heart-joy. My soul has awakened. Life seems the most beautiful and buoyant thing!

"Sister, I feel as though my future was destined to be a very happy one." Again she caught her laughing niece, and whirled her in a swinging dance. A perfect brunette type, her coloring in striking contrast to Doris's vivid beauty; magnetic, full of vitality, and with that soft light in her eyes which tells that for the first time a maiden loves, she made a wonderfully pleasing picture.

"What a gale of happiness!" said Mrs. Marquis, but there was a hint of worry on her face.

This younger sister, not more than ten years the senior of Doris, was very dear to her—and Retlew Baron . . .

She reflected that Virginia had not had a fair chance in her girlhood. Save for the servants living quite alone with her father, who worshiped her, she had but small knowledge of life, and had been thrown far too much into contact with those older than herself; she had had too little normal social life.

Retlew Baron was the son of an old neighborhood family, but, none the less, was more a frequenter of the "new" houses in New Orleans than of the parlors of the old régime; the older families knew little of his comings or his goings, his enemies or his friends. Mrs. Marquis even thought she could remember that at one time he had been attentive to the daughter of a newcomer from the North, named Coles. But she did not let her doubts obtrude themselves upon her sister's joy, instead, she congratulated her, with what enthusiasm she could muster.

They were interrupted by the hurried entrance of old Mammy Rose.

"Julian says you done dropped dis 'ere packet, Miss Fahginya," she explained, her black face smiling in a thousand wrinkles.

"The invitations! How stupid of me!"

"What invitations?" Doris asked.

Her mother laughed. "Why, for your farewell party."

"My—farewell—party! Am I to have a farewell party?"

The girl's surprised delight grew rapidly.

"Why dear, of course you are," Virginia cried. "These invitations are to go out at once."

"We expected to give you a complete surprise, but finally thought better of it," her mother commented.

"You *darlings*!"

But Mrs. Marquis was absorbed in Virginia's romance, as a good sister should have been. "There's one, I hope, for Mr. Baron," she said, mischievously.

"It is the first one in the package."

On the veranda Stoddard Thornton and Colonel Marquis passed the long French window of the room, and Virginia ran to intercept them.

"I've an invitation for you, Mr. Thornton. We're all to celebrate the entrance of our Goddess of the Garden into the wider fields where so-called higher knowledge blooms." She handed him the envelope ceremoniously.

He took it gravely, flushing quickly, and involuntarily glanced at his clothing.

"Oh,—er—thank you," he said slowly, as he opened the envelope and made a quick note of the date. "I— I'm so sorry—I must go to New Orleans that very afternoon." But his face showed sudden relief. "I—I'm to meet, there, a committee. The new bank building, you know."

"Oh, how unfortunate!" Doris cried, and went to him, her face plainly showing the genuineness of her regret.

"But committees never meet in the evening—bank-building committees," Virginia urged.

"This is a most unreasonable committee," Stoddard answered, regaining his composure.

"And you can't get back? We shall have the garden lighted. You have no idea how pretty it will be—lanterns strung about among the roses, with 'fairy-lights' upon the ground to mark the paths! We had hoped you would help to plan the decorations."

"Oh, I can do that, if I may, and perhaps I can return before the lights burn out."

.   .   .   .

"I was so sorry for him," Mrs. Marquis told her husband, afterward. "I'm quite sure he hasn't evening clothes and that was his real reason for not accepting the invitation."

"He has things infinitely better," her husband answered discontentedly. "That chap will be a famous figure before long. His struggles have been ceaseless, and he has not spared himself. He's worth twenty of the young men who will be here, formally clad in the dress-coats which their fathers' money bought for them. But—well, I couldn't offer him assistance. He'd resent it."

"It's too bad. . . . Have you ever met Judge Chapman's son, whom father is to bring, dear?"

"A year ago, in New Orleans, when he was there on business for a day. Immensely rich, but without emotion, I imagine. The judge is very fond of him, however."

Colonel Marquis was sorry Stoddard could not have the pleasure of attendance at the party. He was sure the artist saw too little of young people. He well understood the reason why he shunned them habitually; youth is sometimes cruel, far more cruel than age; but it was a pity the boy must miss this.

.   .   .   .

That evening as they sat upon the veranda, smoking, he added his warm invitation to that of his wife.

The young man was embarrassed. "Really, Colonel," he explained, "I couldn't stay. You . . . know how poor I am. Every cent I have been able to get hold of—well, good marble costs; and the bronze-foundries have no mercy. I'm anxious to exhibit in New York, this winter, and there is the other matter, too."

"If you would let me help you!" The Colonel spoke impulsively; he knew that the suggestion would be gravely, gratefully rejected.

"No; no thank you. Sometimes it seems to me, as if the burden which I have to carry, now, is more than I can bear. You know what those dreadful figures are —thirty thousand dollars, Colonel, and the interest continually adding to them! But it is my burden, and it must be borne."

"It is quixotic for you to assume your father's debt! The men he—owed—can all afford to wait. The——"

Stoddard bowed his head, and, in the moonlight, his companion saw his fingers working nervously upon his knees.

"You must remember that the men he—owed," said he, repeating that significant pause before the word, "were all, quite involuntary creditors. They can afford to wait perhaps, but I cannot afford to let them wait. They—must be paid."

He raised his head and looked off at the moonlit sky. "Colonel," he continued, slowly, "is it possible that I am doing wrong in choosing a profession from which the money returns must be so slow? Sculpture is not commercially profitable. The rewards certainly will be tardy and may never come at all."

The Colonel laid his hand upon his arm reassuringly.

"They will come," he said. "They'll come. Don't you worry about that. For you, who have this gift, to let it lapse and turn to barter for the sake of men to whom you, personally, legally and actually owe nothing, would be madness, no matter what your fine sentimentalism, your keen sense of honor, make you think about inheritance of your father's obligations. I *wish* you'd let me help you."

Stoddard, with his hand, made a little gesture of denial. "I must pay the debt, myself. But I've been wondering about the other. You really think I have a right to go on with my unremunerative sculpture, in the hope that——"

"Of course. Heaven knows you're handicapping yourself enough by fighting so. If you'd let the interest go, a year or two, you could travel, study and win all the more rapidly because of it."

"I shall have to travel, I shall have to study, but, God helping me, I'll pay the interest too!"

"Stoddard, there's not a man whom I have ever known that I admire more, and——"

"Thank you, Colonel. That's worth something, isn't it? No matter how unworthy I may be."

"You're not unworthy, and you'll win. But I'm sorry you won't be here when Doris says farewell to the South. It will mean so much to us—the twinkling of the lights, which, really, will be the farewell lights of her old home—the throbbing of the music, which will be the farewell songs of the old birth-place to her."

"Is she never coming back? You speak in tones of such finality!"

"Oh, she will come back, of course, but she, too, has her ambition, you know, and such artistic fires burn strong, as your own case plainly indicates."

"Her talent cannot be denied but, with her, painting will be an accomplishment, not a profession. She——"

"She's very earnest. And . . . she's very beautiful. That, too, might keep her from the old home after she is finished with her school. You know, Stoddard——"

He saw the young man turn away his head and saw his hands clench tragically. He had watched him, during this visit, and had surmised that there was one prize other than fortune or celebrity for which he would have striven had the burden of his father's sins and debt lain less terribly upon his shoulders.

His heart thrilled sympathetically as he considered him. In Thornton he saw quite different metal from that which formed the gay youth of the vicinity or any others he had ever known. Even in their childhood Doris and Stoddard had been earnest friends. When the tragic crash had come in the affairs of the elder Thornton, quickly followed by his death, Colonel Marquis had wished to help the boy, with the hope, in his own heart, that some day he and Doris might be even more than friends—for Stoddard was so clean, so lofty of ideal, so unremitting in the earnestness of his endeavor. He had been stirred when the boy had announced doggedly that he would repay his father's defalcation, cent for cent, with interest, or would die in the attempt; he had smiled pityingly when he had decided upon sculpture as his life-work; his admiration knew no bounds now that fine things promised in that line. He *would* pay the debt, and he would pay through sculpture!

"And I can't even offer——"

"Thank you, Colonel: I must finish my little fight alone."

"Humph! 'Little fight!' Well, Stoddard, I'm as sure you'll win as—only you mustn't let it cost too much."

"It will cost; but—it will be the first and not the second generation that will bear *my* burden."

"Fine! Fine!"

"And it may not take so very long. If the bank accepts my designs for its façade—you know it is to be a mass of sculpture—the finest bank-building in the South——"

"I'd like to see your drawings."

"Would you, really? I have them here. I'll get them."

He hurried to his room and back again, unrolling great sheets of designs as soon as he had rejoined the Colonel.

"Magnificent!" His host was really astonished.

"I am glad you like them!"

"Like them! They are wonderful!"

The young man smiled.

"Then perhaps, in spite of everything, I'll——"

"Win. Of course you will."

"You're very cheerful and encouraging. Colonel, I——"

There was something so unusual in his voice that it brought the Colonel's eyes back to thoughtful and earnest contemplation of his face.

"What is it, Stoddard?"

Stoddard glanced quickly back of them, as if in apprehension lest they might be overheard, and the Colonel, instantly understanding this, although, of course, not dreaming what impended, rose and started toward the steps. "Come; let's go to the fountain. I love to watch it in the dusk."

They walked to the center of the garden and found seats upon a rustic bench, close to the tinkling spray.

"Now, Stoddard, what is it?"

The young sculptor was dismayed. He had not thought of pouring out the story of his love to anyone; yet would he not be traveling in the straight path of honor if he made confession of it to the Colonel, there and then? Good friend as Colonel Marquis was, it might be that he would consider the elder Thornton's sin a final barrier against the son in his striving for this greatest of all prizes. If so, then nothing but renunciation would be possible, for, above all others, this man had been most kind in the days of grim adversity.

When he had come to full realization of his father's wrongdoing, his boyish heart had almost broken in its agony, but this man had been his comforter; when others in the neighborhood had felt tempted to visit on his head the consequences of his parent's act, it had been the full, unfaltering friendship of the Colonel and his true-hearted wife which had preserved him from what might have developed into general scorn. Surely if ever obligation rested upon any man to be frank with any other man that obligation rested now upon him.

"Colonel," he said slowly, almost faintly, "when I saw Doris in the garden as the sun rose, two things were revealed to me."

"What, Stoddard?" The Colonel was puzzled.

"One was a certainty of my own ability. I had no doubt of it. I knew, at once, that I could represent even her startling loveliness with something bordering on competence."

"That little statuette is wonderful, my boy. It is astonishing. Your art is true."

"You can imagine how good those words sound to me when I tell you what the other revelation was."

"Well?"

"That I love her, Colonel!"

Colonel Marquis gazed sharply at him in the dim light.

"Why . . . Stoddard. . . ."

"I know. It seems presumptuous."

Instantly the Colonel tried to save him from distress. "I did not mean that. But Doris is so young . . . and . . ."

"Colonel, is there any reason why I should not strive . . .? Am I shut out from the right to worship her, to win her, if I prove myself as worthy as the others who will try?"

"Why . . . why . . ."

"Surely what my father did has not influenced you against me in this?"

"No, Stoddard; no!" the Colonel spoke impulsively and very earnestly. The tragedy of the boy's life had troubled him for years. "But Doris is so young, and you, yourself——"

"I know; all that is true; but I know that I shall never change! And, Colonel—oh, it would—help so much to feel that I may fight for her—that, in your eyes, I am not unworthy."

"Stoddard, my dear boy—I knew your father. I have never found it in my heart to blame him very deeply.

He was weak; not wicked, I am sure. And your mother —ah, Stoddard, had she lived, it never could have happened! Poor boy! Life went badly for you all."

The following words came slowly. "No . . . I do not see that I, as Doris's father, would have the right to bar you from any chance that others have. Lad, my confidence in you is exceedingly great." He placed his hand upon the young man's knee. "No; I have not the right; and I surely have no wish. If it will help the great and fine endeavor, you have started on so pluckily, take heart!

"It seems incredible to me that Doris can be approaching so close to womanhood that such talk as this is possible; I suppose all parents feel the same dazed wonder as their children near maturity. I would not consent to let you breathe any word of it to her for years to come. Four at least, must elapse before she finishes her college course, and then more, I hope, before she thinks of marriage. But, dimly, I can realize that it might help you in the fight which is before you to know that if you still wish to try to win her heart when the time comes for such things, you may feel free to do so. I see no reason why you should not, Stoddard."

"Thank you, Colonel." The youth's voice was tremulous and reverent.

"And while it all seems just a bit premature to me, I still recognize the fact that you have done the fine and manly thing in speaking to me as you have, to-night. Don't take it too seriously. Many things may happen. But . . . don't feel that you are held beyond the pale by any of us, here. We all admire you and respect you greatly."

Stoddard tried to speak again, but could not.

They sat in solemn silence a few moments, both lost in reverie. Then the Colonel rose. "Shall we go back to the veranda?"

Mrs. Marquis met them as they climbed the steps. "Stoddard, aren't you coming in to sing, to-night?"

He went indoors with her, particularly glad to sing. The Colonel had been kind; the heavy weight upon his heart was lightened somewhat. This fine and big-souled southern gentleman, at least did not consider him taboo, despite his father's sin and his own poverty. Ah . . . if he could win . . . if he could win! Doris! Doris! his Goddess of the Garden!

Sing? Yes; he would sing. His very heart was singing in his breast.

CHAPTER III

There was a certain melancholy in the preparations for
the family's desertion of the lovely southern home. At
times Doris shivered with the pain of the approaching
parting. How closely all the details of the place were
fixed in her affections! It was as though the very trees
were grown into her heart; the vines and climbing roses
all entwined about it. There were frequent moments
in the next few days when the nostalgia of anticipa-
tion almost made her regret that she was going North
to college. Ah, the cold and barren north! What tales
had she not read and heard of chill, bleak winds, of
driving snows, of tingling, painful finger-tips!

These stories recurred to her as she strolled amidst
the riotous luxuriance of the surrounding woods, or,
with hesitant, lingering footsteps, passed along the
bordered paths of the rose-garden. When, to make the
purchases necessary to her preparations for departure,
she went to New Orleans, lying somnolent beneath the
blazing sun of August, she looked about upon its old, low
buildings, the narrow picturesqueness of its ancient
streets, with fond, sad eyes.

Would rare visits to New York and its vast structures
atone for the lack of constant visits to this wonderful
old town? What could New York's sky-piercing piles
of brick and iron offer worthy of exchange for the
quaint beauties of the old French Quarter? And there

33

was Mardi Gras! How she would miss the carnival! Next winter when showers of confetti fell like snow, amidst a whirling gaiety of happy life and color in New Orleans, she would be where, she had been told, people are too solemn for such joyousness, too distrustful of their fellows to make merry with them if they do not know their names and pedigrees, too cold of heart, to feel real happiness at all.

But her time was not devoted wholly to such melancholy musings. Often there was a definite exhilaration in the work of getting ready. The news that they were soon to leave and that she would not return, next winter, had made a veritable sensation in the neighborly community of charming, cordial southerners, and she would have been far more than human had she failed to thoroughly appreciate the fact that half-a-dozen young men's hearts were fluttering with keen regret at thought of her departure. However there were the planning and arrangements for the farewell party.

Never had the grounds seemed half so beautiful as when all the arrangements for the festivity were completed. Stoddard kept his promise and carefully supervised the decoration of the place; lanterns and fairy-lamps ready for the lighting, were everywhere—in the garden, on the lawn and hung in the trees; while the house was garlanded with evergreen and vases were already in their allotted places, waiting for the fresh-cut flowers which Mammy Rose and Desdemona would supply for them at the last moment.

Doris looked back at all of it with a puzzled blending of emotions as, upon her horse, she started down the graveled drive to bid farewell to distant spots she loved

—to her intimate friends the trees, the views, the charming forest-nooks and woodland bridle-paths, which for several years, at least, she would not see again.

Stoddard, departing for the city, it seemed to her unnecessarily, on the very day the night of which would see the fête toward which they all had labored with such diligence, observed her hungrily, with an artist's keen delight and a hopeless lover's deep depression, as she rode a little way beside the cart which carried him toward town. She had observed the hearty hand-clasp and the look of earnest sympathy and understanding from her father as the two men parted, but, of course, she had not understood them. She was annoyed by his untimely going.

When he reiterated hesitantly his expressions of regret, she complained almost bitterly: "I really don't think it's very nice of you—not to be here for my dance."

Unable, as he was, to explain fully, he answered stumblingly. This still more incensed her, and he smarted under the injustice, but made excuses for her. What could she know of poverty and struggle? he reflected. That a man could be without a dress-coat for a dance would seem incredible to her.

His very hesitations made her annoyance increase. That his heart was filled with love of her, as she chided him and pouted, would have seemed to her a silly statement. Was he not scorning her by his departure? Why had he so worked to help them beautify the house and grounds if he was not to be there when that beauty glowed, resplendent? It could mean nothing but indifference! She became rather angry, and the sculptor, knowing it, was very much depressed.

He yearned to tell her what was in his heart, but put the thought of such a thing away from him with bitter resolution. He was certain of her friendship at least; would he be worthy of it if he should endeavor to induce her to regard him as a suitor, confronted, as he was, by years of struggle? Years during which, with the uncertain sculptor's chisel, he must try to recompense the victims of his father's fraud before he carved out fortune for himself? Ah, what a heavy load the second generation sometimes has to bear! . . . Still . . . if the bank plans were accepted!

"You're the only person within miles who would refuse my invitation!"

"But this Directors' meeting——"

"You know quite well you could get through with it and get back here! Or you could go another time. But, of course, if you don't wish to . . ."

"I *do* wish to. . . but . . ."

She turned a scornful glance on him and hurried into gossip about the woods, the views, the lakes and flowers to which she planned to bid adieu that morning. How unreasonable he was! And how unlike him to be thus!

She had known him since he had been twelve and she eight. He always had been most careful to attend all her dollies' tea-parties—what could have changed him so? She always had made a hero of him, in a way. He had been attentive to her, with a fine, grown-up attentiveness, when the remainder of the world had treated her as a small child. The respect with which he had accepted her pretensions of grownupness had made her often turn to him for serious consideration of her small affairs. When other folk had laughed with joy and tossed her in their arms, forgetting that she was pretending to be aged, untossable, he had been as gravely gallant and respectful as Sir Walter Raleigh had been to Queen Bess in the "history story" which she loved. What had changed him so completely? What could he mean by this refusal? Why was he using formal words this morning instead of chattering with excited understanding when she talked about the dance, the coming northern venture, and the mysteries of approaching college life?

Meanwhile he was absolutely helpless in his dire distress. The very fact that his whole being thrilled with love of her made him less able to explain away the circumstances which annoyed her. He felt tragically hampered and his suffering was acute.

His astonishment at the discovery that she was now a goddess, not merely an entrancing girl, had by no means faded from his mind; he still felt that sense of awe of her which had possessed him in the garden; but his heart was also palpitant with love. To let her feel that he would willingly slight her requests filled him with agony. Yet he could not explain!

Ah . . . perhaps . . . after his drawings were accepted, that day, in New Orleans . . . her father might . . .

He was not egotist enough to feel positively that he could win her love; but, ah! he longed to try. Still . . . it would be unfair for him to try until . . . of course, he was on honor!

She was rather glad than otherwise when they reached

the by-path into which she must deflect to reach her forest goal. There was something of relief in it for Stoddard, too. He had feared himself while he was with her, feared loss of self-control, the outburst of his love in spite of all—and this, he knew, must not occur. He was not only conscious of the obligation he was under to his friend and benefactor not to lay siege to Doris's heart until he had won his spurs; but he was conscious of the danger to himself which would arise from letting his impetuous heart crave with too great an ardor this being who, in the whirligig of fate, might conceivably prove unattainable.

She was further from his reach, he warned himself, than ever princess of a fairy tale was from a pauper lad. Would not the avowal of a definite resolve to win her add agony to an existence which, at best, seemed now to promise little but a desperate struggle for that which probably could not be won?

But the thought weighed upon him until, suddenly, he feared with a tremendous terror, that should he allow his heart to throb too warmly with his longing, and should this end in disappointment, the courage necessary to the other task would die—the other task which was a task of honor, and which must be accomplished if it cost his life, or, worse, even if it wrecked his happiness.

So, as he left her and Julian drove him on beyond the by-path, he solemnly abjured all further thought of love until the last cent of his father's debt was paid, and, thus abjuring, turned to get a final glimpse of her —and thought of love and nothing else.

After she had disappeared, but before he turned his eyes to the front again, he saw a young man, dressed in smart riding clothes and superbly mounted, riding hurriedly, as if to overtake her.

How little had his abjuration counted? Although he fought against it, a pang of painful jealousy cut through him like a knife at thought of the fair field such rivals had, while stretching out before him lay a road so full of obstacles that to declare even to himself, determination to surmount them all, seemed akin to madness.

But, against the judgment of his reason, his depression lightened when he chanced to look down at the box he carried. His "Goddess of the Garden!" Ah, but it was good! He knew it to be good! The fingers which had modeled it could mold the clay of fortune, chisel the hard marble of his destiny into what form they would! And if he won the contract with the bank——

He shut his teeth determinedly, and, half-an-hour later, when Julian chanced to look at him, he was still staring straight ahead, now into the outskirts of the city, with an expression on his face which made the darkey wonder what could possibly be "a worryin' of Marse Thornton, anyhow"?

But Julian's complacent thought that Doris had achieved a new conquest—the servants of the family gloried in her unconscious victories over the young men she met, and knew more of them than she knew herself—was less vivid than it would have been had the worried victim been one of the section's own gay youths. This young person from the outside world, who brought very little luggage when he came to visit, did not impress Julian as a conquest worth exulting over.

" 'N' 'is father were a bank-robbuh too!" Julian

mused scornfully. He had not heard the tale in its real truth. He had no mental standard to enable him to know the difference between a man who goes with dark-lantern and jimmy to despoil a vault, and one who, mastered by the insidious temptation of the possibilities of speculation, and driven by a mad desire to give advantages to an adored son, "borrows" first a little, then a little more, then more, more, more, hoping constantly to win at the tremendous game, but ever loses, until the crash comes, rushing on him in an overwhelming tumult of discovery, exposure and disgrace, and the son for whom he made the effort is burdened horridly, not helped upon the way.

The darkey did not know, nor could he know, the bitterness of the remorse which came too late and weighed upon the broken culprit until he sank into the grave; he did not know, nor could his simple mind have understood the horror which had flooded the son's mind, as soon as he was old enough to comprehend the nature of his father's crime and had inspired him with his mighty resolution to make restitution; he did not dream of the tremendous days of terrible depression which continually crushed Stoddard as he realized with growing vividness the futility of the profession he had chosen, and which he seemed not to have strength sufficient to abandon for more promising life-work.

Having left Thornton at his destination, Julian, while driving from the court-yard of the small, picturesque hotel in the old French Quarter, looked scornfully at the young man's back. His lip did not cease curling till he had made the purchases with which he had been charged, and returned to the gay, smiling house among the roses.

In the little dingy hotel-room which Stoddard entered, meanwhile, he almost succeeded in throwing off the melancholy which had depressed him during the long drive after Doris had been left behind. That was the glory of his art. Alone with it, it ever caught him to its breast and soothed and comforted him, so utterly absorbed him that the irritating worries of the outer world were soon forgotten. Now his fascination became so earnest that his engagement with the bank's building committee almost slipped out of his mind. But remembering it in time, he hurried to the meeting-place.

His drawings, spread flat and weighted at the corners to prevent the material from curling, lay upon the long directors' table, as he entered.

"Ah, Mr. Thornton," said the President, and warmed the sculptor's soul by rising cordially to take his hand. "Glad you are here so promptly. We've been looking at your drawings."

"I hope," said Stoddard, almost choking with his joy as he observed the interested faces all about the room, "that you have found them satisfactory. I hope——"

"Can you make these figures look as life-like and inspiring in the marble?" asked the President. "Why, they almost seem to breathe! They're different from the stiff images which usually appear as decorations. If in marble——"

"Oh, these drawings are only rough sketches," said the sculptor. "They are intended to convey the general idea, rather than the details of the finished work. The marbles will be more complete."

"And life-like, as these are?"

"Far more so; oh, far more so."

"Then, I, for one," the President said heartily, "am decidedly in favor of arranging with you, if we can come to terms. Jarvis, the architect, is more than satisfied; he is pleasantly astonished. Aren't you, Jarvis? What do you say, gentlemen?"

The smiling men around the table all agreed; the architect especially seemed enthusiastic. Such decorative work as this would be, could not be found in the whole South!

"And now as to terms," the President said, genially, while as in a mist, the table, the directors, the whole room swam before the happy eyes of the young sculptor. What would this contract mean for him? Two long years in Europe and a big payment on the dreadful debt! Ah, what a step toward her! The mere thought thrilled him.

He named the price which he had figured out in fear and trembling.

That an expression of surprise went round the table did not escape his anxious eyes. Had he set his price too high? He could not name a lower one and make any profit from the work. "Is it—more than you were thinking of appropriating?"

The President laughed more genially than ever. "No, Mr. Thornton. To speak quite frankly, it is a good sight less than we expected you to ask."

His heart bounded in relief. "It is my first large contract," he admitted. "Later, I have hopes that——"

"That you'll be able to lay on the prices," said the President, and laughed again.

"And you will, too," said the architect.

"Well, when our work is done," the President declared, "we hope you will. Always glad to see the other fellow pay a fancy price for what we've managed to get cheap. That's a detail of the banking business."

Everybody smiled. It was a very genial group, intent on very pleasant business.

The President drew a pen and paper toward him.

"Well, let's sign some sort of paper on the job. You might want to raise your price, you know, on second thought."

"No," said Stoddard, "but we ought to have a contract, I suppose. I'm not a capitalist and shall need credit in securing my materials. A contract will enable me to get it."

"Full name, then," said the President.

"Stoddard Thornton," was the answer.

As the President wrote busily, a director at the far end of the table started, suddenly, as if at mention of the name.

"You are not a relative of Richard Thornton, are you?" he inquired, his brow contracting in a frown. "If I remember rightly, Richard Thornton's wife's name was Stoddard when he married her."

There was an antagonistic timbre in his voice which instantly caught everyone's attention.

Stoddard's spirits sank. He paled slightly, but did not waver in his gaze when he turned to his questioner. Instead, his head became more erect, defiant.

"I am Richard Thornton's son," was his reply.

"Gentlemen," said the director, now scowling fiercely, "I move we reconsider for the moment, and take a little time to talk this matter over privately."

There was general surprise, but it was plain enough

that something of which the others did not know was in the air between these two.

Ten minutes afterward, the unhappy sculptor was not in the least astonished when a boy brought to the outer room where he had waited, a cold, polite note from the President, announcing that the Board had changed its mind; that there were other drawings which they thought would please them better.

"Oh, Father! Father!" Stoddard mourned, as he went back to his hotel, bitterly disappointed and disheartened, his high hopes supplanted by despair.

The kindly old Frenchwoman who was mistress of the little hostelry (much frequented by artists and others of small means) during his absence had guarded his low-ceiled apartment against the glaring rays of the afternoon sun, with partially drawn shades and lowered awnings. The place was almost dark when he arrived.

Therefore he did not at first observe the cloth-draped figure of wet clay upon the table. Finally, however, his eyes caught it as it stood there, like a little frozen ghost. He went over to it, raised the cloth and looked at it. Hurrying to the window he thrust up the curtain, then pulled madly on the awning-ropes and raised the shadowing canvas. Turning to the now well-lighted figure, he regarded it thoughtfully from every side.

His face slowly hardened in resolve.

"The Goddess of the Garden!" he reflected sadly. "The goddess of a garden into which no sorrow, no disgrace, no stern necessity for bitter striving ever has intruded! . . . God helping me I shall not ask her whom I love to share with me the weeds and wreck and ruin which oppress the sorry garden of *my* life!

"With the shadow of my father's sin upon me; with the heavy burden of his debt upon me, I would be a sad companion for the glory of her youth and happiness."

He decided not to attempt to reach the house among the roses before the lights he had help place for Doris's party had burned out.

CHAPTER IV.

The wild-canary, if he watched, saw strange, man-made blossoms budding in the rose-garden that afternoon, man made to bloom with the radiance of caged flame when night came. From the veranda in the center to the trees which sentineled the borders, colored lanterns were swung gaily. The oval walk about the fountain, the four broad graveled paths diverging from it and the wide promenade about the glowing spot of beauty, were all lined with "fairy lights," ready for the match to set them twinkling. On the terrace at the veranda's edge, dainty tables were arranged; the gleaming floor of the great drawing-room was bared of rugs in readiness for the swirl of dancing feet.

Mrs. Marquis watched the tumult helplessly from such points as she could find where she did not obstruct the paths of caterers with baskets, the musicians with muslin-swathed instruments, or the florist's men come from New Orleans to rob the garden with judicious skill and transform the rooms within into bowers of greenery and bloom.

Luncheon was a somewhat hurried ceremony, as the preparations for the evening had become absorbing. But discussion, even of this topic, stopped, when from the butler's pantry came one of the most amazing figures ever seen in that or any other dining-room. Mammy, at the moment, was standing at the buffet while the butler

46

served. The startling apparition was the bearer of fresh strawberries.

Mammy was the first to note its appearance, and, as she did so, nearly dropped the plate she held in her hand. Incredulous astonishment almost overcame her, but she recovered herself quickly, and whispered, breathlessly, as she stared:

"Bress de Lawd, ef dat ain't Sis' Desdemona! Where'd she git dat lookin' thing she's weahin' on huh haid?"

She stared at her obliquely, with face turned away, but with her great eyes rolled toward her until their whites gleamed uncannily.

Teddy, the only dog allowed indoors, began to bark frantically, not recognizing the small negro maid, whose head was now enveloped in a large red wig. Jack was the first of those at the table to catch a glimpse of the amazing sight, and, after an instant of dumb astonishment, saluted her with a glad shout.

As the others turned to look, the little darkey-girl, too much embarrassed to endure their gaze, departed hastily.

From the back porch, a few moments later, came the sound of Mammy, sermonizing her.

"Ev'yone de white folks was a'laffin' at yo'—even Massa Jack. Yo've made yo'se'f de laughin' stock ob de plantation. Yo' ought to be ashamed ob yo'se'f! Ah tells yo', Desdemona Snowball, yo' is nevuh gwine to git to Hebben wif dat red thing on yo' haid! De good Lawd won't nevuh have yo' 'roun' de golden streets a-lookin' dat way, sho's yo' bo'n. He wouldn't resignize yo'."

Desdemona's voice came, answering, half-scared and half-defiant.

"Wouldn't make no diff'ence to de Lawd. He kin see *t'rough* wigs! Heah Ah is, be'n sabin' up mah money fo' a yeah, so's to git some haiah mo' lak Miss Doris's; de Lawd He wouldn't make me suffah dat way an' den buhn me up in hell-fiah, too!"

That afternoon occurred a great commotion. A shriek was heard, there was a rush of hurried feet and frantic calls of "Teddy! Teddy! Heah, you Teddy!"

But Teddy, pausing not for the calling, dashed merrily, instead, into the center of the family group now on the veranda. In his mouth was Desdemona's wig. He had been the only witness when the little black girl, impressed against her will by Mammy's sermon, had hidden it out in the stable, and his recovery of it had been prompt.

In hot pursuit of him, embarrassed, wrathful, rushed the maid, but paused, abashed, at sight of the small dog's astonished spectators.

Tarrying when he had found an interested audience, Teddy tossed about and tore the weird mass of puffed and braided, straight red hair excitedly, and Desdemona shrank back in keen shame, distressed. But when the onlookers yielded to the irresistible humor of the situation, and laughed uproariously, she tried to snatch the wig and run. The little dog was far too quick for her, however; she could not catch him. Ashamed and woe-begone she quickly gave up the pursuit.

Virginia was the ruling spirit of the afternoon, her face aglow with that new happiness which had kept it radiant since she had told of Retlew Baron and the soft words he had whispered. It was she who saw that Mammy Rose was rigidly upheld in her entreaties to "Miss Dawiss" to lie down, so that she might be rested for the evening; she who kept the army of employees, foreign and domestic, to their tasks; who remembered to send the car for Judge Marston, her father, and George Chapman, his guest. Everywhere and watching everything, supervising here, encouraging there, she gradually brought order out of dire confusion, and finally, with a happy sigh, at five o'clock, she sank limply into a chair, having, after a long and searching glance, decided that no preparatory detail had been neglected.

At half-after-seven, Julian, with a long taper like a magic wand, went about cautiously—a black genii dressed in livery, arousing into scintillant beauty the "fairy lights" which gemmed the ground-level and the multitude of colored lanterns swinging from the trees, half-hidden in the shrubbery, and hanging from invisible wires stretched high in open spaces. After his visitations the rose-bushes gleamed with a pervading, soft effulgence which made them positively incandescent.

A deep orange after-glow from the late sunset still tinged the western sky; but slowly died away as, one after another, the artificial lights gained strength to twinkle in the garden and on the lawn, outlining the pillars and the railings of the veranda, the eaves, the walks, the drive.

With the first stroke of eight the earliest guest arrived. Others followed in carriages and motors, while Mrs. Marquis, erect, distinguished-looking, with her habitual calm unruffled, personified fine, welcoming matronhood. At her side, Doris was charming in pale pink chiffon. For the first time sharing his father's duties as host, Jack made a gallant figure of young southern hospitality.

By nine the soft strains of the orchestra tempted young feet to the waltz, and Doris's farewell party was well under way.

"Orlando, look at her," exclaimed the fond mother, extending a restraining hand as Colonel Marquis passed, "I have never seen so many pretty girls together, and she is quite the loveliest of them all."

Her husband smiled, indulgently. "You need only to look into a mirror, dear, to see where she found her beauty."

She glanced at him almost shyly. "You never will cease to be the lover, dear, will you!" Then: "She has certainly set hearts fluttering."

"There's not a young man here who's not bewitched," he granted. "Ah, there's the Judge."

A handsome, white-haired gentleman, erect despite his years, stepped from a motor, and, followed by a younger man, came up to the veranda.

"Doris," he said, presenting his companion, "this is Mr. Chapman, son of my old law-partner and best friend."

In the network of fine wrinkles about his strong, handsome old mouth, never grim when she was near, an expression of true satisfaction grew as he observed the instantaneous effect her beauty and charm had upon his guest.

This young man was of a type unusual anywhere, and in the South, almost unknown. Not more than thirty at the most, there were details of his face suggesting,

none the less, the man of fifty. His gravity belied his
youth; his habitual expression was a little cynical. Thus
early his hair was graying at the temples. None could
mistake him for one of those misguided ones, who, living at too high a pressure, grow old before their time;
rather he suggested one who had not known youth at
all in the true and joyous sense.

He was one of those men whom one is intuitively sure
will do well whatever they may undertake—if sentiment
be not included in it. He sobered Doris when she took
his hand, but her knowledge of Judge Marston's tradi-
tional affection for his father and interest in him, made
her more than ordinarily anxious to be cordial. She
danced with him frequently enough to incense more
than one of the young men who found his name repeated
several times upon her card.

"Who do you think snubbed me, just now?" Jack
asked, as he paused near his mother for a moment.

"I can't imagine anyone who'd be so foolish." Her
eyes dwelt fondly upon his fresh, young face.

"Well, Doris was. I tried to be in fashion and get a
dance with her, but she didn't even have a split for me.
She says she's split almost every number, too!"

Virginia was scintillant. Early in the evening her eyes
began often to rove involuntarily toward the entrance
and the receiving party, and, seeing this, Mrs. Marquis
smiled at her, thinking reminiscently of her own court-
ship days. The influence of her first real love affair
upon the luster of her sister's eyes, the color of her
cheeks, even upon the vibrant timbre of her voice, had
given even her new loveliness.

Virginia had had fewer heart experiences than most

women of her position in that section, perhaps because few men appealed to her, but more probably because of her extreme devotion to her father, who, early left a widower, had tacitly permitted her to take far more of care upon her shoulders than most girls of her age would have been willing to undertake, or be capable of taking.

But Retlew Baron was not one of those arriving early; he did not even come within the first hour.

Virginia became anxious as the later moments passed. Mrs. Marquis noticed it and Doris guessed it, although it was hardly probable that any of the others were aware of it. She stood a little more erect, if possible; her brilliant smile, perhaps, was brighter even than it had been; when she danced it was with added animation. Even to the eyes of those who loved her she was the gayest of the gay when mid-evening had arrived and Retlew Baron was still absent and had sent no word. She was not one of those who wilt, helplessly, beneath a slight.

About this time Colonel Marquis caught his wife's eyes as he made his hospitable rounds, and, unseen by the others, signaled that he wished to speak to her. She saw worry on his face and instantly connected it with the real agony she was certain poor Virginia was enduring.

"My dear, my dear!" he said softly, but excitedly. "I have just learned that the engagement of Retlew Baron to Marguerite Cole has been announced, to-day. If she hears of it—Virginia—without preparation——"

"*Orlando!*" cried his wife, appalled. "It is incredible! Incredible!" Her hand went to her lips in a gesture of worry. "Are you sure there is not some mistake?"

He nodded, most unhappily. "No; it is true. It will be announced in to-morrow's newspapers."

Unnerved, they stood together, a moment, overwhelmed by the painful tidings. "What shall we do? What *shall* we do? The poor, poor child! How can I ever tell her?" she whispered helplessly.

"She must be told," he warned. "I know, my dear, that it will be a real ordeal, but you are the only one to break the news to her." His face was seamed with sudden marks of worry. For a moment her eyes melted into tears, and when she spoke her lips were tremulous.

"And she was so happy! How can I? Oh, how can I?"

He pitied her, as the bearer of such tragic news, almost as much as he did poor Virginia, who must receive it. A gleam of wrath for the one who was responsible for the situation mingled with the soft glow of sympathy in his eyes, but he urged her not to lose a moment.

"I'll get to my room, somehow," she assented, in a whisper. "Tell her, very quietly, to come there to me."

"At once. And—shall I come with her? Would it make it easier for you?"

"No, no; you must remain here with the guests."

Trying to conceal her agitation with a smile, she left him.

Virginia had been dancing with Arthur Armsby, while Doris's partner was Northrop Reese, his somewhat heavy face so aglow with satisfaction that it seemed almost lightsome. As Virginia sank into a chair the Colonel went to her.

"Virginia," said he, "Frances wishes to speak to you a moment. She is in her room."

Instantly apprehensive of bad news, she glanced quickly at him, then assented and hastened to her sister.

"Virginia, dear," said Mrs. Marquis, when they were together, "I—I don't know how to tell you. I—have heard something which will——"

"What is it, Frances? Oh, what is it? Is it—something about Retlew?"

"Yes. Dear heart—dear heart——"

For a moment the unhappy girl, finding her indefinite apprehensions plainly on the verge of tragic confirmation, stood, too dazed for speech; then, falteringly: "Is there—has there been an accident?" Her tone was tragic and her eyes implored denial.

Gently Mrs. Marquis broke the news to her.

Virginia sank almost fainting upon a couch.

"Be brave, Virginia; be brave!"

But as she urged it, she was conscious that the revelation could not, possibly, have come at a more unfortunate time. Virtually one of the hostesses at Doris's ball, its victim must maintain at all cost, a demeanor of unruffled calm for her own sake. The conventional rules of life, as she must live it, demanded of her that she take this blow without a single sign; her pride required of her that even those whom she loved best must glimpse her agony but dimly.

"Dear, dear Virginia," said Mrs. Marquis miserably. "Bear up a few moments longer, so that no one may suspect what has occurred."

She turned apprehensively as the door opened. When she saw only Mammy Rose, she sighed, relieved. The old negress hurried forward in distress.

"Why, Miss Fahginny! What's de mattuh, honey?" Ever the comforter in time of trouble, she knelt beside the couch, speculating wildly. "Somebody hu't yo' feelin's, chil'?"

For a moment, certainly, Virginia almost yielded to a fierce outbreak of emotion under the strong temptation offered by this proffer of poor Mammy's sympathy; but she did not quite give way. Developing in this emergency, a strength of character which amazed her sister and awed Mammy Rose, although, as yet, the latter did not know what had happened, she rose, and, like a queen, with her head up and smiling as though nothing of unusual import had occurred, started toward the door.

"No one shall know," she said without a quiver in her voice. "No one *must* know."

A moment later she found her place once more among the guests. A new note had come into her beauty; a note which more than one of her admirers wondered at— a spiritual, ethereal note, which only sorrow, accepted as a burden to be carried without plaint and without bending can impart.

But she looked on the assemblage, and was conscious that, in days to come, she must look upon the world with a new vision. Something was now lacking from the merriment about her which she knew would never exist for her again. Realization had sprung into being in her soul that underneath the gayest smiles might lurk a hidden woe such as now crouched back of her own. The questions which were clamoring for answer in her tortured brain were tragic queries for the brain of youth to ask of life. Could any happiness be genuine? Was there in the world, a lasting, perfect joy? Was not every happy heart poised on the brink of an abyss of sorrow, into which, at any moment, an unexpected trick of Fate might plunge it?

Within ten minutes of her reappearance, the names of Retlew Baron and the Coles were announced, and she swept forward with her welcome, her congratulations and good wishes, among the foremost of the laughing, chattering group which instantly surrounded them.

She could see, as she looked unfalteringly, straight into his eyes, that Baron himself was in a fever of anxiety as to how she might accept the situation, but she smiled at him and gave no sign.

When he urged her to one side and whispered that there were things he must explain, she answered in a quiet, unexcited voice:

"Explain to me? Why, how diverting! But to-night we are so occupied. Sometime, perhaps; but, after all, why, ever? You will have so much to do and we are leaving for the North so soon."

He regarded her with weak amazement. He had been unable to find a good excuse for a refusal to escort the girl he did not love, but, finding he could marry, wished to, so that he might add her father's power to his in a commercial enterprise. But he had come unwillingly. He had not expected Virginia to make a scene, but, being unable to appreciate or understand her, had thought there was a possibility of one.

Now, finding her so calm, he found her altogether too calm for his liking; learning that he need not fear too much emotion, he was incensed because she showed so little. Cheap in every detail his pride was sorely hurt. She saw this and it comforted her.

CHAPTER V.

Ignorant of what had happened, Doris smiled across at Virginia with unaffected joy in the pleasure of the moment. She was intoxicated by the pure delight of living. All her world was doing homage to her. It was her first experience of that feeling of real power which girls know at an age which finds boys still nebulous and humble.

Her quick eyes caught a subtle change in Virginia's expression. Vaguely worried by it she was almost on the point of starting toward her; but Virginia, reading her intention intuitively and alarmed for the safety of her secret, fearing that some unavoidable expression might reveal her agony to such intensely sympathetic eyes, waved her away with a gay gesture and went merrily and speedily into another room—went merrily although her heart was breaking, speedily although her feet seemed leaden.

Doris looked after her with puzzled eyes but was given scant time for reflection. An instant later Arthur Armsby whirled her away in a waltz and she became absorbed by the exhilaration of the moment, lulled by the soft strains of the instruments, and fascinated by the slow pulsations of the dance.

"So you are going north to college!" said her partner when the waltz was ended and they had stepped out to the veranda.

"Away—up—north!.." she gaily answered.

"It's tragic for the other chaps, but it's jolly good luck for me. We always spend the autumn in the north, you know."

She laughed quizzically. "Then you must be sure to come to see me."

"I shall be sure to. Why do you laugh?"

"It will be rather fun to have you come, because you won't be given admission. They tell me no boys are allowed to call upon the freshmen. I shall be a freshman for a whole long year, you know."

"And you laugh at thought of my terrific grief, of my heart-rending disappointment?" His tone was full of mock reproach.

"Grief-stricken, heart-rent boys are always funny," she admitted. "But you can avoid your grief and spare your heart, you know."

"How?"

"Why, you need not try to see me."

"Do you suppose mere fear of grief could stop me?"

She smiled, delighted by his easy gallantry. "Oh, the college rules are very, very strict!" she warned.

"But I shall be, oh, very hard to turn away," he countered. "However, on the chance that they may over-power me, bind me, bludgeon me, keep me away by force, give me for remembrance the rose you carry, won't you? Possession of it might ease my exile." His voice fell to low, ardent tones. "Please, Miss Doris! Early in the evening, I decided that I'd ask you for it."

It was a gorgeous flower, especially selected from the whole wealth of the garden. She had worn it, for a time, but it had been torn out of its fastening, and for

ten or fifteen minutes she had been holding it in her
hand. The little pin of gold which had secured it to her
gown still glistened on its stem.

His pleading thrilled her; such experiences with boys
were new to her; she did not understand why everything between her and this youth should have
changed so suddenly. He was no longer the good playfellow. Somehow, he was different. Something had
been taken from the joy of their companionship—but
something, also, had been added to it. At first she had
wondered if she liked the change, but now, glancing
shyly at his pleading face and imploring eyes, she decided
that she did.

But she did not give him the rose immediately. That
instinctive coquetry, dormant in every woman since the
creation of the world, awakened within her consciousness. So many new emotions stirred in her to-night!

"Wait until to-morrow," she suggested, smiling, flushing, tantalizing. "I'll pick a fresh rose for you, then.
This one has begun to fade."

"It has withered in your hands, as we all would yield
up our lives to you, if you desired," said he. "That
makes this rose—this especial rose—desirable above all
other roses."

He smiled pleadingly at her, half joking, half in earnest; but there was no pretense about his attitude of
adoration; it was only that his own enforced change from
playfellow to suitor had been so sudden, puzzling him,
perhaps, no less than it did her.

"I . . . don't . . . know," she said. "I'm
not sure you deserve it." She was very much in love
with life as she was finding it; she was anxious to pro-

long these new experiences. They made her tingle, half with fun and half with a fear which she did not understand.

"Please! . . . . . please! . . . . ." he pleaded. Then suddenly, he looked away from her flushed and radiant face. It was annoying to have Northrop Reese come up to join them at that moment.

Doris, smiling, turned to the newcomer, genuinely cordial. She had always liked him, in a way, but not quite in the same way in which she liked the other boy. He was of good family, but was awkward, ponderous of movement, slow of thought. While she found the new game Arthur had begun to play with her highly exciting, it was so new that it confused her. A change from it was already welcome. Northrop aroused in her no such pleasant, but disturbing qualms, as those which Arthur stirred.

But the look on Northrop's face was as unusual as the look on Arthur's. The latter's novel attitude of gallantry had pleased her; Northrop's intensity of real emotion was as strange and frightened her a little. The youth was very grave; in his eyes was a queer earnestness which she had never seen before. Everyone seemed different, to-night, she marveled—and not least of all, herself.

The newcomer did not grant even a glance to Arthur; it was as if he did not know that he was there. He kept his gaze resolutely upon her face.

"It's goin' to be right lonely hereabouts, Miss Doris," he said, awkwardly. His broad Southern accent fell on her ears with pleasant softness, after the more cultivated speech of Arthur, who had been schooled almost as much abroad and in the North, as in the South.

She did not know why, but the smile died from her lips, and was replaced by an earnestness almost as grave as that on Northrop's face.

"I shall not have the heart to go if you all keep telling me such lovely things."

Arthur, rather angered by Northrop's intrusion, stepped back, and stood in silence, slightly frowning, waiting with impatience for the moment when the uncouth youth should go; but, far less fluent than his rival, Northrop had to strive earnestly for words, now that he stood in the presence of the incarnation of his heart's desire, and, striving, found none to his liking.

The pretty speeches which he had prepared laboriously for the occasion, had departed wholly from his mind. Appalled entirely beyond his understanding by the news that she was going north, he had looked forward to the opportunity this party would present, with hopes of— he knew not what, but at least of saying something big— so big, that in their lives it would be epoch-making. He had planned for a private talk with her; assuredly he had not thought to blurt out what he had to say before another boy.

Confronted by this situation, his wits almost deserted him, but suddenly the longing to obtain from her before she left the South a small memento became insistent; he wanted to receive it from her own loved hands, and the desire that it should be the flower which she had worn and now twirled carelessly between her fingers, rose paramount above all other things.

"I came over hoping for a keepsake," he said, slowly,

but without a glance at Arthur, whose quick southern temper was fast accumulating fury.

"A keepsake!" She was really surprised.

"To ask you for that rose."

By this time he had quite forgotten Arthur; his big, pathetic eyes were fixed hungrily on hers; his mighty hands, so large that they seemed almost like real deformities, worked nervously, with a spasmodic play of strength which sent their finger-tips into his palms until they hurt him. His face was tensely strained and eager.

The situation began to worry her excessively. From the corner of her eye she had already seen the angry flush on Arthur's face. She did not know exactly how to manage things. She could not give the rose to both.

Arthur stepped forward, looking hard at Northrop. "I beg your pardon," he said, coldly, "I have just begged Miss Doris for that rose. My claim is first. I fancy."

He stared steadily, unsmilingly, straight into Northrop's eyes. Northrop, glanced slowly at him, but although dimly conscious of his deep hostility, turned quickly back to Doris, quite ignoring him.

"How very silly you boys are!" she said, reproachfully. "Come here to-morrow and I'll give you each a dozen roses. This one is ruined, anyway. I shall give it to neither of you."

Impulsively she tossed it back of her across the porch railing, hoping thus to end the tensity of the unpleasant situation.

But she had taken the wrong course. An instant the boys stood glaring at each other. Then, young and impetuous, not gauging the right thing to do, Northrop turned to the near steps, leaped rapidly down them and hurried toward the spot where the discarded rose had fallen. After a second's dumb surprise, Arthur, with a lithe agility in striking contrast to the other's massive power, placed a hand upon the railing, quickly vaulted it and alighted close beside the rose, just as Northrop reached it, and, in a moment more, would have stooped to seize the flower.

Doris, by this time, had become definitely angry, but she admirably controlled her dismayed astonishment.

"You must not touch that rose!" she said, quickly, leaning across the railing. Then, with a new finesse which she was conscious would have been foreign to her yesterday, but which was natural to-night: "You're both acting like little boys. Come back here and—be nice to me."

The altered tone in which she spoke the last four words destroyed the tension. It changed her speech from a command to an appeal. It did not lessen the boys' anger toward each other, but it shamed them, bringing realization of the fact that they were behaving boorishly before her.

"Now, not another word about that poor, old, withered rose," she ordered. Then she laughed. "I believe I'm more grown up than either of you. I'm going to rob my brother Jack of the next dance—his only one! and split it between you. You must be friends, and match with coins to see which is to have the first half of it. Jack won't mind when I tell him I did it to prevent bloodshed. **Really you ought to be ashamed, you two! You've almost spoiled my party.**"

After the last half of the dance, which had been his

portion, Northrop said farewell and departed. She did not know it, but, as he went, he passed within a foot or two of Arthur, quite by chance. Wrath rose in his face. He flushed, tried to speak, but could not. Arthur's temper was not proof against his look. Some quick, half-whispered words were passed between them.

At the moment, Doris's attention was focused on George Chapman, who was advancing toward her. She watched his adroit progress through the throng of dancers with a certain grudging admiration. There was a polite precision about every movement of his body, a sophisticated polish in the smiles accompanying his apologies to those who brushed against him, which marked him as a man apart from those whom she had known. Their courtesy was invariable, a fine quality innate in most southern gentlemen. His was not more genuine, but, somehow, it seemed more elegantly finished. He was of a type new to her. One does not find the calm, impeccable young bachelor among the older southern families. He sank gracefully into a chair beside her.

"Do you never tire of dancing, Miss Doris?" he asked gravely. "I seldom dance. My sister never does. She doesn't approve of it."

He did not say this as his sister's partisan. He spoke with a grave gaiety as if there were a joke somewhere. Doris could not quite make up her mind just what it was. Here was another new sensation. Arthur and Northrop had aroused in her a sense of power; this man made her feel a weakling, he baffled her. But the unwonted sense of dawning womanhood, of having stepped across a threshold, was as strong as she gazed at him as it had been when she had looked at them. How many curiosities were being roused in her! This, too—this study of the northerner, was thrilling. What fascinating mysteries men were after all!

She was amused, yet hampered by a feeling of restraint. Light gaiety would be difficult in this man's presence, she felt. "I should like so much to meet your sister," she remarked inanely.

"I am not sure of that. She's coming out to-morrow, though, and you will have the opportunity. She did not come to-night because she does not care about participation in such gaieties."

"Does she dislike parties, even if there is no dancing?" Doris knew there were some people who thought dancing sinful, but even they had parties—very dull affairs; she had attended one of them.

"She thinks them a waste of time. The only gatherings of which she really approves, she calls 'meetings.'"

"Meetings?"

"Yes; where weighty matters are discussed. She is a suffragist—a 'suffragette' to the irreverent."

"Really?"

"Yes, she believes that women all should vote, serve in Congress, and lead opinion. Do you?"

"I know so very little!"

"Doubtless you will be more interested after you have been in college."

"Information, I believe—information upon many interesting topics—is what I am going to try to find there." She was achieving ease with him and that elated her far more than she could account for.

"Jane has a plan for you. She wants you to become

the center of what she calls a 'Freshman Suffrage Group.'"

Doris laughed. "It would be fun! I'd like to."

"Tell her you'd like to; don't say it would be fun." He smiled engagingly; she answered with a charming frankness. It was as if they had become partners in a secret.

"Would that offend her?" she queried innocently.

"It would make her think you frivolous. Frivolity, she says, means uselessness."

"Usefulness is such a bore."

For the first time he really laughed. "That remark would make Jane faint—if she *could* faint."

"Couldn't she?"

"I think not."

"I didn't mean it quite. Usefulness to those one loves is not a bore; I suppose it is the greatest fun there is." She did not know just why she said this.

"Are there many whom you love?" He looked at her, as if awaiting her reply with actual curiosity. It was as if "love" might be a word with which he had not been especially familiar.

"Oh, I *adore* people. Father says I am a friend of friendship and in love with love."

"I've never known so very much about the latter."

"But there's your sister."

"Yes; there's Jane."

"She loves you, doesn't she?"

"I think so."

"And you love her, of course."

"Love Jane?" He paused a second, as if the thought were novel. "Oh, certainly; of course."

"And she'll be over here to-morrow?"

"She's sure to be."

"We shall be very glad to see her."

"If you promise her to start that Freshman Suffrage Center she will like you very much."

"I don't believe I could be serious enough about it," Doris answered smiling, "if she really is as earnest as you say she is."

"Jane certainly is earnest."

Doris at first could not decide just what she thought of the son of her grandfather's old friend. He was fascinating and attractive, certainly, but was he likable? She made a difference in the meaning of the words, as she considered him. He had none of the small social arts, with which she was familiar among Southerners, although he practised some which they had never learned. His politeness was not gallantry; it was, instead, a somewhat cold and very studied courtesy; but finally she decided that it none the less attracted her. His attitude toward women—toward herself—was novel. It was not completely subjugant, but, was rather that of tolerant submission. His interest in her seemed very real, though possibly somewhat amused, yet he seemed without a sense of humor, as she knew it; there was no twinkle in his eyes. But there was something puzzling in them, something, though they were gray and almost chill, which attracted her intensely, half hypnotically. But in spite of this queer sense of power in him which was so plain to her, she still was, somehow, a little sorry for him, too. The emotions he aroused in her were contradictory.

But she did not let the problem worry her. Life

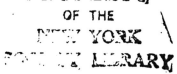

was too personal that night. The quarrel between Northrop and Arthur; the strange expression she had seen upon Virginia's face; this unusual person from the North—all these, amidst the excitement of her farewell party, became but parts of a bewildering mosaic, and, despite the somber coloring of certain elements, its dominant note was gay and cheerful.

.   .   .   .

Virginia had made her escape as soon as possible; but this was not until the last guest was gone. She found the silence of her room a great relief. Even as she felt this she kept up tensely for a moment. But soon she yielded to the inevitable emotional reaction and fell upon her knees at the broad window, praying for strength and wisdom to help her endure the sudden, incredible sorrow which had come upon her.

Thus Mammy found her when she stole softly in.

Virginia turned, and after one glance at the old, sympathetic, wrinkled face, burst into heartrending sobs. Mammy knelt beside her and put her arms around her, comfortingly, trying to hide the fright which the outbreak aroused in her.

"Don' yo' cry, Honey, an' spoil yo' pretty eyes," she tenderly implored. "Ah dunno what's happened, but ain't nothin' wuth no teahs f'um Miss Fahginny."

But Virginia's sobs, once started, were uncontrollable.

She was not to be comforted. She pressed her face against old Mammy's shoulder in an abandon of despair.

"Hush, Honey, hush! Don' yo' cry. Let ol' Mammy cry fo' you. Won't make no diff'unce with huh ol' brack face."

CHAPTER VI

When Arthur came to her to say good-night Doris saw something in his face which worried her. His lips when in repose, after forming the pretty, cultivated compliments which were so frequently upon them, and which interspersed his leave-taking, were set closely in tense, straight lines.

"You were dreadfully angry with poor Northrop!" she reproached him.

"Oh, for a moment," he admitted; "and I am sorry I was rude. Won't you forgive me?"

It had always been among his charms that his contrition, after he had erred, was quick and frank. She could not remain vexed at him; no one ever had. That may have been one of the handicaps which hampered the good natured, gallant, handsome, popular and wealthy boy. Praise of him was always sincere; blame was generally coupled with a smile and an excuse.

But Doris did not at once yield to the strong appeal of the big, earnest eyes. She stood looking at him with a little frown, which, however, she presently found it difficult to maintain.

"I wanted that rose so much!" he added, his eyes now definitely imploring.

That she must relent was certain, but she tried to make forgiveness seem a grudging matter, tried to hold it back a little. "I never heard of anything so utterly absurd as the commotion you boys made about it!"

His quick wrath at Northrop rose again, and, for a moment replaced his gay, but still impressive evidences of devotion. "Some chaps need lessons in good manners."

This helped her to retard forgiveness. She answered his change of manner with an instantaneous alteration of her own from mere reproach into severity. "Yes; two, —whom I know—not one but two! You almost spoiled my party."

Wrath faded from his face, as quickly as it had come into it. Now he was all the culprit, begging her forgiveness, not the critic, making a complaint. "I'm so sorry; indeed I am—tremendously! Won't you tell me I'm forgiven?" he implored.

She hesitated. The look of pleading on the handsome, boyish face, the vibrant supplication of the high-bred, almost tremulous voice, were irresistible. "Well, perhaps," she said, endeavoring, without much success, to make the words seem grudging.

"I shall try to find that rose, when I go home, and if I do I'll treasure it."

"You must do nothing of the sort. You must promise me to let it lie exactly where it fell—to let it lie there until Julian comes to-morrow morning. He will destroy it with the other rubbish. I mean that. You must promise!"

He did so, with reluctance, and a little later said good-night. As he turned away, she saw him hurriedly glance at his watch.

Weary from the dancing, she sank into a chair, idly wondering if he could have an appointment at that hour.

Undisturbed, she now luxuriated in her relaxation following the excitement of the evening. She had become aware that life was very good to her. She did not understand, but wondered at and gloried in the changes which had metamorphosed her. New emotions had been flooding through her being. Her mind was filled with many wondering "whys"? Romance had grown real; it was no longer the intangible web and woof of other folks' experiences and imaginings. She, herself, was involved in it.

She asked questions of herself which she had never asked before, and which she could not answer. She knew she captivated those of the opposite sex; but why? Wholly novel, unexplainable emotions had made her vibrant all the evening, especially when she had been with Arthur and, to a less degree, when at her side had stood the dignified but pleasantly devoted Northerner. What was their meaning? Even memory of them somewhat confused her and that further puzzled her. Why had Arthur flushed so as he led her out to dance? Why had her own cheeks answered with a flaming signal? What was the reason for the leaping turmoil in her breast when George Chapman's eyes had rested on her face? She was nonplussed by many things. For the first time in her life she that night had been definitely conscious of her own charm of personality. She had known that she was "pretty"; now she knew that she was beautiful and that beauty does more than please the eyes of men; that it stirs their pulses.

So absorbed was she in her reverie that she was conscious presently that the mere intensity of thought was wearying. She rose and sighed, definitely grateful for a sudden breeze which breathed on her and cooled her cheeks and throat.

Vaguely she speculated as to where her father and her mother might be. The full significance of the disaster which had fallen on Virginia, did not yet impress itself upon her. It did not occur to her that they were with her, doing what they could to ease her intolerable distress.

She looked about the veranda for Teddy, who had disappeared, in agonies of fear, after a whirling, dancing foot had bruised his friendly little toes. She did not see him, and rose, standing by the porch rail a moment.

Then she saw Arthur start down the drive in his light, racing runabout. She knew that he had loaned his chauffeur to some helpless neighbors and presumed that to be the reason why he was last to leave the Marquis garage. The glimpse took her mind from Teddy, and she watched his driving with a glow of admiration, as the brilliant moonlight revealed his careless, but complete control of the low, high-powered car on the abrupt curves of the drive. He scarcely seemed to watch the road and had but one hand on the wheel as he adjusted his magneto and arranged his robe, yet the car made the half circles with all the accuracy of a bird in winged flight.

Starting, he had thrown off the muffler, and, even after she had turned her eyes away from him to search for Teddy, she could mark his progress by the noise of the explosions.

Suddenly they ceased and, attracted by the subsequent quiet, she turned. He had brought his car to a standstill fifty yards from the gate which would have taken him to the highway.

A moment later she saw the machine start on, this time fully muffled, not through the gate and out into the high road, but into a narrow, tortuous way which branched there—a little used, but more direct route than the public road, to the main highway of the section, serpentining through dense woods which were a part of the great Armsby property bordering the Marquis place along its southern boundary.

"Someone called to him to go by the woods-road," she thought, surprised. Then, a little later, she began to feel indefinitely worried, "He ought not to risk it, late at night, in the pitch dark."

But she was not greatly interested, for although she called her little dog persuasively, he did not come bounding to her side as usual, and this bothered her. Could Teddy have run away?

No servants were about, and, as the moments passed and he still did not come to her, despite her most persuasive trills and enticing whistling, she went down the veranda steps into the roadway.

The moonlight was perfect, as moonlight can be only in the soft nights of the South; the moist air was refreshingly cool and caressing. She strolled slowly along the drive, signaling for the truant now and then, reveling in the bewitchment of the mystic out-of-doors after the intoxicating indoor tumult of the evening.

Suddenly, in answer to her calls, the little dog appeared, scampering from the shadow of the woods. He jumped joyously about her feet capering his welcome. It was plain enough that he believed she had come out to join him in a midnight frolic. But, having found him, she turned back.

For an instant Teddy watched this action with surprise, his head cocked to one side in disappointment. Then, in a way which she knew well, he gently caught her skirt-hem with his teeth, and pulled a little. It was his signal that she was to stop and turn the other way about. He sometimes urged her thus, when, in their play, a ball fell into some position from whence he could not move it without her aid.

"What do you want, Teddy?"

He gently tugged again.

"Something over there?"

He looked up and wagged his tail with furious assent.

"Where, Teddy?"

He ran a few steps toward the forest edge, and then stood looking back at her, his head eagerly side-tilted, every muscle in his little body tense, ready to guide her with a rush if she showed any indication of following.

She looked about her hurriedly. What could he be after? She knew she ought not to enter the dim aisles of the forest at that hour of the night, but she was unafraid and followed.

A dozen yards beyond the border of the woods, he stopped, a silvery patch of moonlight falling on his tiny, active form as he began to tug violently at something. She stooped to see what it could be, and, to her astonishment, discovered—Desdemona's wig.

Teddy had been burying it, as he did all his dearest treasures, but some of its bright strands had caught upon a branched twig just above his reach, as he had shaken it in canine joy, and he could not loosen them. He was asking her for help.

She bent to disentangle the lodged tresses, and, as she did so, heard, from a little way within the copse, two voices. One was Arthur's, angry but subdued, the other, Northrop's, so vibrant with the wrath it carried that its words were half choked and mumbled. She caught enough of them to know that he was urging Arthur to some sort of duel, and that Arthur, though apparently quite calm, not frightened, was protesting that such an episode, that night, so near the Marquis place, participated in by two young men who had just left her party, might especially distress her, Doris, and later cause unpleasant gossip.

She could not hear distinctly all that was said, so, for an instant, she did not fully realize the seriousness of the situation.

Its truly startling nature was revealed to her when she heard Arthur say, somewhat contemptuously, that he was unarmed and that the other must be quite aware that in these days gentlemen did not carry pistols with them when they went as guests to the houses of their friends.

Then, to her amazement and dismay, she heard Northrop declare loudly, blusteringly:

"I expected you to make some claim of that sort. I can supply you. Here's a pistol. I brought *two*."

"You must be insane, Reese," Arthur answered.

"Are you a coward?" The words were hissed, insultingly.

She tried to scream, but could not. For an instant she was spellbound.

Then she heard the crackling of dry twigs beneath a

quick, impulsive step, and knew Arthur had been angered beyond the limit of his self-control; she knew he was advancing on the youth who had insulted him. Such things are very likely to end tragically in the South, even in this calm, commercial age. Again she tried to scream; again she could not.

She abandoned Teddy and his treasure. Her frightened eyes peered searchingly into the deep gloom of the woods.

She began to run in the direction of the voices, terror adding fleetness to her flying feet, although the path was rough and barred continually by tangled shrubbery. Indeed, although it was bright with moonlight, she could not force her eyes to watch the way, and made uncertain progress, often stumbling; but she hurried—desperately.

Before she actually reached the glade in which the two boys stood, the widening path gave her a view of them. Northrop was a terrifying spectacle. His deeply shadowed eyes seemed of abnormal size—black blots against a face whose ghastly, wrathful pallor was accentuated by the nature of the light in which she saw it; his almost bloodless, tightly compressed lips were scarcely visible. His attitude reminded Doris, horribly, of a picture in her Fairy Tales—the picture of the monster in the story of "The Beauty and the Beast."

The boy's heavy head was thrust forward from between high, massive shoulders, his knees were bent, his abnormally long arms contracted slightly, at the elbows. In each hand he held a revolver. How wickedly they glittered in the moonlight!

She paused, too terrified to move.

"Take one of these!" she heard Northrop urge, his voice choking with the passion in it.

Arthur merely shrugged his shoulders, without further words, keeping himself well in hand, although it was apparent that he did so with great difficulty.

For a moment Northrop glowered at him; then, with a choking cry and one revolver held by the barrel and raised high in the air, he suddenly ran toward his enemy and struck him a crushing blow.

Without a moan Arthur sank before the onslaught. Northrop bent above him in exultant frenzy. He seemed so changed, so terrible, that Doris shrank, aghast, as looking more than ever like the beast in the old tale, he gripped his victim's throat with his great hands.

With a cry of horror, Doris now rushed forward and cast herself upon her knees beside them.

"Please don't kill him! Please don't kill him!" she entreated in a pleading tone, her wide eyes raised appealingly to Northrop. There was an intensity in her voice which reached his understanding—even through the real insanity of wrath which held him. Then, as he caught the tense appeal upon her face and in her attitude, the madness quickly left him.

He dropped his hands, quite overcome, inwardly revolting at the deed which she had saved him from committing, and staggered to his feet.

She bent slowly over the unconscious Arthur, in an agony of fear, until his tremulous eyelids showed that he was gradually struggling back to consciousness.

Rising after she had made sure that he still lived, Doris caught at a tree, for her limbs were trembling beneath her. "I'll send someone to care for him," she said, her voice hesitant with sobs.

"No," said Northrop, slowly. "Please do not. He's not dying—I thank God for that! You've saved his life; you've saved me from a dreadful crime. I must have been—insane. I'll care for him. I'll——"

His voice broke.

"Can I—trust you to care for him?"

"Yes, you can trust me now."

"I am almost afraid to." Shuddering, she looked down at his hands, which, she knew, forevermore would be dreadful to her. "Northrop, you must go away at once. "

"But how can you, alone——"

"I don't know; but in some way I will. Please, please go, Northrop . . . quickly . . . quickly!"

After another dazed look toward her, the boy bowed submissively, as might a guilty prisoner, admitting justice in a judge's sentence, and strode off among the trees, following neither road nor path, crashing blindly through the undergrowth. A moment later Arthur had sufficiently revived to struggle, with her help, into a sitting posture. He looked at her with eyes from which the incredulous confusion slowly cleared. The memory of that dreadful grip upon his throat was uppermost in his shocked brain, and he raised his hands, touching the bruises carefully, investigatively.

"He choked me! A—h! He choked me!"

"He has gone, and you must go."

He realized, for the first time, that it was Doris who was with him.

"Doris! Doris!" How did you come here?"

.

"I was trying to find Teddy, then I heard you boys; and—oh, you have been so foolish! Between you, you might have ruined my whole life and lost your own, over a foolish quarrel about a rose!"

He was beginning, now, to reason things out clearly. "You saved my life! He struck me with a pistol and was choking me to death! Ah . . ."

"You must get into your car and go away, as he has done—if you are strong enough."

"I'm all right, now. I was a little—weak—when I woke up."

"You might never have awakened. But now hurry. No living soul but we must ever know a thing of this."

"I was a fool! I should have utterly ignored him."

"Yes; and now make haste—you must go quickly."

As she hurried toward the house the small dog suddenly recalled himself to her.

She had entirely forgotten him since she had first heard the voices in the wood. Now, as they approached the veranda steps, he ran triumphantly ahead of her with Desdemona's wig—his spoil of victory.

He almost stopped as he trotted by the discarded rose, which still lay by the graveled drive. He saw the glitter of the pin thrust through its stem, and that aroused his canine curiosity; but he had worked hard for the wig and he could not manage both the wig and rose; his mistress was apparently in haste. He let the rose lie where it was and followed Doris blithely, as she went swiftly into the house through a side-entrance.

Half-an-hour later Stoddard Thornton, returning from New Orleans at a time when he felt sure all the guests would have departed and the family would have retired, approached upon the moss-thick grass beside the drive, avoiding carefully the least disturbance of the noisy gravel. His heart was drowned in gloom. His disappointment over the directors' action in the matter of the sculpture for the bank-building was shadowing the whole horizon of his future.

How distant, now, how very distant must be the days which, that very morning, he had dreamed of as so close at hand!

He, too, saw the rose, and caught the glitter of a moonbeam on a facet of the tiny brooch still clinging to its broken stem. He stooped, picked it up, recognized the brooch as Doris's, and caught his breath reverently. Ah, she had worn the rose!

It was as if the gods, an instant kind after a day of cruelty, had thrown it in his path. He disengaged the ornament and thrust the rose into his breast, taking a sort of savage joy from the discomfort of its penetrating thorns. A sleepy servant, who had been awaiting his return, opened the front-door, admitting him, and he laid the pin upon a table in the hall, with surreptitious care.

CHAPTER VII

Doris awoke late in the morning still weary from the excitement and exertion of the night.

Hearing voices underneath her window, just before she went downstairs, she glanced out and saw Stoddard and her father coming from the garden in earnest conversation. The conference was so absorbed, the faces of the men so solemn, not to say sorrowful, that a sense of some impending disaster suddenly oppressed her. Already worried by a vague knowledge of Virginia's suffering, this indication that the young sculptor she admired and liked so much was also troubled, doubly distressed her.

She hurried down, but when she reached the veranda, her father was discussing poor Virginia's troubles with her mother, his face heavily lined with marks of worry. When she spoke of Stoddard he explained that the artist had been forced to start away, regretfully, without awaiting her appearance. He had left farewells for her.

Of Virginia's trouble the Colonel and Mrs. Marquis said as little as possible before her, so Doris's mind was principally fixed on Stoddard. She was puzzled, worried and possibly a little piqued. Mrs. Marquis soon left them, making an excuse of commonplace affairs, but, really, hurrying to her sister.

After she had gone, Colonel Marquis, glad of a subject of conversation which might keep Doris from thinking of Virginia and from asking questions which he would not care to answer, explained that Stoddard had decided to go north; that, indeed, things had occurred which would take him away at once.

"Aren't we to see him again before we leave?" she asked, her mind busy with the mystery of this sudden going.

"I think not. He feels that he must leave the South at once for fields which possibly may offer better opportunities."

"Then he is not to do the bank in New Orleans?"

"No; and I am very sorry. It was a bitter blow to him."

She had not felt certain that his absence from her party was quite to be forgiven; her sense of slight because he had departed that morning before she had appeared, had been very real at first; but as she observed her father's face, the feeling grew in her mind that only something very serious had forced upon the sculptor the course which he had followed. Perhaps she had been doing him injustice. Her heart thrilled with something deeper than mere disappointment. It was rather gloomily therefore, that after breakfast, she took up the work of preparation for departure, at the point where arrangements for the ball had interrupted it.

Mammy, too, offered something of a problem. She was immersed in gloom because of Virginia's trouble and Doris's imminent journey. In the family discussions it had been decided that she was scarcely strong enough to endure the long trip to the North. Of the servants only Desdemona and Julian were to go. This weighed heavily on the old nurse, and Doris tried hard to comfort her. Had the old woman's grief been less acute, Doris, herself might have yielded to depression. It was indeed a tragic time for both of them, for never since the girl's birth had they been separated longer than a few days at a time.

Doris sought relief in the little studio built for her in a corner of the grounds. With a northern exposure; free from shadowing trees, but prettily embowered in flowering shrubs not high enough to shut away its light; shingled with hewn cypress, which, in two years' exposure to the weather, had come to look almost like frosted silver; charmingly designed, the studio gleamed in the midst of flowers and greenery, a veritable gem of beauty, the scene of many happy hours before her easel.

Mammy, her eyes swollen from much weeping, soon appeared with a light wrap. The day was far from chill, but her sense of service was the dominant motive of her existence, and her "Miss Doris" was soon to be beyond the reach of it.

"Bettuh wrop dis 'roun' yo', honey," she advised, with a brave effort to disguise her grief.

"It's as warm as toast, to-day," said Doris; but she took the wrap and smiled at the old woman. It was a little difficult to keep back the tears. Of course, she did not know about the ceaseless vigil of the night beside Virginia's couch, and this morning Mammy seemed so infirm.

"Seems like it nevuh ain't real wahm, no mo', like it was wunst, yeahs ago," was the old woman's comment.

"Stay here with me, Mammy. I'll work on your portrait."

This was the most ambitious one of many pictures of

her devoted old attendant which the young artist had attempted—a wonderful conception of the subject's dream of her own self. Mammy in her youth, had been the belle of a plantation, and her vanity never had lessened. Doris was planning to present this portrait to her, just before her own departure.

That childishness of mind which is especially an attribute of the old southern darkey, had, in Mammy's case, found its most characteristic exhibition in connection with this picture, as Doris, understanding her completely, had felt sure it would. With decided ability the young artist had depicted on the canvas precisely what the dear, aged woman most wished herself to be—not young, exactly, but very far from old.

It was an extremely formal portrait, and showed Mammy without a wrinkle on her face, dignified of mien, gorgeously appareled in a gown the like of which had not existed in this world, but which had been devised for illustrative purposes during many a long conference between the artist and the sitter; it gave Mammy's hair a raven gloss and only a slight curl, no kink; the pictured skin was an extraordinary olive—painted with a color mixture which had been prepared beneath Mammy's careful supervision and frequently revised upon the insistent plea that maybe it was "jus' a teeny mite too brack." The old negress dearly loved to pose while Doris worked upon this wonderful creation: it might well have been completed long ago, had not the painter understood this, and seen to it that the work was long drawn out.

But there was another portrait of which Mammy knew nothing. The artist had worked surreptitiously on it whenever Mammy went to sleep upon the model's stand. It expressed the best of the young painter's ability, and was a really worthy likeness of the fond and faithful companion of her babyhood and youth. In this, she had put forth her utmost effort to place upon the canvas a record of dear Mammy Rose exactly as she was, with no exaggerations, save, perhaps, those born of love—an excess of that kindly glow which really illuminated Mammy's face whenever she was with her, possibly a little increase in the snowiness of the white aureole of wool which ringed the strong but wholly simple, deeply lined and wonderfully loving countenance.

She was working on the first and formal portrait when the visitors arrived, for Mammy had not yet sunk off to slumber in her high-backed, easy chair.

They were Judge Marston and his guests, Miss Chapman and her brother. Their coming was a great delight to Mammy, who was proud beyond all limit of the fact that Doris cared to paint her portrait, and of the nature of the portrait which she painted. But, of course, she rose, curtsying, pretending readiness to leave the model-stand, although she had been almost upon the point of dropping off into her usual slumber.

The Judge was a bit annoyed at finding Doris busy upon this particular task. He knew about the portraits —who among them did not? He enjoyed, as much as anyone, the little joke in them, but he had been anxious that the Chapmans this morning should witness something more expressive of the artist's real ability. He was too considerate of her, however, and even of old Mammy, to complain, and, at the first opportunity after the greetings and Doris's welcome to his friends, he took them aside and explained matters to them. Mammy, in the meantime, settled back with fine pride into the attitude of rigid grandeur which she was wont to hold upon the model-stand until the sheer weariness of her old joints made her relax.

Doris did not wish to stop work for the morning, if she could avoid it without discourtesy, because the time of her departure was so close at hand, and the real portrait of the aged colored woman was not quite complete. She explained this to the party hurriedly, outside, and then again took up her brushes, while they sat about her, carrying on their conversation in low voices, as she had carefully suggested.

The drone of those low voices, the heat in the low building, the weariness of her vigil at Virginia's side through the long night, soon set Mammy nodding, despite the presence of the strangers; and when she slept soundly, Doris, with extraordinary care to avoid waking her, drew from a safe place of concealment, the real portrait of her ancient nurse.

At the first sight of it Judge Marston's face broke into smiles of pride and real appreciation, and, in pantomime, he called the visitors' attention to its undoubted excellencies. Even Jane Chapman, who, plainly, was not by nature an enthusiast, gave it approval grudgingly. Her brother in its praise would have been emphatically approving had not Doris stopped his outburst with a smiling protest and an upraised warning hand.

It was just as the artist had actually made the final brush mark upon this work of weeks, that Mammy stirred uneasily, with that absurd preliminary snort which ever meant that she would soon awaken.

Doris hastily hid the one upon which she had been working and substituted for it the other canvas. The sequestered portrait was not a caricature, but brought out fully, with tender understanding and love, the kind simplicity of the old face; but she would not have had Mammy see it for the world. She was hard at work upon the formal portrait when her old nurse roused completely.

"Huh," said Mammy, embarrassed by the thought that she had yielded to her weariness in the presence of the visitors, "mos' asleep, I wuz. How yo' gittin' on wid dat dere pork-rate, honey?"

"Mammy, it really is finished!" said Doris, with enthusiasm, partly assumed and partly genuine. "I don't believe there is another thing to do to it. I am so glad to have completed it before I go!"

"And it's splendid, Mammy," Judge Marston smilingly assured her.

"Perfect!" said George Chapman, with enthusiasm.

Doris noticed, without giving it much thought, that Jane did not join in the praiseful chorus. Her brother also saw this, and seemed chagrined by it.

"Don't you think so, Jane?" he asked.

"Oh, quite," she answered. "Quite, I am sure." But Doris noted that her lip curled slightly.

It curled more definitely ere they left the studio, for George showered almost fulsome praise on the young artist, as, now that Mammy's somnolence was over and it was safe for them to move about, she showed them other bits of work.

"George," Jane said, severely, when they had left the studio and she had a moment's private speech with him as they passed toward the house, "you'll turn that young girl's head."

He looked at her with something surprisingly like real annoyance, and then laughed. "Jane," he answered solemnly, "I am afraid she has turned mine, already."

"George Chapman!" said his sister, definitely shocked.

For him to speak a word in praise of any woman, had filled her with apprehension ever since he had attained a marriageable age. His marriage certainly was not included in her plans for their joint future. The mere thought of a young sister-in-law distressed her beyond measure.

When he announced, the following day, that they would travel northward with the Marquis party, she was much disquieted, but there was a determined look upon his face, not often there, which warned her that a protest would be futile.

Doris's voice was choked with sobs, when she bade farewell to Mammy, and with eyes winking back the tears, ran swiftly down the veranda steps, to spring into the waiting motor.

"Don't come down, dear," she called back across her shoulder, mindful of the unusual "mis'ry" in Mammy's "laigs" that morning.

"S'pose Ah's gwine to let yo' staht off away f'um home widout Ah tucks yo' in?" said Mammy. "Ain't gwine have yo' ketchin' col' befo' yo' leaves de place, honey."

And so, though the late summer day was almost insufferably hot, Doris, submitting with a grateful little smile and brimming eyes, left the grounds, wrapped carefully in every robe which Mammy could lay hands upon. She did not venture to unwrap them until the motor was well down the road and out of sight even of the glimpse of roof which was the last sign of the old home which she could see upon her journey out into the world.

Her final sight of Mammy showed the faithful creature as she raised her arms in a despairing gesture of unutterable woe, and, heart-broken, turned to sink upon the veranda steps. Doris's eyes were shining with not wholly uncontrolled tears, until, in the big train-shed in the city, she found herself surrounded by a group of laughing young folk, come to wish the best loved of their number Godspeed on her journey.

Arthur was among these, as a matter of course, and the flowers which almost filled her section in the sleeping-car, were largely gifts from him. On the outskirts of the crowd, Northrop Reese was hovering, evidently most unhappy. He did not try to penetrate the seething, youthful group which clung closely about her, so she made her way to him and took his hand, her heart filled with sympathetic understanding and pity for the conscience-stricken boy.

"I hope you will have every possible success and all the good times on the list," she declared as she smiled at him forgivingly.

He was standing, gazing dully after the departing train, when she drew her head in from the window, after the last wave of her hand at the young friends who had formed so large a part of the delightful life which, she reflected, she was leaving, possibly, forever.

The long day on the train would have been intensely wearisome, if the traveling party had been less complete; as it was, the trip probably bored no one, but

Jane, whose worry increased with every passing moment. Upon one occasion, it even drove her to open declaration that she wished her brother smoked. As her previous objection to this vice had been rather notable, he looked at her in some astonishment, and asked her why she had so suddenly lost her aversion for the habit. She did not answer him; it remained for Desdemona, who, wondering at everything she saw, still had attention for the smallest detail of the "white folks'" actions, to probe the real secret of the northern lady's strange remark. The maid was talking at the time to Julian, whose attendance to the party's comfort was an insult which the porter of their car deeply resented.

"Ah'll tell yo' why dat ol' maid wishes dat her clammy brothuh wuz a smokuh," she confided.

"What's de reason?" he inquired.

"It 'ud sometimes take him away f'um ouah Miss Doris," she explained.

The matter of the family's residence during the years when Doris was to be at college, was finally decided while the journey was in progress. A general removal to the college town had been planned, at first, but a letter from the college president had hinted that it sometimes seemed a good thing for the students to be separated from their families and home-surroundings during the working years of college life. This had appealed to Colonel Marquis, but his wife had hesitated. Now, she yielded, to the not unmixed delight of Doris. The thought of new scenes and new faces was appealing, but it also was a little terrifying when she reflected upon being left alone among them. However, the entire experience was too absorbing—and delightful—to let her apprehensions become really acute.

Judge Marston had decided, earlier, that a northern year would benefit Virginia, whose sudden change from bright, exuberant vitality, to saddened, listless inanition, amazed and alarmed him, and he had settled on hotel life for them; Colonel and Mrs. Marquis now resolved to take a house, and, to Jack's inexpressible delight, to start him at once on preparation for Columbia.

In accordance with these various decisions, only Jack and his mother went upstate to the sleepy college-town with Doris when she started to matriculate. They remained at a nearby hotel till she was comfortably settled in the sunny room allotted to her and another student in an ancient gray-stone building swarming with lovely, happy girls.

CHAPTER VIII

"But, my *dear*!" Miss Brush exclaimed, as she gazed at Doris's work after her first week in the art-class. "You must have had some training."

Doris flushed before the praise. When she had been put at drawing casts, she had not murmured. She had drawn casts for a year at New Orleans, before she had been admitted to a private life-class, but had not dreamed that such work would give her real advantage over all these other brilliant girls, by whom she now found herself surrounded. There was a certain poise about these northerners, a glitter in their talk which had at first impressed her mightily with their superiority; their cleverness had made her rather humble. Now it was with distinct surprise that she saw Miss Brush lingering above her work much longer than over that of any of the others, and saw upon her face and heard from her lips, such unqualified expressions of approval.

"Yes; I've had a little training," she admitted.

"You must go into a life-class. Your time would be wasted, now, on casts."

"Really, how lovely!"

"Come with me," she was invited, and, before she knew exactly what was happening, she had been led into the Presence.

The Presence was no less than Miss Devine, the President, whom some girls called, in pique (and private)' Miss De-vil (with strong accent on the final syllable), and some, more fortunate, denominated Miss Div-ine. It was to the latter name that Doris leaned from the first moment, for, with that democracy which made her short reign famous among the reigns of all the Presidents of Welleslar, Miss Devine obligingly laid down the fancy-work with which she sought occasional relaxation from the trials of managing some hundreds of young angels, and joined Miss Brush in an immediate pilgrimage to the region of the "Junk Shop," which was what irreverents had dubbed the plaster-cast room of the art school.

Much less demonstrative than the art-instructor, she still showed real surprise at sight of the large, charcoal drawing which Miss Brush pointed out as that of Doris. "Ah," she said, *"Ah!* Very good *indeed*, my dear; oh, *very* good."

It was at that moment Doris's nickname had its birth in the impulsive brain of a young class-mate, who, toiling near, was the recipient of no such praise.

"You would have thought she was a little female Michael Angelo," she indignantly declared to the other girls, that night.

"We'll call her 'Mike' then," one of them suggested, and thus it came about.

At first Doris did not know exactly what to make of this. She had not been thrown in company with girls so free and unrestrained. She had rather a bad night of it, after the whole class had, one by one, from time to time, addressed her pleasantly as "Mike." She wondered if they might be making game of her because they did not like her; she began to have that feeling—most tragic to a girl or boy away from home among strange young people—that she was really an outsider, and that she did not belong with them, and never could.

But next day a room-mate was assigned to her, in the person of a slim brunette named Lillian Spencer, who was rather fond of self-analysis, and, therefore, mentioned, thrice in that brief day, that on various occasions she had felt "mixed emotions."

"Don't you mean mixed pickles, dear?" one of the girls inquired, winking at the others—and to Doris's vast delight, including her among them, which gave her a fine sense of fellowship and of "belonging." Lillian gazed at them, her lips parted in completely voiceless wonderment, but from that moment she was known as "Pickle-lily."

This gave "Mike" much comfort.

"Well," Doris told Lillian with a fine philosophy, "if you can stand it to be 'Pickle-lily,' I can surely stand it to be 'Mike'—begorry!"

The reply brought forth a scream of laughter, which became applause, and did wonders toward enshrining "Mike" in the young hearts there assembled.

"Was it worrying you, dear?" asked one of her new friends, who might have been tormentors. "The President of last year's senior class was called 'The Ape' by everyone who truly loved her."

Thus Doris's college-life began, and after that, she had little time for worries. Certain of her studies were absurdly easy for her. English and the languages, civil-government, literature and logic, she found simple, even fascinating; but in the realm of mathematics she floundered hopelessly.

"The brilliant artist, young Mike Marquis, who is in our midst," the college paper said, one day, "is worrying herself slim about the problem of how many girls Room Sixteen held yesterday, when two came in to visit two who normally were there. Two and two make four, dear. You will find it in the logarithms table at the back of your Greek dictionary."

She read this gibe with flaming cheeks, and, for a moment, after she had read it, her white teeth were set firmly, and the thought ran in her mind that in the future she would "cut" "Pen" Haslam, who, she knew, had been responsible for it; but she did not make this sad mistake. Instead, she caricatured her vividly for the next art-show in the basement of Big Hall, and had a most satisfactory and sweet revenge.

But she was tender-hearted to a degree which puzzled some of the young female savages enrolled at Welleslar. Looking at "Pen," conscience stricken, as the latter stood with wrinkled brow and gradually flushing cheeks before the awful portrait, Doris suddenly ran to her and put her arms around her neck.

"Pen, dear," she exclaimed contritely, "I never would have done it if you hadn't really been such a tremendous, raving, beauty."

"Pen" looked at her and smiled. "Were you thinking I felt cut up over it?" she asked.

"For a moment, I thought possibly you might."

"Well, Mike, me little Irish darlint," "Pen" replied, "I might have been just such an idiot if you had not come up to pour these honeyed words upon my wounds. Run up to my room after all is over. I'm going to make fudge, illegally."

When the end of the first year came, Doris had made a record in everything except mathematics, and had passed by half a point in that. In pictorial art, she was supreme. The girls begged for her caricatures, and her portrait of Miss Brush in the annual exhibition of the Pen and Paint Club, sometimes locally known as the "Pig-Pen and Fresh Paint Club," an organization of the students of the various art-courses, attracted "Prexy" so that she begged for it—almost on her knees, according to the sworn report of "Pickle-lily."

Every girl selects some one instructor, in her college life, to worship beyond reason, and Doris chose Miss Brush as her divinity. She bowed before the august "Prexy" with respect and awe; metaphorically, she cast her arms around Miss Brush's neck with adoration.

And Miss Brush, who also was emotional, as artists ever are, loved her in return, with real devotion, predicting great things for her; even going to the length of writing to her parents a long letter, telling them that Doris's art-work must not be abandoned when her college days were over, because, if this occurred, the world of painters in America would lose in her a bright and shining star.

Her parents, her grandfather and Virginia, were considering this recently received letter when she came upon them, the first night of vacation, on the veranda of the handsome Newport cottage of which Judge Marston had secured the lease for a term of years exactly corresponding to the years which Doris was to spend in college.

"And she doesn't seem puffed up with pride, at all," Jack mused, as he gazed speculatively at her.

"Prithee, lad," said Doris, looking at him with those high, superior graces which a maid who goes to college may exhibit toward a brother who has had one year in "prep," "why should I not be haughty? But what is the especial matter which has come to your attention, now?"

Her mother handed her Miss Brush's letter.

"The *darling*!" cried the girl, with delightfully flushed cheeks and misty eyes. Then, with that charming earnestness of manner which had developed in the college year and helped to make the girls adore her: "She suah is good to me!"

Her father, looking at her with those slightly puzzled eyes with which a parent studies the development of children who have been long away from home, burst into laughter. "But isn't everyone?" he asked.

Doris nodded brightly, throwing him a kiss. "What do you hear from dear old Mammy?" she inquired. "I've written to her, printing all the words, so that Amanda Jane could read the letters to her, but, of course, no one has answered me, and all the news I've had has come from you."

"What she calls her 'mis'ry' is no better," Mrs. Marquis answered. "I had rather hoped that we might send for her to come North to us, but it would be unwise, I fear."

"When I waken, mornings, I'm always so acutely disappointed because she isn't there to tell me that the sun is shining! and I've not stopped missing her at night, a bit."

"Why don't you ask about the boys? Armsby, for example?" Jack inquired, and grinned. He was at that age when instinctively he felt more or less disposed to tease.

But Doris's new-found poise was proof against the slightest sign of confusion. "Why, yes, how is he?"

"I assumed you had forgotten that such a chap existed?"

"The name, somehow, seems familiar to me," Doris answered, puckering her brows. Then laughing, "But you haven't told me how he is."

"Bully; and he's coming North. He's coming on the yacht."

"How very nice!" This with complete, unruffled calm. "And who has heard from—" she continued carefully, inquiring for all her other southern friends.

It was not until she learned that Northrop Reese was doing rather badly; that two of her girl friends were soon to marry; together with all the details of a Mardi Gras romance in which a third had been concerned, that she inquired for Stoddard Thornton.

Her father's face grew grave. "Poor lad!" said he. "I hear from him occasionally, and he always asks to be remembered to you. He's fighting hard to win against big odds, as he has been since he first took up his burden."

"What is he doing?" To her surprise, it was only with an effort that she made the question seem entirely casual.

"He won the marbles for a public building in some western city in an open competition. This winter, I believe, he plans to work, in New York city. I do hope——"

The arrival of Judge Marston and George Chapman here interrupted talk of Stoddard.

The Judge's guest remained with him two weeks. He even came again before vacation days drew to an end, and Doris had to hurry back to Welleslar. His devotion was complete, although so unassuming that it scarcely claimed the family's notice; only Doris felt entirely aware of it, and wondered whether she was really pleased or bored by his attentions. She decided, in her analysis of him, that he was somewhat colorless, but that she rather liked him, nevertheless. "There's no commotion in this man's devotion, but still, it's not entirely unpleasant," she wrote Pickle-lily. And he kept herself, her mother, and Virginia constantly supplied with flowers.

The change in poor Virginia was the one sad note in the vacation, which was continually crowded with the most charming and satisfying episodes. To the other members of the family this change was not so marked; to Doris, whose last memories of her, except for the few busy and confused days following her party, and immediately before the journey to the North, were of a gay, vivacious girl, it was most apparent, and proved exceedingly distressing. Doris did not understand it, but refrained instinctively from asking questons, even of her mother, and never mentioned Retlew Baron's name. It made her heart yearn toward Virginia, though, even more affectionately than it had before. She spent many hours with her, always showing sympathy by means of small caresses and continual little services.

Virginia's love for her was manifested more plainly than it ever had been. Especially she watched Doris with large, shadowy, almost worried eyes, when she was surrounded by adoring boys, as she was very frequently. This puzzled Doris not a little, and once, when both George Chapman and Arthur (who had arrived, yacht, motor-car and all) were calling, Virginia's regard of her and them, from a half-lighted corner of the broad, rug-strewn veranda, was so unwavering, so almost uncanny in its alert intentness, that Doris asked her, later, if she disliked either of the visitors.

Virginia started, as if someone had surprised her in a secret. "Dislike them? No," she answered. "I was only wondering——"

"Wondering what, dear?"

"Oh . . . nothing . . . really."

"Aunt Virginia is so strange, sometimes," said Doris, later, to her mother.

"She isn't very happy," Mrs. Marquis answered; and Doris, noting some sign of restraint in her reply, made no further comments.

.   .   .   .

"Pickle-lily" had the carpet up and an incredible rug upon the floor of their joint room when Doris reached the dormitory early in September. Doris looked at the new gorgeousness with speechless joy.

"Has Mr. Rockefeller left ten millions to endow Welleslar with rugs? Or am I having pipy visions?" she inquired.

"No; he still confines his generosity to co-ed institutions. Ours is not oil-burning." Pickle-lily answered, very gravely—but did not continue the explanation. Plainly she wished to be questioned further.

"Then where . . . how . . . who . . . eh?"

"It was a little gift from an admirer," Pickle-lily granted nonchalantly.

"A . . . a . . . which? From . . . what?" Doris, with her fascinated gaze upon the glories of the Oriental carpet, was unable to express herself with fluency or grammar.

"A gift," said Pickle-lily.

"Go on, please, very slowly and distinctly, so that I may clearly understand each syllable. Don't nibble at your words. E-nun-ci-a-tion is—I am consumed by curiosity. I have only gifts of flowers and candied fruit to tell about. Oh, yes, there were some salted peanuts, too. But no admirer gave *me* any frabjious rug. Hurry, child. Can you not see how I suffer?"

"It was a gift," said Pickle-lily.

"You said that before, dear. And I know the man. We had him in mythology, last term. You are referring, I suppose to Mr. Croesus, late of Mount Olympus, or some foreign place like that. Fancy! That ge-or-ge-ous rug a gift!"

"No, it wasn't Mr. Croesus; it was an Armenian." Thus Pickle-lily gave occasion for wild dreams of romance.

"The king of that domain, of course."

"I don't believe Armenia has kings. At any rate, if he is king he didn't mention it."

"But still, he gave you . . . that!"

"Well," said Pickle-lily weakly, "he said, at any rate, that at the price it was a gift, and nothing else, when my dear nunkie bought it for me, 'cause I am a real dood dirl. He swore that it was just like giving it away to take so little money for it."

"You are a fraud, of course; but how much did your nunkie pay for it?"

"Little one, I dare not tell you till the gym-medico has pronounced you free from cardiac disturbances and sound in wind and limb."

"I'm not free from cardiac disturbances. I'm so in love with our new rug my heart throbs awf'ly. But I was having dreams of invitations to a country-place in Zenda, as soon as you were married."

"No," said Lilian, "I believe I shall invite you to Milwaukee. You see, I met this summer, the most stunning thing! He looks just like the clothing advertisements in the back of Munsey's. He——"

"Say no more, I pray!"

"It was really he, not beer, that made Milwaukee famous."

"Milwaukee! How prosaic! A man came up to Newport to see *me*, in the most graceful yacht! He——"

Miss Brush came, interrupting them. "Doris, dear," said she, "I wonder if you'll really pass any of your exams if I let you serve on the Insane Committee of this year's High Jinks."

The "Insane Committee," it must be explained, was that which had in charge the art exhibit of the annual frolic in the vaulted basement of the central building, known to the students as Low Room, High Hall.

CHAPTER IX

Miss Mohonk, instructor in political economy, was known as "Votes" to the student contingent of college-life, but Doris, noting the excitement of her eye when it was searching for some suffering girl to call upon, whom she could feel quite certain had not given the subject of the recitation any study whatsoever; observing, too, her keen apprehension lest she should not find a victim who would fail when questioned; bearing in mind her picturesque, unusual waddle; considering her wild flights of rhetoric, and more than all, impressed by "Mohonk" as a name, re-christened her, in the privacy of Pickle-lily's exclusive company.

"Mohonk—honk, honk!" she murmured, as this thought was born in her unusually active brain. "Honk —honk! Wild duck!"

"She's *not* a duck," said Pickle-lily, with somewhat savage emphasis.

"But you'll admit she frequently is wild, dear."

"She did dreadful things to me, to-day, revealing to the world my ignorance of civil government and the duties of the ladies of the South Dakota Legislature in a manner which will shame me till I die."

"Wild goose, then," Doris tentatively suggested.

"Oh, perfect!"

The trouble is, about such matters, in a female college, that they cannot be kept wholly quiet. The name

103

for Miss Mohonk spread through the glad ranks of the girls like thrilling news from home; so, when Jane Chapman went to Welleslar, on a visit to her old and close friend, Miss Mohonk, that lady had some sad, sad tales to tell of the young southern student.

Miss Chapman was not much astonished and made this fact quite clear. The truth was, that Jane's jealousy of Doris had increased with every day since her brother George first had seen the young girl.

Thus, when Doris was adventuring through her second year at Welleslar, she found a hostile spirit on the platform of the classroom of political economics. She did not at all understand why this should be abroad, and talked it over with Lillian, late one night, while their one electric bulb was muffled in a rain-coat, so that it threw its rays only upon the printed pages, which the girls pretended to be studying, with heads close together to save lighted area, and therefore minimize the chances of discovery. Neither she nor Pickle-lily suspected that George Chapman could have had aught to do with Miss Jane Chapman's faint but unmistakable enmity. As they talked it over in cautious whispers, the rubber in the rain-coat slowly melted from the heat of the electric bulb.

"Moreover, I promised I would organize this college into busy bands of suffragettes for her," Doris said in bitter, discontented tones.

Lillian sat back in her chair, and although her face was now in darkness, smiled a smile so satisfied that Doris, though she could not see it, felt it to be there.

"Well then, my dear Watson," Lillian exclaimed triumphantly, at length, "is it possible that you do not comprehend the motive for this crime?"

"I confess, Mr. Holmes, that I do not."

"She is mad as hops because you didn't organize them."

"Mr. Holmes, can it be possible!" Doris was the one to sit back in her chair, this time.

"That might be it," Doris finally admitted. "I supposed the promise was enough to prove to her that I am crazy for the ballot. I would never have believed that she would be so foolish as to think I really would organize those clubs. I haven't any very clear idea what woman's suffrage is about anyway. Have you?"

"I've not the faintest notion in the world but we both know what clubs are."

"Would any of the dear girls join such a silly thing?"

"They all would if they thought it might help you in days of trouble."

"Let's organize, right now," said Doris. "To take Time by the bangs is the first symptom of real progress."

"Bangs? Bangs? Where have I heard that word before, I wonder?"

"In 'The Life and Times of Cleopatra,' by Charles Dana McCutcheon, illustrated with real etchings made upon the pyramids by P. Rameses Gibson, or some name like that. Bangs were things the Ptolemy ladies wore upon their foreheads, so called because of the explosive effect such hair-dressing had upon the hearts of men."

"And how can one take Time by the bangs?"

"By organizing, here and now, the first Woman's Suffrage Club of Welleslar."

"Suffrage or suffering?"

"Both, dear. I shall be president. You shall be vice-president, Molly Meadows shall be secretary, and our generous little friend, Tight-wadine McCullough, she shall be the treasurer. She's safest, for she never treats and doesn't care for sweets."

"What shall be the object of the gay association?"

"To impress Miss Chapman with the fact that I have kept my word unflinchingly, in the face of dreadful odds. I wish her to believe that I would die for suffrage. Votes for woman, from this moment, are the chief ambition of my sweet young life."

" 'Tis well. And when shall this club meet?"

"It is in session now. Do you agree to these things?"

"Violently, and with my hand upon this German grammar."

"Then, the Club is now adjourned until we get a chance at some few other faithful spirits on the morrow."

" 'Votes' will be delighted."

"You must call her the Wild Goose when you are here, behind locked doors; it will help to make us happy."

"Doris, dear, please tell me what you are really meaning to do?"

Doris daintily and silently munched fudge, thinking deeply, meanwhile. Lillian did not question her insistently. She knew that in her own good time the oracle would speak, and she was rather happy, as she waited, for the light was concentrated upon Doris and she always loved to watch her—to try to pick flaws in her and completely fail. Doris's beautifully delicate hands toyed with a fudge-spoon, and the odor of the melting rain-coat had not yet become apparent.

"They are slender, tapering, divinely white, and graceful," Lillian mused.

"Are you speaking about votes for women?"

Lillian made no answer, but let her eyes stray from the hands up to her chum's amused and smiling face.

"She is flower-like, delicate and dainty. Her arms are wonderful, and her feet would rattle in a fairy's shoe. But oh, those slender, tapering, divinely white and graceful hands!" said Lillian. "Mike, heaven made you for exactly the same reason that an artist paints a picture—the mere love of doing something beautiful!"

"Pickle-lily," Doris answered, "do be serious. Endeavor to be sane. You yourself, are beautiful of mind and person, and your lovely eyes see charm where no charm really exists. We were talking of Miss Chapman."

"Gadzooks, odds bodkins, and what ho!" said Lillian. "Why invite me to consideration of a tragedy when there is a summer-dream like you at hand? And you haven't told me yet what you really want to do."

"I'm not quite certain," Doris answered. "But Miss Chapman has a brother——"

"Murder will out!" cried Lillian—very carefully.

"I rather like him."

"A-h-h."

"Not very much—just rather."

"I am not so deeply interested, now."

"He likes me very much, I fancy."

"The subject once more becomes fascinating."

"And that is why she is inclined to scratch my eyes out."

"Such lovely little eyes!"

"She doesn't care for any lovely eyes, except her

brother's, and they're not lovely—only cold and interesting—except sometimes when they are not cold."

"How paradoxically entrancing!"

"And so—you see——"

"I see."

A band of sweet, but not sincere young women, self-dubbed the "Welleslar Woman's Suffrage Cohort," was organized the following day, and when Miss Chapman came, within the month, to call on the Wild Goose, they assured her that they doted upon votes. The Wild Goose talked about them to her friend, with not a little pride.

"I'll venture that our little southern girl is not one of them," Miss Jane asserted confidently.

"Upon the contrary, my dear Jane, she organized them."

Miss Chapman almost doubted her friend's word, but, finally, deciding that the information might be accurate, elaborately called on Doris in her room. A friendly scout preceded her in wildest haste and gave Doris time to put away a chafing-dish, a pink shirt-waist, a powder-box and puff and, most carefully of all, a water-color portrait of George Chapman, which she had produced from memory to satisfy her room-mate's curiosity.

"My dear Miss Marquis," Jane exclaimed, "I am so gratified to hear that you are really interested in the future progress of our sex."

"Oh, very deeply," Doris granted, wishing fervently meantime that that portion of the sex, consisting of Jane Chapman, would take up its progress toward the haunts of the Wild Goose, conveying from her own immediate vicinity those small, keen, gimlet eyes.

"I shall send you all the latest literature upon the subject."

"How sweet and good of you! We are so bothered here, to get improving reading." (Any girl who read the literature advised by the instructors would have needed days of forty hours apiece.) "I shall be so glad to get some books on suffrage!"

The Welleslar Suffrage Cohort grew apace, as time passed. Its various young lady members were unanimous in declaring that nowhere else in college could they invariably have such ripping times as in the room of Mike and Pickle-lily, and that nothing offered such delicious details for discussion as the fudge and suffrage mixture which was ladled out there.

The young ladies' knowledge of the suffrage question did not materially increase, perhaps, but their bills for sugar, chocolate, molasses and shelled nuts did, and they achieved remarkable attacks of indigestion. Miss Chapman became an almost constant visitor at Welleslar, and the Wild Goose frequently addressed little meetings in the now busy room of the two chums.

Everything, apparently, went well. Miss Chapman winced whenever Doris sent a message to her brother George, but evidently decided that a maid so full of real ambition to advance her sex and to preserve her country could do nothing really wrong. It was only when, through a sad inadvertence, Wilhelmina Vandergilt (well known as "Guilty Billy"), revealed the fact that never at a meeting, so far as she had noted, had the word "suffrage" been mentioned without giggles, while fudge and boys were ever taken seriously, that the Wild Goose began to dream of treachery and communicated her suspicions to Miss Chapman. Miss Chapman instantly began to worry about brother George, and Doris knew it and was very wrath.

The last term of a certain year was drawing to a close, and with it the college life of Doris, when she originated the idea of an art exhibition in the basement. It was necessary to raise money, in some way, for an infants' home to which the senior class traditionally sent an annual contribution, and no suggestion so clever as this occurred to anybody else.

Her group of intimates was much amazed when Mike announced that she would paint, for the great exhibition, a portrait of Miss Chapman, and, for a time, it was believed that the hostility, which all had known blazed in her heart toward the Wild Goose's intimate, had finally expired.

This impression was strengthened when it was discovered that Miss Chapman sat, every day, for half-an-hour, while Doris painted busily, in one of the big, vacant rooms, once prepared to house an expected curio collection which, after all, had not been bequeathed to the Institution. A favored few were bidden to inspect the work, and all who saw it called it wonderful; and incidentally (having seen the portrait privately with Doris, who had had a chance to talk to them while they were viewing it), went from its presence with the knowledge, imparted under strictest seal of secrecy, that Miss Chapman had her "cap set" for Professor Adzit, instructor in the higher mathematics.

"He doesn't know a thing about it," Lillian argued.

"He doesn't know a thing about a thing except the higher mathematics," Doris answered. "If he knew a thing about a thing other than the higher mathematics, could he do a thing like falling in love with anything like dear Miss Chapman?"

Lillian looked at her with dazed admiration. "I don't think he could," she answered.

When she had been fined a bottle of vanilla extract (the fudge flavoring was almost gone, and Doris's money was exhausted, for it was but a week before remittance day) Doris went on very gravely:

"I shall have to put a stop to it forever."

"A stop to what?"

"Her young romance. I rather like old Adzit."

"And how can you put the kibosh on her young romance?"

"I am a magician. Stop! Look! Listen! Do you remember that we lost the new tea-strainer? Wait! I'll find it through my magic, and you'll understand how very magical I am."

"If you find it, I will swear your name is Madame Houdin-Hermann."

Mike arose and made some passes over a large band-box which contained Pickle-lily's newest hat. She was always having marvelous new hats, to the excited envy of the other maidens. That rug-producing relative had further solved the chemistry of maiden's souls, discovering that hats, also, form a precipitant of amazing quantities of love for uncles.

"If you will look into that band-box," Doris said, with a triumphant air, as if her magic had won victory over mighty difficulties, "you will find that by my wondrous art, I have produced the missing tea-strainer, and caused it to appear inside the lining of your newest hat."

"You awful villain!" Pickle-lily shrieked, her brows intensely corrugated with keen apprehension. "If it dripped on it! Oh, if it dripped on it and stained that baby blue! You'll need all your magic for your own salvation!"

"It didn't drip on it a drop, dear," Doris reassured her. "I had to hide it rather hurriedly, for I was using it in study hours, and the Troglodyte was at the door." (The Troglodyte, be it understood, was Miss Eliza Spence, professor of geology, a favorite at times, but much opposed to too much tea among the girls.) "I wiped it on my best silk stockings."

"Where were your stockings at the time?" Pickle-lily was suspicious.

"Where are my stockings usually, when they are being worn?" asked Doris with some dignity.

The tea-strainer was in the hat, exactly as the conjurer had predicted.

"Now," said Mike, "do you doubt that I am truly magical, and can accomplish the destruction of the schemes of the fierce Wild Goose against the heart and hand of Old Subtract-and-Adzit?" (Which was what the girls occasionally called their deep well-spring of knowledge of the higher mathematics.)

"If you put *him* in my hat, I never *shall* forgive you!"

"He is already hidden in his own abstractions. And therein lies a paradox. It has made him even easier for the Wild Goose's pal to—to——"

"Jolly?" suggested Pickle-lily somewhat timidly.

"Very shocking slang, my dear, but it will do. I shall arouse him from his trance, and prove to him that Jane is a coquette."

"Miss Chapman a coquette!" Pickle-lily sank back on the cosy-corner couch and kicked her heels astonishingly.

"Mind the electric bulbs, dear," Doris urged. "And after you have minded them, and have once more assumed a lady-like position, wait and see, sweet child."

And Pickle-lily waited—for she was obliged to wait whether she wanted to or not. That was one of the most fascinating things about her room-mate.

The night of the Great Art Exhibition was announced in flaming bills, hand-painted in the basement, with lamp-black and vinegar, cheap products, both of them, and therefore possible to the class-funds remaining at that late day of the month. The Ten Cent Store gave credit for a carriage-painter's brush.

Even freshmen were graciously permitted to contribute to the Great Art Exhibition. Freshmen almost always are permitted to contribute anything which means real work to the enterprises managed by the upper-class girls, at old Welleslar. Upper-class girls are extremely fond of managing, but they are not particularly fond of making contributions.

The exhibition was divided into groups, shown "Plainly," as the bills said, in "Three Separate and Distinct Rooms, All Under One Great Roof, and to be Seen for the Ridiculously Small Admission Fee of Fifty Cents or Half-a-Dollar, to be Devoted to the Clothing of the Poor Upon Fifth Avenue—One of New York's Most Automobiled Slums."

The three groups, the poster added, consisted of "High Art, the Higher Art and Highest Art," and those who did not think the show was worth their money would

"Have Their Criticisms Cheerfully Returned to Them on Application to the Board of Damagers."

The High Art Room was devoted to the portraits of the college founders; and other valuable pictures loaned by members of the faculty, residents of the very cultured little college-town, and various rich alumni of the institution.

The latter, according to a custom which had grown throughout the years, gave great consideration to this exhibition, and sometimes loaned real marvels to the show. There were, for instance, this year, two actual Rembrandts, a Sir Joshua Reynolds, and a "Dutch Girl" by Franz Hals, delivered with the utmost care by tremulous expressmen, accompanied by especial guards supplied by a great surety company.

In the Higher Art Room was discovered by the wandering spectators an exhaustive display of the best work of the year's classes in the college courses, and in the Highest Art Room, were the "fakes."

Here flamboyantly appeared casts from the cast-room, variously decked—as Julius Caesar in a picture-hat, a cigarette between his lips, with gauze smoke wired to it; the Father of our Country, rising from a pedestal upon which a diaphanous shirtwaist had been adroitly buttoned and artistically stuffed; Foxy Grandpa (borrowed from a toyshop) crowned with laurel, and Shakespeare in a Mother-Hubbard, denominated "Ella Wheeler Wilcox." Here also were cartoons by students. Mike's work predominated, consisting of amazing caricatures of her beloved classmates, identified by actual names, which had been drawn at random from a laundry-bag. One end of the room was given over to a "Holy Show

of Sculpture" made up of clothing stuffed and sur-
mounted by amazing heads. Oh, there were many things
there in the Highest Art Room, "and," as Pickle-lily
said, "then some."

It was the favorite among the visitors, and there were
times when the High Art Room held few spectators.

In the "Higher Art" room, where the students' serious
work was shown, there was more interest this year than
usual. Among the multitude of really careful and often
highly meritorious landscapes, portraits and decorations
done by earnest students in the classes of the year, the
work of Doris attracted much attention; some of it drew,
from those who knew, really surprised comment on its
worth. And of her pictures, none occasioned more remark than her portrait of Jane Chapman.

Jane's face, in repose, was rather pleasant—high bred,
somewhat too aquiline, but very delicately featured, and
Doris had not only reproduced, but had accentuated all
its good points, avoiding every shading of expression
not quite admirable, with a true portrait painter's skill
of seeing nothing but the worthy, when at the easel.
She had, herself, carefully arranged the lighting, which
was perfect—the portrait being deeply set in a gold
frame guarded by a rail which kept the spectators at
four feet distance. Jane's eyes were reproduced in an
especially flattering manner, the addition of a bit of
hazel to the steel-gray of their reality giving them a
charm upon the painted canvas which they never had in
life.

Jane herself was utterly delighted. The portrait quite
completed Doris's capture of her heart, which the organization of the Suffrage Club had really begun.

"Its gaze at the spectator is so direct and fearless!" she told Doris as she stood with arm about her, looking at the picture. "It is the sort of undismayed and penetrating contemplation of the world to which I earnestly aspire, but which, because of the great imperfections of my nature, I am sure I have not achieved."

"I tried to make the eyes entirely true," said Doris. "I am glad you like them, but really they fall short of their originals. I worked carefully on their expression; I am sure there is no flattery in it."

But there was something else in it, for, after Jane had passed along, and a new group had gathered, in which Professor Adzit formed the center of a carefully selected and instructed bevy of girls—instructed, but not thoroughly informed—the portrait looked straight in his eyes, with such appeal that it almost embarrassed him.

He had been wondering much about Jane Chapman. He loved dignity in women, and Jane was ever dignified; he loved spirit in the fair sex, and Jane was surely spirited—her talks upon the suffrage question had quite stirred him; he hated all frivolity in women—this being, probably, the strongest of his emotions—and surely Jane was never frivolous.

"There," he was saying to the group of girls about him, some of whom, he had observed with an especial horror, had been smiling rather pleasantly at the fortunate young men there present, "is one whom you young ladies may well emulate. Miss Marquis has with admirable skill depicted in this striking portrait the serenity and calm of a delightful countenance, behind which may be seen no symptom of frivolity. Thought, thought, my dear young ladies—it is thought which makes the world go round, and, in the future, it must largely be the thought of woman."

"Miss Chapman is so sensible!" sighed Lillian. "She is my ideal, but I find it extremely hard to take life seriously."

"Yes," was Mr. Adzit's comment, "it is doubtless hard at times, but life is very serious, and the young girl who is frivolous will miss many, many lessons which, if properly heeded, would be useful to her in her after life. Now observe the study which Miss Marquis has created of Miss Chapman's face. Can you imagine the beautiful woman who is thus depicted, wasting time upon the idle occupations?" ("Idle occupations" was Professor Adzit's favorite paradox.) "Can you imagine her, for instance, neglecting proper study of the higher mathematics, in her college days, for tea-drinking or what you girls call 'fudging'? I certainly cannot. Can you imagine her—I hate to mention this, young ladies, but I have had, as I am required to have, a watchful eye upon some of you, here, this evening—can you imagine Miss Jane Chapman—er—um—flirting?"

None could, and he smiled upon the group with a pleased air.

"Flirting? No!" he said. "She has always had much better things to think about!"

He turned back to regard, once more, with keenest satisfaction, the portrait of the serious Miss Chapman— the portrait of the admirable lady whom he could not think about as ever having flirted.

And as he turned back to regard it, lo! that portrait winked at him three times! Winked saucily, flirtatiously, amazingly!

CHAPTER X

The scandal was not very great; Doris had achieved too many powerful friends among the faculty, and the bars of discipline were always somewhat lowered to the leaders of the Art Exhibition, for its object was so worthy. Certainly much should be forgiven true friends of the orphans. Besides, Miss Chapman was not generally popular with the Institution's heads, neither were these good folk entirely devoid of humor.

Doris's group of pals, who, with Professor Adzit, had been the only ones to witness the extraordinary action of the portrait's eye, remained discreetly silent; Professor Adzit, after all, was really a man, and said nothing. Doris had been certain he would do exactly that.

Careful use of strong adhesive plaster on the back, and fresh paint on the surface of the portrait, concealed the wound through which the eyelid, pulled by a string running down back of the picture to the floor, along it through tiny screw-eyes to the post, and there upward, had given Doris's apparently careless hand an instrument with which to close the eyelid and produce the first half of the wink. A rubber band had yanked the eyelid out of sight again, producing the last half of the operation, and Doris had the canvas backed with other canvas, heavily shellacked, before she forwarded it to the original.

In her ignorance, Miss Chapman smiled, thoroughly

pleased when the portrait, a gift from the young artist, reached her New York residence. She even spoke with high approval of the painting and the painter to her brother George.

"The development of Doris Marquis, my dear George," she said at breakfast, the morning after the arrival of the picture, "under the fine influence of the higher education has been remarkable."

He looked up from his newspaper with a glad smile. His intentions had become concrete. He had definitely decided to make the girl of whom his sister spoke so well the mistress of his home if he could manage it.

.   .   .   .

"Mike," said Lillian, one spring morning, "do you know what's coming?"

"Keep quiet, can't you?" Doris bitterly retorted.

Her head was wrapped in a wet towel; her elbows were firmly planted upon either side of a large book. She was "boning" for examinations, and she had been thus busied through the livelong night.

"I suppose my general appearance indicates that I do *not* know what is coming!" she said pettishly. "No intelligent observer, looking at me, now, would guess, of course, that I am studying like mad for just exactly what *is* coming! The casual mind would not infer from my demeanor and this towel, that I am mighty well aware of what is coming!"

"What strange nick-names some people invent for persons," Lillian mused.

"*Now* what can ail the child?" asked Doris of the rising sun, visible at that moment, through the open casement. "Nick-names? Her mind certainly is wandering!"

"No; I was thinking of the fact that your delightful family are wont to call you their 'Miss Beautiful.' An admirer statuetted you as the 'Goddess of the Garden,' I think you once conceitedly explained. You did not pose for him adorned as you are now, with towels, neither could your eyes have been thus swollen from an effort to make amends at the last moment for four years of idle life. Your tresses could not thusly have been tousled, nor your costume have consisted of an antique pink kimono split into ribbons on the gory fields of pillow-battles."

"Pickles," Mike begged earnestly, "be still, please. You take my mind off logarithms. Of course I know what's coming. Examinations, then *examinations*, followed by EXAMINATIONS! Examinations, dear, are just exactly what are coming."

"Your intellect is immature," said Pickle-lily. "It grasps but a small detail of the whole. The vast, basic fact escapes it wholly, as Miss Prex would say. Examinations, to be sure, are coming; but after them— then what?"

"More of them," Mike responded cheerlessly.

"And then?"

"You repeat things like a parrot! Hush, child," Doris cried. "Hush! But if it will cheer you, I will tell you the glad tidings of what is coming after—if we're lucky. Commencement, and diplomas—perhaps; and applause, maybe; and the end of this long grind—if we are lucky. But it will never come for me, dear—never, never—if **you** don't let me work."

"You must stop work, and get all freshened up," said Pickle-lily, "or they'll know we have been up all night, and chide us.

"There is something coming after the examinations and commencement day, which you apparently have never thought about, although I had imagined, from divers things, which you have said during our four years' association, that you had ever and anon considered it. Life, dear, is coming afterward . . . Ah! . . . LIFE!"

"I feel more like its opposite, this morning."

"Poor child; you look as if you'd been prize-fighting and knocked out. You should have studied steadily throughout the years, and then this 'boning' at the final moment could have been avoided."

"Some pickle-lily comes in bottles," Doris said with a sad glance at her, "and that cannot spout foolishness. You, unfortunately, were not bottled properly, and so inflict your platitudes on me. But you have spoken truly about Life. It's . . . coming! Just wait until I lave my fevered brow, and then we'll snuggle on your lovely rug and carefully discuss the matter. There are a number of grave details in this thing called human life which long have needed some expert attention. Let's settle them. It's Sunday morning. We can cut chapel and lie lazily slumbering when we ought to be at worship. You're letter-perfect on the last word we have studied for four years, and I know just enough so that I may worm through if everything is smooth and fortunate. Anyway, I can't grind any more just now."

This plan was put into operation.

"So there have been three men in your life!" Pickle-lily commented, enchanted, after an hour of somewhat giggly reminiscence.

"Four—two men, two boys," said Mike.

"I like to call all my boys men."

"Four men then," Doris granted. She rather liked to call them "men," herself. It is the way of college-girls.

"Name them again."

"Well, there's Arthur Armsby. He's the handsomest! Pickles darling, if you'd only seen his face that night— so white and rigid, after that terrific battle! Oh . . ."

"I think that was the most romantic thing! Nobody ever fought for me! I——"

Doris had never told anyone but Lillian of the struggle between Northrop Reese and Arthur; but it was one of her pet recollections. The horror of it had not died entirely from her mind, and, often, she found it deeply exciting to recall the stealthy search with Teddy through the night-bound woods, and the events which followed fast upon it.

"It was like a scene upon the stage," she gloried, with a touch of what her friend immediately called "conceit." "And Northrop very nearly killed him!"

"Will they both be here at commencement? Suppose one should kill the other while Miss Prex is at her prayer!"

"Oh, no; Northrop won't be here. Poor boy, I have never heard a word from him since the day I saw him in the railway station at New Orleans."

"Has he committed suicide, do you suppose?" Pickle-lily's eyes were big with her imaginings.

"No; he's working his plantation. Father tells me he's

not very nice, these days. He drinks, and things like that."

"But Arthur is to be here?"

"Yes; but you must call him 'Mr. Armsby.' Don't forget that, please. I have some rights!"

"How very snippy! . . . And the great Jane's brother?"

"Yes, he's coming."

"He's too old for you."

"Why, he's not so very old; and he's enormously good looking and—and eligible. His face is absolutely classical."

Lillian nodded gravely. "I knew it. And I'm jealous —frightfully, because your Arthur's handsome, too. May I call him 'your Arthur'?"

"If you're sure to put in the 'your'."

"Oh; I don't want him. I've got Billie. He's not handsome. He looks like a Chinese mask designed to frighten devils from the Temples of Confucius; but he *is* a *half*-back."

"Isn't it the most extraordinary thing that all your men are—er—such brutal creatures? Half-backs, and on the Yale Baseball Team, and that Harvard person is a champion long-distance runner isn't it?" Doris's face was full of scorn.

"They're not brutes, they're athletes."

"When you marry them, they'll doubtless beat you to a pulp."

"This isn't Turkey," Pickle-lily said indignantly. "And I shall marry only one of them. Besides, can't I fight, myself? What, do you imagine, has been the object of my work upon the basket-ball team all these years?"

"Training for the matrimonial altar? I never once suspected it. You are so far-sighted!"

"Don't let's be amusing," Pickle-lily protested. "Let's get back to pure romance, unmixed with brickbats. You haven't even mentioned your dear Artist-man—the sculpist. I love to hear you tell of him. Tell me the sweet story again, love? I adore it."

Pickle-lily snuggled up as might a child, waiting for a favorite tale.

Now it was rather strange that Doris rarely spoke to her chum of Stoddard Thornton, even in her most confidential, sentimental moments. She loved to rattle on to her of Arthur and George Chapman and all her other admirers, but, somehow, the struggling artist, with his heavy burden, did not seem to her a fitting subject for light chatter. She had not the least idea why this was. But, this morning, dreamy from her lack of sleep, yet in no wise inclined toward slumber, imagination stimulated by reaction from the effort of hard study, she spoke freely.

"Well, once upon a time, a beautiful young girl—oh, she was very beautiful—too lovely for mere words to tell about——"

"You insufferably conceited prig!"

"Yes; am I not? Well, she was standing in a garden, and——"

"I think he must have been the loveliest thing that ever lived to be so stricken by your beauty! And you *are* beautiful, you know. I never seriously deny it. It's only when I'm joking or when I have a grouch."

"I'm not as beautiful as you are!"

"How perfectly absurd! You make me look like a cartoon. But please go on about the statuette!"

"And I haven't heard a thing about him for a whole long year," said Doris, when she had completed her recital.

"I think it's too romantic for words!" her chum exclaimed. "And there's nothing in my life but halfbacks! Oh, I'm simply cheated! I really dote on artists."

"One of your athletes may become a sign painter in after-life, dear," suggested Doris cruelly, and then went to sleep.

She was sleeping rather heavily when Pickle-lily's hand upon her shoulder, shaking her, aroused her.

"Mike," said the disturber, as Doris awoke, "I've just thought of something awful!"

"Wh-what is it?"

"This is our last year together."

Doris sat up suddenly. "Why, so it is!"

"And our last in Welleslar."

"Good gracious!"

"And the last of our—girlhood!"

"Heavens, Pickle-lily!"

"In a month, we shall be—women! Young, no doubt, but nevertheless, women! Girls no longer, Mike."

"I can't—believe it!"

"It just came to me—as suddenly!"

"And, being women, even young, I suppose we shall be forced to cease our frivolings. We shall have to take life seriously."

"Dreadful, isn't it?"

"Unspeakable. No one will make excuses for us on the ground of youth. We shall have responsibilities."

"It sounds almost like an ailment."

"It is one—fatal, sometimes."

"We shall have begun to—age!"

"Don't; you frighten me."

"It's very serious.. What are you going to do about it?"

"There's nothing one can take for it, is there?" begged Mike.

"Nothing except poison, and that's likely to have bad results, I'm told. Oh, yes there is; there's occupation. If the dose is not too large it's said that occupation cures age wonderfully. Have you chosen your vocation?"

"Certainly, my art."

"Oh, no; that will be your avocation. Note the difference. You learned it from Miss Vocabulary."

"Vocation—avocation—yes; there's a difference," mused Doris. "An avocation is a side line; vocation's what you really do. Well, art——"

Pickle-lily smiled, full of extraordinary wisdom. "My dear—you artist—you delight—you—you little villain—art, as I have said, will be your avocation. Your vocation will be boys, for a few years, then men. They will occupy your time to the exclusion of all other things. You won't want them to; they merely will. Let me see your palm."

Doris held her palm out, feigning fear. "If it's too dreadful, keep it dark," she begged.

"I see," said Pickle-lily, "in this palm, cart-loads of fun!"

"You're the kind of fortune-teller I approve of."

"And tremendous stacks of sorrow."

"I shall change my fortune-teller if you talk like that."

"For, you see, you are the kind whom people, when they love, love half to death. I do, myself. And everybody else does. It's all right when it's only girls. Their love is harmless. But when it's boys—excuse me, men—well, then, you see, it is more serious and you're doomed to trouble—trouble—trouble!"

Her eyes were big, her tone was ominous of dreadful things. She sat back on the rug and paused. Presently she continued: "But it will be nothing to the trouble you will give the men. Now stop and think." She feigned to trace the names in Doris's pink, moist palm. "Here's that poor Northrop Reese, with the ham-hands. See, he ends here."

Doris traced the little line where Northrop ended, but was not impressed. "What, at my thumb?"

"He's under it, they all are, and they always will be. But he's out of the reckoning. We'll let him die, or anything he chooses. But see these other twisted lines. I don't know anything in this wide world of palmistry, but if I did, I'd prove to you that these three, all crisscrossed, mixed-up and fighting, are your other slaves—your Arthur, and your Chapman person, and your Stoddard sculptor-man. I——"

"Don't tell me any more, please. You don't even keep me wide awake."

Mike turned over, and endeavored to resume her slumbers. She pretended to, in fact; but really she was thinking of the three who had been named by the young palmist. What—who—how—oh, what did it all matter,

anyway? Examinations were at hand—THE FINALS
—and—then . . .

But, still, there were those three——

.   .   .   .

"Did you get through, do you think?" her room-mate
asked after all was over.

They were extremely neat as far as clothing went,
for the finals were a ceremony, but there were some
pencil smudges upon Doris's cheeks and a blot of ink
upon her nose. The matter was reversed in Lillian's
case—the ink was on her cheeks, the smudge upon her
nose.

"Of course not."

"What did you flunk in?"

"Everything. Did you get through yourself?"

"In 'math,' I think; in nothing else. I may have failed
in 'math.' "

Nervous, worn out, apprehensive, without hope, the
two girls fell into each other's arms, sobbing in unison.

"This cosy-corner fairly drips," said Doris, presently,
"Let's try to find a dry spot."

"Why bother?" Lillian inquired. "It soon would be
afloat."

But no dreaded rap upon their door next morning announced the tragic coming of a proctor with little notes
to tell of failure, and, before they knew it, commencement day had dawned serenely.

.   .   .   .

No member of the Marquis family was missing from
the softly lighted, dim old college chapel, fresh with the
perfume of a thousand roses—roses tied with wide,

white satin ribbon, every bunch of them, almost like a bride's.

Jack, whose freshman year had ended but the day before, believed himself exceeding wise. He regarded the soft femininity of this commencement ceremony with a little pity, but he was forced to the conclusion that college didn't seem to hurt girls' looks much.

Virginia, whom the years had changed remarkably, but whose face no longer bore the sharper tragic traces of her sorrow, sat, sweetly sympathetic, smiling with the soft reflection of the joy which everywhere around them lighted faces, brightened eyes.

Colonel and Mrs. Marquis were both a little tremulous. This mile-stone in their daughter's life was, to them, a very solemn monument, as mile-stones in their children's lives are, ever, to the men and women who have lived, as completely as they had, in their maternal and paternal love.

As Doris stepped upon the flower-banked platform to receive that wondrous thing, the diploma of her finished college education, her mother, who never had doubted for a moment that Doris was the loveliest of this world's creatures, gasped, almost painfully, with new realization of her charm. When she turned to Colonel Marquis, she saw him gazing toward the sweet, white figure on the rostrum with almost fierce intentness, his love plainly magnified into a veritable hunger to have her home with them again.

As he noticed his wife's study of his face, he turned his eyes away to look out of a window at the freshness of the wonderful June day. And she was certain that a shaft of sunlight, entering just then, sparkled, when it reached his cheek, upon a tear. She smiled softly.

But as she turned again to look at Doris's slim young wonder, her own eyes filled, until the image of her darling swam and wavered through a falsifying lens of tears.

CHAPTER XI

At Newport, out of consideration for Virginia's re-
tiring tastes, which the passing years had but confirmed,
Judge Marston had taken a cottage, well separated from
the gayer groups of summer dwellings. Doris's months
there were quiet, uneventful; it was a dream-like period
of readjustment. One of the great cycles of her life had
passed, the next had not begun.

There were few visitors, save certain sailing, golfing,
swimming college-boys, who thronged about Jack for a
time, until he disappeared, returning visits.

Doris's state of mind was illustrated by the astonishingly mature attitude she took toward his young friends.
Plainly she thought of them as charges, rather than associates; and did what she could to entertain them, for
Jack's sake, but gave them little thought.

She rode rarely; sailed almost none; eschewed golf, of
which, at college, she had been a devotee; studied her
elders with a new attention, and more understanding
than they dreamed, and spent much time in meditation
on the rocks, where splendid crevices gave shelter from
the winds, and where the sun was almost as warm as
had been that dear southern sun which seemed, now, a
part of an existence which had ended, ages upon ages
gone.

She was scarcely conscious of her beauty, which had

131

ripened wonderfully. The ability of unaided thought had come upon her unawares, and she reveled in it.

Only twice was she aroused from what amounted to abstraction. Once when Arthur Armsby's white-winged "Albatross" quietly came into harbor in the night, and when she looked out in the morning, lay there, almost as if it had been, indeed, a great bird which had alighted on the ocean swell for a few hours rest from flying.

She caught sight of it as early as half-after-ten when she went out to the rocks, ostensibly to read, but, really to ponder the delightful problems which life suddenly presented to her. The recognition made her heart beat with unwonted vigor, and, to her own surprise, sent her homeward long before the luncheon hour. She did not go out again; neither did she mention to the other members of the family that "The Albatross" had "arrived in."

When Arthur drove up in the later afternoon, extremely handsome in white yachting clothes, with a suit-case on the seat beside the weather-beaten Newport hackman, and begged, immediately, for a dinner invitation, she was almost cheated of the real delight of seeing him again, by the annoyance of the consciousness that the blood had mounted richly to her cheeks.

"What ripping color!" he exclaimed, as, with both her hands in his—he had insisted upon that—he stood looking hungrily at her.

After this, for some strange reason, there was a restraint between them, which they had never known before.

He had gone to Newport with the definite intention of discovering whether his vague fear of Chapman as a

rival had fact for its foundation; but he went away with
nothing added to his knowledge, upon this or any other
subject appertaining to Doris, except the growth of his
conviction that she was the loveliest of all created creatures.

That she was really earthly, he distinctly had his
doubts, when, on his evening of departure, he had them
all for dinner on the yacht, and caught the smile she
gave his bo'sun who had quickly dived from the high
deck into the sea to save for her a breeze-blown handkerchief.

It was a gallant thing to do—but Arthur told the
bo'sun afterward that he might look out for another
berth as soon as they arrived in New York Harbor.
What presumption for a mere sailor to have dived after
Doris's handkerchief before he, himself, had had a
chance to think of springing for it! At New York (be
it recorded to his credit) he went ashore, and, at the
club, found a better job for the presumptuous sailor.
Moreover, this occurred before the rather spirituous
dinner which he had ordered for himself and one or two
young friends.

It was after he had gone that Doris found herself
increasingly considering Virginia. She did not in the
least know why, but an acute appreciation of the sorrow
which had fallen on her lovely aunt was hers for the
first time. That it had not come before was not surprising, for the tragedy had happened when she was but a
girl, and furthermore, had been concealed from her as
far as might be; but now she suddenly began to comprehend with a sharp-sightedness which she, herself,
could not quite understand, the sadness of the disap-

pointed woman's life, and to try to mitigate it with many thoughtful, loving acts.

Beneath the influence of Doris's unspoken sympathy, Virginia told her briefly the sad story of her disappointment.

That young girl is fortunate into whose life enters a sympathy so whole-souled and complete as that which resulted in this instance. The sweetening influence of such emotion will notably augment unselfishness and thoughtfulness, directed not only toward the object upon which it is especially spent, but toward mankind in general. With a fresh appreciation, now, Doris saw her grandfather's devotion to Virginia, and, through understanding of it, was drawn closer to him than she ever had been.

It was a period of appreciations with her.

She recognized with real astonishment, the perfect beauty of her parents' wedded life, and even looked with approval, rather than amusement, at Jack's increasing manliness and growing sense of a protective responsibility toward her. During these few months, indeed, the full young fountains of affection in her heart poured in increasing abundance for the members of her family. Until this time, she had taken their unceasing love as a matter of course; now she placed a generous value upon it and returned it with intense earnestness.

In other words, Doris had matured with startling speed, as is sometimes the way with girls when once the boundary between careless youth and early womanhood is passed.

When George Chapman, with his sister, came up for a week-end, she even took occasion to be genuinely considerate of the extraordinary Jane. Once or twice, she almost went so far as to confess the dreadful secret of that winking portrait, but took thought in time, and did not rise to such towering heights of righteousness. Had she obeyed her first impulse in this small matter, a great change might thus have been worked in her subsequent life, but, like the rest of us, she failed of prophecy sufficient to know that.

She hugely enjoyed Chapman's company, and, when she saw how much it pleased her grandfather to have her do so, sometimes actually sought it. But Chapman did not often give her the opportunity for this. He was continually with her when he could be, and it was not until half-an-hour after they had gone that she realized how much this had distressed his sister.

Jane had been very glad that they were going; it was plain to Colonel and Mrs. Marquis and Virginia, and perhaps to Doris, that nothing could have dragged her from the spot, if George had not gone also. Her jealousy of Doris, which was afterwards to reach proportions of real moment, had even then begun to be conspicuous.

Nor was she the only one who was intently studying the friendship of this man and this young girl. Virginia watched every step in their acquaintanceship with a studious care. Even Doris caught the earnestness of her close observation, and, possibly, was a little worried by it. She had already seen her Aunt observing Arthur with a sort of desperate analysis. She wondered why this should be. It did not once occur to her that, mindful of the tragedy of her own life, the loving woman was filled with fear for her, almost amounting to a panic, when any man exhibited an interest in her.

Taken all in all, Doris found it a really delightful

summer. She was sanely happy in her perfect health, her growing understanding, the undeniable and blameless satisfaction which accrues to girls when they wake up to certain knowledge of their own charm and beauty.

She was but dimly conscious of the great change which had come into her existence with the ending of her college years. Her vacations, after the spring terms had finished, had all been spent here, and the charming idleness of this summer did not seem very different from that which she had known in the hot months of the three preceding years. Her greatest pain, perhaps, was the discovery of the magic comfort which grows out of sympathy for others and from service.

It was not until they had returned to New York in the Autumn, and, instead of going back to school, she found herself the center of much talk about a formal introduction to society, that she fully realized herself to be upon the threshold of a new epoch of life. When this realization came, the rush of its arrival was tremendous, overwhelming. It almost intoxicated.

If the sensation of adventuring had been strong in her when she started from the South for college, it was doubly strong one crisp, cool, bracing morning in New York, when she was riding in the park. Virginia was beside her, Jack squired them on a mighty roan, and she, herself, was on a mount sedate and sure, for bridle-paths in Central Park are not places for great equine spirit, be the horsewoman in whose hands the reins repose ever so accomplished.

Jack pulled a newspaper clipping from the pocket of his riding coat.

"Honey, I forgot to show you this before. You were so slow in coming down to breakfast."

"What is it, Jack?"

"Why, it's the official news that you are—well—grown —up."

"In a newspaper?" She smiled at him, believing that a joke was hidden somewhere in the matter. "What *is* it?"

He pulled his horse into a walk, then to a halt, and she was soon close by his side.

"Wait, please, Virginia," he called. "Doris insists on knowing why the great, wide world is showing especial interest in her at the moment."

"Is it in the newspaper?" Virginia said, annoyed. "We wanted it to be a real surprise."

"Oh, I'm sorry," Jack exclaimed contritely. Then, finding comfort in the thought, "But the swarm of girls which gathers round her every afternoon would be quite sure to see it, anyway, and chatter of it to her in their innocent young way."

"But what is it in the newspaper?"

"Shall I tear it up, or show it to her, or feed it to a squirrel?" he asked Virginia.

"Oh, let her see it, now that it has been printed."

He reached across the little space of road between them, and handed his sister the clipping, while a queer, almost quizzical, smile was on his face—that smile of a superior maturity which proved his masculinity, and sometimes amused, sometimes puzzled her.

" 'Mrs. Orlando Marquis,' " Doris read, and, as she read, flushed slowly, " 'will formally present her daughter to the social world next Tuesday afternoon, at their home — Riverside Drive. Relatives and friends will assist in the reception, and in the dining-room, five of Miss Marquis's college friends, among them Miss Lillian Spencer, will pour tea and serve at tables. Ferns and American beauty roses will form the chief decorations of the house. A dance will be given in the evening. The second evening following, the debutante's aunt, Miss Marston, will give a dinner and a dance in honor of her niece.'"

Doris, after reading this, looked at her companions, her eyes shining with delight. Especially she beamed upon Virginia, and, urging her horse nearer, reached for her hand and pressed it lovingly.

She was unusually silent during the remainder of the morning's ride, and, as they cantered through the Park, looked about her almost as if she had but just awakened from a slumber.

A sense of the intense reality of life—a new, complete sense of reality—was in her soul. She saw things with new eyes. The splendid trees, which New York has collected from the four corners of the world for its great pleasure ground, beginning to blush rosily beneath the compliments of Autumn, seemed startlingly clear-cut and actual to her vision; the nurse-girls and the babies on the foot-paths and at crossings had an added tangibility; the riders whom they passed upon the road were newly vital, strangely personal. Hitherto all these had been mere properties in a stage-setting, into which Life, greatest histrion of all, had not yet made an entrance.

She drew a great breath of the crisp air.

"What is it, dear?" Virginia asked, as if that breath

had been a speech. She had been watching Doris intently.

"I'm not quite certain: but it's something most magnificent, and not a little mystifying. It's tempting; it is terrifying: it is promising and it is threatening; it is——"

She lacked words to finish.

"Womanhood, my dear?" Virginia asked, smiling, but not very gayly.

"Yes, it must be that," Doris assented gravely.

Mrs. Marquis was not at home when they arrived, and Doris, with thoughtful tread, climbed to her own studio. This was beneath the very roof, where servants' rooms had been torn out and joined, so that she might have a spacious skylight. But to-day, she did not raise maulstick or brush, although there was an uncompleted canvas on her easel. Instead, for a time, she sat before it, intensely motionless, gazing, unseeing, at the flat and formless landscape which had been blocked in.

Virginia went at once to her hotel. On this journey, down the drive, and through the park, she saw even less than usual of the beauties of the foliage and landscape gardening. She left the limousine and entered the wide doorway of the Plaza, almost without consciousness of the obsequious attendants or the thoughtful clerk (who told her, as she stopped for mail and cards, that Judge Marston had gone downtown). Even the upward hurry of the elevator did not rouse her. Once in her room, she was more restless than was Doris in her studio, although not less absorbed in thought.

What . . . what confronted the dear girl whom she so idolized? Would it be weal, for her, or woe? Ah

. . . ah . . . the weave of Doris's life must not include the threads of Tragedy!

She looked about her discontentedly. The hotel apartment was symbolic of her own existence. With all its elegance, despite the little touches she had given it, it still lacked the semblance of a home. Home! She could never have a home, again! She shuddered at the thought of the associations clustered round the place down South; it made no appeal to her. She wondered if the years had soured her; she knew she never had recovered from the miserable ending of her only love-affair, and, when she was occupied, as she often was, with efforts to forecast the future of her beautiful niece, she looked on all men, save those of her immediate family, with far too much suspicion of their motives and sincerity. It was torture even to consider that Doris's life might hold suffering as acute as that which she had known.

Virginia had been attractive, too; remarkably attractive. She rose and peered into a mirror. The face she saw had lines upon it which never should have marked a face of thirty. Thirty? She felt that she was ages older. Age progresses, not as years accumulate, but as youth dies. Her youth had died. Love had killed and not rejuvenated, in her case; and at every hazard, from such a fate as that Doris must be saved.

She sighed wearily and sank back in her chair, intent on careful thinking. Marriage, she admitted, was the only life for women; she had no illusions on that score; Doris must not know the loneliness which had made her ineffective, purposeless, and had made existence colorless and dull for her. Her analysis of the situation, though much overdrawn, was not without its accuracies.

Two suitors who must be considered seriously were already in the field—Arthur and George Chapman—and of these it was Arthur who most engaged Virginia's thought. As a man he was as handsome as he had been as a youth; too handsome, possibly, she feared. A danger lay there, for the handsome man is rarely strong in character. He was honest and high-minded, that she did not doubt; but was his integrity of purpose founded on enough stability of character? Upon his smiling, mobile mouth expressions sometimes came which she feared indicated weakness; his large attractive eyes were softly brilliant rather than alertly earnest. And in her anxious searching of her memory for everything which she had heard about his past, she found some bits of trifling gossip attributing to him too great a love for wine.

Going back to these, which she acknowledged might be but idle rumor, she recalled his father's history. It was not a pleasant one for her to contemplate, although Major Armsby, while he lived, had been probably the most popular resident of their section. But his popularity had been established on good nature and a hospitality which might be called excessive, rather than upon a solid worth of character. He had been the hardest rider to the hounds of any of the desperately hard riders who were in his set; he had left a record of a score of duels behind him. She could not remember that he ever had been charged with being other than unvaryingly faithful to the young wife who had died at Arthur's birth; his faithfulness, indeed, had extended even to her memory; but during their brief married life, the poor girl had been miserable, because of his hard drinking, his hard riding, and his high play at the gaming tables.

These reminiscences gave Virginia's anxious mind much food for worry about Arthur.

She turned from him to Chapman with scarcely greater satisfaction although the mistakes which, with some show of basis, Arthur might be expected to make, and in a measure be excused for making, were those particular errors into which this man could never fall. He was older than the handsome boy, much older than the lovely girl Virginia was so sure he loved. It was impossible to think of him as ever having been particularly juvenile. He was rather coldly critical of men and things, almost ponderously able, and with a full appreciation of his own ability, although this could be charged to egotism, rather than to conceit. She could not think of him as anxious for the world's approval.

That he loved Doris, she was certain. There had been no demonstrative, impulsive signs of it, such as had been plentiful in Arthur's case, but in Doris's presence, Chapman's eyes invariably dwelt upon her with a satisfied approval, and his attention was never distracted from her by other young and lovely girls. Frequently their presence seemed annoying to him. And he studied Doris's likes and dislikes with devoted care. The nature of the gifts he showered upon her, with as much lavishness as the conventionalities permitted, proved that.

The conventionalities themselves he never violated. If minute propriety may be considered the ideal husband's most essential requisite then George Chapman certainly fulfilled the most exacting matrimonial demand; but Virginia wondered if a girl like Doris would be satisfied, through life, with a companion of such limited qualifications.

Having considered this, her mind reverted to one long almost forgotten. Colonel Marquis had told her about Stoddard Thornton's unselfishly concealed devotion. He had let his liking for the sculptor help to make impressive his description of that moment, enveloped and made dramatic by the sweet rose-garden night, when the young man had told him of his burdens and his almost hopeless aspirations. She reflected that, of course, he had been crowded from the race; but she felt this to be both unfair and tragic.

She told of her reflections upon George Chapman and young Armsby that evening, when, with Mrs. Marquis and the Colonel, she sat upon a balcony looking out across the Drive and the Hudson.

Far across the river glittered the massed lights of a pleasure park; only the red and green and white lamps of the multitude of passing craft visually revealed their presence on the water, for there was no moon. The shrill, staccato whistling of small boats or deep, reverberant tones from larger vessels came to them occasionally. On the drive before them, motors flitted almost noiselessly, heralded by the blinding glare of searchlights, their departure modestly announced by far less obvious tail-lamps. Across the Drive, upon the benches, dim, paired figures showed lovers to be taking full advantage of what would surely be one of the season's last really hot evenings. A great stage, double-decked and thunderous, came with labor up the hill, stopped to drop a passenger and then went on about its ponderous business.

Her companions were somewhat aghast.

"But, my dear Virginia," her sister protested, "Doris is too young to marry, or to think of marrying. These things need not be considered for—oh, years to come! Let her have some youth and freedom, dear! She——"

"She is nearing that same age at which tragedy came into my life," was Virginia's reply.

It impressed them sharply, almost startled them. It was true!

For a time they sat in silence; then:

"She seems still a little girl," Colonel Marquis somewhat weakly protested.

"You cannot prolong her childhood until she is as old as I," Virginia answered evenly. "You cannot stay the march of years, the progress of development—life's normal course. I know how earnestly you wish you might; how the wish is parent to the thought that possibly you may. But no—time passes. Ah, how fast it passes!"

The Colonel rose and put his hand affectionately on her shoulder. "We understand, dear: and you may be right." He thrilled with sympathy for her whose life, despite the span of years which it had yet to run, seemed to have passed, so far as joy went. "It is your love for her which makes you anxious. Perhaps we ought to be considering these things; but it is hard for us to realize that she will ever wish to leave the home. Of course, she will—she will emerge into her own and broader life, and I suppose we must begin to think of it."

"Father has been thinking of it," said Virginia. "He often speaks about her marriage."

Mrs. Marquis forced her lips into a smile. Doris's marriage! How strange the two words in conjunction sounded to her! To the mother's heart it seemed but yesterday when she had seen her in short frocks, pursuing butterflies about the rose garden.

"But, dear, at any rate," she urged apprehensively, "we must be careful not to put such thoughts into her mind. Let us keep her young as long as possible. What a blow to all of us the loss of her will be!"

"Father," said Virginia, "believes George Chapman is the one to make her happy. The thought that they will marry has become a fixed idea with him."

"I cannot even bear to think of it," replied Mrs. Marquis.

"Well, for a time, at least, we won't then," declared the Colonel, glad to dismiss the subject.

In the meantime Doris was not thinking of it. Life, as it was, was too delightful to give her time for speculation upon what it might develop into later. The devotion of young men had become a commonplace with her. She accepted it as a princess of the blood accepts the right to rule.

Arthur's yacht was now in New York waters, and, an evening or two later, a party of young people cruised in her through the magic moonlight down to Sandy Hook and back.

Had the chaperone known of that conversation on the balcony, between Virginia and Doris's parents, she would have realized that observations which she herself made, this night, confirmed Virginia's estimate of Arthur's feelings.

As the host, he was the essence of devotion to all the girls on board, but his especial preference for Doris was clearly indicated. Nor did the clever-eyed young matron fail to observe that Chapman, quiet, watchful and missing no opportunity to further his own cause, was definitely his rival.

Once or twice, she saw a glance flash from the handsome Southerner toward his deliberate and persistent guest, which made her romance-loving heart—that heart which made of her an admirable chaperone—leap pleasantly to the suggested memories of her own days of youthful popularity, and, finally, through sheer delight in the tenseness of the situation, she called Arthur for a few moments to a seat beside the wide-armed wicker chair in which she lounged. She nodded mischievously toward Doris, who, in the full radiance of a deck-light, showed to marvelous advantage, as she was talking animatedly to the older man.

"I don't see why you asked him," she said confidentially.

Arthur glanced quickly at her. Then the slight, unconscious frown which had creased his almost Grecian brows, vanished, and he laughed. "Your eyes are quite as sharp as they are lovely," he replied.

"You must save your compliments for younger guests. Still I am duly grateful. But tell me, is it really a race?"

He sobered instantly. He knew her very well, and was certain she was fond of him, as matrons are of all nice young men. "If you think he's not too old to enter, then it is," said he. "Tell me your opinion. I've been worrying about it. Could a—could an elderly individual, of that dry-as-dust description, possibly— er——"

"Possibly be a rival to a youth as rich and handsome as yourself?" she finished for him. Then she answered:

"You over-estimate his age. Youth has a way of doing that."

"You talk as if you were a grandmother!" he ridiculed.

"I must be very old," she chided, "for I am senior chaperone to-night. Your other married women are mere girls. I like you, Arthur; you are charming. But you know very little about women, young or old. Had I been in your place, I would have scuttled this delightful yacht, before I would have asked George Chapman to sail on her through the moonlight, when Doris Marquis was to be a passenger."

"You don't really mean it, do you?" he exclaimed dismayed.

"I really mean it, my dear boy."

It distressed him amazingly, but he tried to laugh it off. "I shall take the wheel myself, run the 'Albatross' upon the nearest rocks, and rescue Miss Doris with thrilling bravery," he fervently declaimed, but it was evident that he was busy with more serious thoughts.

"I have no doubt you'd drown the rest of us without the least compunction if you thought you might win her that way. And we'd be dying in a very worthy cause. But it might not be effective after all. You, yourself, are not much of a swimmer, while she's a perfect mermaid. I saw you both at Newport. She might have to rescue you, which would be most humiliating; or she might leave you to your fate and rescue the grave Chapman man! The experiment would be risky. But—" others were approaching "— don't forget my little warning."

They caught the swell from an enormous, swift excursion-boat and it was the exquisitely courteous, somewhat reserved George Chapman who was at the side of Doris in the general turmoil instantly resulting.

The young chaperone derided Arthur about this. "See how you miss your opportunities!" she laughed.

"You are very—stimulating," he said, smiling. "I shall miss no more opportunities this evening." He hurried away to bring order out of general confusion.

Having come up at the rail, laughing, Doris held Chapman's arm, while she smiled brilliantly at Arthur, as he hastened here and there, making certain that the lurching had not given anyone real discomfort. Unquestionably she was interested in both men.

Later, as she whirled uptown, from the landing-pier, in the motor with which Virginia had gone for her, Doris was unusually quiet. She caught and held Virginia's hand, after a rather longer interval than usual between remarks, and, subtly, the elder woman knew she had been right in thinking that the time was close when things of mighty import were certain to transpire in the girl's life; she was sure Doris was, at last, considering men and their relation to the future—to her own future.

Analyzing anxiously with definite deliberation, she tried, upon this ride, to sound Doris on the subject of those who had been mentioned in the talk upon the balcony. She reached no satisfactory conclusion as to which, Armsby or Chapman, most interested her niece, but, without surprise, discovered that she was to a degree interested in both.

It was on the moment's spur that she brought forward Stoddard's name. She was not sure that Doris ever thought of him.

"We were talking of an old, old friend, this evening," she ventured.

"Who, dear?" Doris did not seem keenly interested. Difficult dancing on the yacht's deck had somewhat wearied her, and she had been rather busy with her thoughts, as well.

"Stoddard Thornton. You remember him?"

She was, perhaps, a little pleased by the girl's immediate response.

"Oh, you have heard from him? I should like to see him! Remember him? Indeed I do."

"No, we haven't really heard from him. But he is here, in New York city."

"Really?" The interest now, was definite enough.

"Yes; in New York city."

"Then why has he not looked us up?"

They passed, at the moment, into the bright glare of an electric lamp, and, with a queer exultation, Virginia saw real eagerness on Doris's face and there was distinct grievance in her voice.

It might be a dreadful wrong to all concerned, she reflected, were Stoddard led to think himself quite hopelessly disqualified by poverty? Strangely enough, Virginia had no doubts about his worthiness; that was something which it would not have been easy even for an enemy to question.

"I suppose he has been rather cramped by the enormous problems of his life," she commented. "Perhaps he has not found it simple, with no tool other than a sculptor's chisel, to chip away the barrier which he feels exists between him and a proper peace of mind; perhaps he has not found it easy to transmute his modeling-clay into a fortune, and perhaps this fact has kept him from us."

"As if money mattered in one's friendships," said the inexperienced girl.

Virginia laughed. "You, at least, remain unmercenary in a too mercenary age! . . . But he will not come to us until he has worked out the money problem. I am sure of that."

"It is not very nice of him to take that attitude."

"You think not? It seems rather fine, to me."

But the merit of unselfish sacrifice, so apparent to Virginia, was hidden from the girl. Unversed in the stern realities of life, she had small understanding and, therefore, small appreciation of this suggested mental attitude of the young sculptor.

"Crabbed, I call it," she commented, and sank into silence.

The real resentment which Doris put into the words illuminated her aunt's mind, convincing her that she, and not the Colonel and Mrs. Marquis, had been right in analyzing the girl's feelings. Of course, Doris thought of men. What girl does not? Modestly, and, no doubt, almost unconsciously, she considered some of those she knew as matrimonial possibilities. Virginia wondered if by any inadvertence, a hint had ever reached her of Stoddard's declaration that he looked upon her as the chief incentive for fighting in his cruelly unequal battle with the world.

"I think I could get his address," she suggested. "I am sure the only reason he has not communicated with us has been the feeling that until he sees some signs of victory ahead he has no right——"

She caught herself adroitly. She had almost slipped into a declaration of his life's aim, as he had revealed it to the Colonel.

"—to take time for social interests," she added, somewhat lamely.

"How absolutely silly!"

"Would you like to see him?"

"That doesn't seem to be the question," Doris answered with some spirit. "Apparently his High and Mightiness is not anxious to see me—or any of us!"

And there, the conversation ended, for the time; but Virginia was not deceived. She was sure of the existence of a vivid curiosity at least, and, perhaps, something more, behind Doris's pique at Stoddard's silence, when he was so near. Then and there, she formed the firm resolve to bring these two together.

Within a day or two, she learned the street and number of the sculptor's studio, and, one afternoon, made a lone pilgrimage to it. It was hidden in a quaint part of New York with which she was unfamiliar, lost in the maze of streets to south and westward of Jefferson Market.

He was in blue denim blouse and duck trousers when she found him, his hands white with plaster, struggling to make something new of "Justice" for a western courthouse. Virginia saw little of the studio, except that it was very meager, very littered. She had eyes for him alone.

The years had left their marks upon him. The boyish flush was gone from cheeks no longer round and smooth, but hard with muscles born of his determination. He was much thinner than he had been when last she had seen him. There was a hint in his appearance that he even might have known privations. But his eyes were keen and calm, his hands were steady and his smile undimmed. His lean height gave somehow the impression of a large reserve of strength.

He met her with delight, of which she could not doubt the genuineness, welcoming her simply—a large part of the real charm of his manner lying in its utter frankness. There was something fine, she thought, in the unconscious way in which he quite ignored the poverty of his surroundings, making no apologies for them. He had not inflicted them on her; he had not asked her to come from her world into his to visit them.

His delight could not be doubted; plainly it was as keen as it could have been had he been greeting her in the magnificence of a Fifth Avenue studio. The best chair he could offer had a broken back, but he conducted her to it as if it had been a throne. In his eyes gleamed the same fire of earnestness and unwavering resolve, which she remembered seeing in them in the old days in the South. There was a satisfying firmness in his handclasp.

Her first question was almost exactly that which Doris had asked her concerning him, the previous evening, in the motor.

"Why have you not been to see us?"

"I have been very hard at work."

"Too hard at work to find time for old friends?"

His face flushed. "I've only been trying to make

sure if I am worthy of old friends—or new," said he. "Success, you know, is what proves worthiness."

"No; in that you are mistaken," she declared. "Worthiness is its own proof, with or without success." He had explained the "Justice" to her. "But you have succeeded, or you'd not be getting orders to make 'Justices' to put on court-houses—even court-houses in very little cities, 'way out West."

"The fact that I must make them proves that I have not. But I am not in the least discouraged. I——"

"Of course, you're not discouraged. I'm sure you're not the sort to get discouraged."

There was other talk about her family, about his work, about old times—and then Virginia put him to a little test. Had he lost interest in Doris, or was he trying to conceal a greater, more mature and intense interest than he ever had known before?

"Only last evening, Doris and I were talking of you," she said, trying to be casual, but with a covertly careful examination of his face.

"How beautiful she has grown to be!"

She could see that he regretted this remark instantly. That he had seen her, clearly was an admission which he had not cared to make.

"Then you have seen her?"

"On the street, one day." He was visibly embarrassed.

"And you did not let her know that you were near?" There was reproach in tone and words.

"She was in a motor, and—whirled past too rapidly." The little hesitation in the middle of the sentence convinced Virginia that, for one reason or another, he had been careful not to let himself be seen, or at least, had felt relieved because he was not seen.

"You didn't *wish* her to see you!" she exclaimed reproachfully.

He hesitated long before he answered. "Perhaps . . . not."

"Why?"

He waved his hand. The gesture called attention to himself and everything in the great, meager room. It was a sort of high sign of the surrender of his pride. Not unwillingly, but perhaps not readily, it took her into his confidence. It was an abnegation of reserve.

She knew this and valued it. It added to her respect for him; no respect is keener than that which we are compelled to feel for revelations that are forced, not voluntary.

"This is not, exactly, what one would call prosperity," he said with a queer smile, as if remembering days when the slight mitigations of the room's bareness would have seemed luxurious to him, "but—well, it is the height of easeful plenty, compared to——"

He left the sentence incomplete, knowing she would catch his meaning.

In his frankness there was nothing of complaint; no appeal for sympathy; the expression of his face, the hard, lean lines of his energetic body, the calm, untremulous capability of his artistic, but strong hands—all these impressed her with the force of his determination to compel success. The care with which he curbed his evidently great desire to ask questions about Doris, and the eagerness with which he caught up every crumb of information which apparently she let fall by chance, seemed somewhat pathetic.

As, the motor threaded its devious homeward passage through the crowded streets of the poor quarter near his studio, this pathos more and more impressed her. There was a dignity about the course which he had followed that strongly appealed to her. Virginia again compared his struggling pluck with the easy lives of Doris's other suitors. Chapman never had been forced to fight, save when he had found it wise to bring the weight of his great capital, the force of his peculiar genius for finance, into somewhat ruthless play in business matters. Arthur never had been compelled to fight at all. Chapman, probably, was selfish; successful business men are likely to be. To Arthur, giving never had entailed any self-denial; therefore, although he was now full of generous impulses, he also might develop selfishness if the time should come when generosity meant sacrifice. But in her thoughts she could not link selfishness with the young sculptor.

She determined that if Stoddard wished to join the race for Doris's favor he should have the opportunity. She wished to have him enter, and decided to confront him with temptation, in the hope that he might yield to it.

Stoddard had captured her anew, and all sorts of wild schemes flitted through her mind. She even considered giving him commissions for extraordinary work (of course, through a third party) so that he would be able sooner to discharge the debt he had assumed, and have a fair start, not only in the contest for Doris's love and hand, but in life's struggle generally. It is even possible that if she had not been sensible enough to give full value to Stoddard's evidently abnormal sensitiveness upon this particular subject, the gentle, generous, disappointed woman might have attempted this, in her great anxiety that her dear niece should not be robbed of life's greatest joy, as she herself had been. Remembering this, she realized that should he ever learn that she had followed such a course, it might, while not arousing real resentment, still rob him of a great deal of satisfaction and comfort.

"I will take Doris down to see him, anyway," she finally resolved, "since he will never come to us."

"Whom do you think I went to see, this afternoon, dear?" she asked Doris, when she had reached home.

"I can't imagine. You so seldom visit anyone."

"A friend of mine who is a sculptor."

"You don't mean——"

"Yes, and I'm going to take you down, to-morrow." She quickly veiled the deep intent of this design with casualities. "Have you ever seen a sculptor's working-quarters?"

"No; and I should rather like to."

It amused Virginia to feel that Doris, also, was speaking with restraint. How mature the girl had become!

"It's really most interesting," Virginia went on, carefully. "Casts everywhere, and clay in almost agricultural quantities strewn universally upon the working-platform underneath the skylight; no luxury in any part of the big room."

Doris seemed unusually thoughtful, as she commented: "No; I should not expect much luxury in Stoddard Thornton's studio. Has he——"

"Paid off that enormous debt? Oh, no, not yet; but I think he will soon. I know little about sculpture, but it seems to me he shows great talent." She paused a moment, studying the girl as carefully as possible, without allowing her close scrutiny to become obvious. "Do you really think you would be interested?"

"Yes; I should love to see a sculptor's studio, and I should be glad to see him, too. It has been years; and we were—such great friends!"

"Well, then, come to the hotel at two to-morrow. I'll not let him know our plans. He might try to scrape away the clay and clean up the debris. It would be an endless task."

It was before two the following day, when Doris called for her—which Virginia thought an interesting sign. The girl was in extraordinarily high spirits. The drive downtown was a gale of laughter.

The queer old section of the city, where the studio was hidden in a three-story building which once upon a time had been a private dwelling, but now housed on its ground floor a grocer's shop, and on its second, his family, offering space for Stoddard's studio on its third and highest, was of itself a novelty to Doris. The delicately nurtured girl had never visited so poor a neighborhood, and with a little sinking of the heart wondered if it might not be a slum. As a matter of fact the little street was not so very humble, although quite unpretentious. Nearby, although they had not known it, they had passed the studio of one of the world's greatest sculptors—the lodestone which had drawn Stoddard to that particular neighborhood.

Indeed Doris gained confidence when she saw that

nearly every one of the old houses near had in its slant roof a big sky-window, planned to catch the north light in good volume. Her heart thrilled strangely, as she stepped to the sidewalk and, for a moment, stood waiting for Virginia to alight.

When they reached the studio-door, Doris and Virginia were confronted by a card, hung on the knob. Doris stooped to read it, glad of an opportunity to keep her face concealed from Virginia, for she feared it was revealing strange emotions; she certainly was feeling some which much surprised herself, and she thought would surprise her aunt much more, no doubt.

The legend on the card was:

OUT FOR A FEW MOMENTS:
S T E P   I N   A N D   W A I T.

Doris straightened, looking at Virginia. "Shall we?"

"Why not?" Virginia answered. She was beginning to feel very pleased. "The invitation is so general, it surely includes us."

They waited twenty minutes, that for the girl were crowded with emotions so unwonted as to be almost startling.

The studio, itself, which, after a few moments of timidity, she investigated superficially, was full of fascinations. It had, for her, many messages, of that art, sister to the one toward which she had such pronounced tendencies. She touched the oily clay gingerly, examined the queer tools, held her skirts free from the dust, and even for a moment sank to rest upon the Grecian bench (built of pine boards) upon the model's stand.

And this was where Stoddard worked; where he was carrying on the battle against fate which she but dimly understood, but of which she was keenly conscious none the less. What had the years made of him? She was astonished by the strength of her desire to know. Was he as handsome as the early days had promised? Had the expression of his eyes changed? Were his long, slim fingers still as nervous in their strength, still as insistently eager to feel the touch of clay, or maul, or chisel? What a wonderful companion he had been! She so much wished to see him.

But he did not come, and, after half-an-hour had passed, Virginia decided that they could wait no longer.

"*Must* we go? I'm sure he'd hurry if he knew we were here."

Virginia wondered if he would. She was vexed, not with him, perhaps but with their fortune. She wondered if he had not been a little stupid in maintaining so steadfastly his purpose not to—no; she did not; it was that which she most admired in him.

"We will come again, less unconventionally—some time when we have made sure that he will be here," she suggested.

"Perhaps he does not wish to see us!" The girl's voice sounded queerly thin and disappointed.

"What nonsense! Of course he does."

Doris reluctantly arose, and slowly made the round of the great, disordered, shabby room, while Virginia stood admiring the startlingly chaste head of the "Justice," which had appreciably progressed since she had seen it on her previous visit.

Doris's heart was sinking as if a ruthless hand had

drawn a curtain, shutting from view some new and pleasant vista which had just been shown to her.

"I'm not sure that he does," she said, continuing her inspection of the studio while Virginia struggled with a stubborn glove.

Beside the door, just where the light from the roof-window fell upon it, was a little india-silk curtain, exquisitely embroidered, hanging by rings upon a short, brazen rod. It was the only bit of elegance in the room, and stood out in striking contrast to the general dinginess. They both had observed its beauty and remarked upon its probable age and rarity; now it occurred to Doris that a mere hanging would not be likely to be suspended upon rings. She reached out idly, touching them. The delicate silk slid back.

It was with difficulty that she stifled a cry of sheer astonishment and delight, as she saw the content of the niche which the curtain had concealed. It was one of those narrow recesses bending inward to a depth of eight inches or a foot, and curving at the top, in which our ancestors were wont to harbor dreadful bronzes in the days now happily gone by; but this one now served a better purpose.

Lined with green India-silk, dull with age, and shading mysteriously to red in rich, Oriental tones, it shrined a tiny statuette on a slim, long pedestal.

Amazed, she gazed at it, for, beyond a question, it was a marble portrait of herself, full length, and marvelous in its sweet girlishness, wonderfully chaste in the soft white of the Carrara marble from which it had been cut; exquisite in its vivacity; chiseled with a delicacy of art which made her gasp. Upon the little ped-

" . . . beyond a question it was a marble portrait of
herself. . . . "

estal, from which sprang the mere suggestion of a branch of blossoming rose-bush, had been cut, "Goddess of the Garden." It was a finished replica of the delightful clay Stoddard had modeled for them in those far southern days. And it was enshrined as might a worshiper enshrined the statue of a saint!

With eyes which suddenly grew misty, she looked quickly at Virginia, making sure, with unaccountable relief, that her aunt's attention had not been attracted by the episode. She softly drew the curtain close across the niche.

"Shall we go, now, Aunt Virginia?" she said, almost in a whisper.

"Yes; but we must come again. I want to see him."

As they left, Doris took from her corsage a single, purple orchid, and looking here and there about the place, decided on a broken pitcher as the best available substitute for a vase. She placed the flower in it after Virginia had passed through the door and then quickly joined her on the stairs.

Dressed in an old smoking jacket and duck-trousers a man just then took his place at a window opposite, and his laughing eyes looked down at them with an extraordinary interest, as they emerged from the stairway leading up to Stoddard's studio.

It was Whilk, who made a specialty of "kiddies," in water color, and so spent as much time at the window as he could, watching the gay urchins of the neighborhood.

He had seen the same motor pause at the same place, the day before, and had seen Virginia leave it, but Stoddard had been silent on the subject afterwards, and

Whilk had not mentioned it. Now he saw her standing on the sidewalk with a young girl, wonderfully lovely. Here was Romance, surely—or a big order for his friend. For a moment, speculating idly, he sat watching the beautifully gowned pair, and then realized that Stoddard was in the back room where there was a cooking-range, experimenting with a composition metal with' which he hoped to find it possible to cast small figures without aid from foundries.

"You'd better hurry home, old man," he called across his shoulder. "The Queen of Fortune has been again to see you, and this time she brought the princess with her. Of course, they didn't find you; and they're just leaving."

He took one more look at Doris, as, delayed by a group of children ere they could cross the sidewalk, she stood beside Virginia.

"A *royal* princess, too! Steam up! They've evidently seen the note upon your door, and are about to go. Hurry, or you'll miss them!"

Stoddard made haste to the window. As he saw who was standing on the sidewalk, there was an expression on his face such as his friend never before had seen there—a look of delight and eager longing.

"He knows them very well, indeed," Whilk told himself, observing this. Then, shrewdly, as he saw him hesitate: "He must be tremendously in love with that young girl."

Indeed, the sculptor seemed like one entranced. He merely stood at the window, gazing.

"Well, why don't you hurry?" Whilk inquired. "They'll be off, if you wait there much longer."

With a quick step, Stoddard hurried to the door, but, at that moment, the crowd of children parted, Virginia and Doris stepped across the sidewalk, vanished in the car, and the chauffeur moved his lever.

CHAPTER XII

Julian had learned ambition in the North, and decided to progress in rhythm with the world. With rare intelligence for a southern darkey (and much to Desdemona's admiration) he had mastered motors, and was now a full-fledged and reliable chauffeur; indeed he was at the wheel when Doris, delighted because Lillian had come visiting, decided on a run into the country. Doris very much desired a brisk hour in the crisp autumn air. She felt that it would be a stimulant to thought, and realized that even in her rose-strewn path of life, she had reached a point where careful thought was necessary.

It was a gorgeous day. In the brilliance of October sunshine, New York basked as near to sleepiness as New York ever does. The Drive swarmed with motors.

"I know what I like about New York," said Lillian.

"What, dear?"

"It's so snappy. Lives here are like rubber bands stretched just about as far as they can stretch."

"They break sometimes."

"Yes; but if they do, they are at once thrown into the waste-basket—they're put entirely out of sight. No doubt there are rubbish heaps in New York city, but we don't have to look at them. We only see the bands of —new, live rubber."

Doris wondered if the neighborhood where Stoddard

Thornton's studio was located, would seem one of the rubbish-heaps to Lillian's eyes, but did not mention it.

That rush up the Drive to 125th Street and over the Fort Lee Ferry was wonderfully invigorating, made as it was at a speed of thirty miles an hour, when Julian's now understandingly developed eye saw that the coast was clear of blue coats and brass buttons.

As the boat swept from the slip, they left the car, going to the upper-deck, which at that hour was not crowded. There they gloried in the sparkle of the sunshine on the lordly Hudson; watched the soft, multishaded blue above New York; considered the delightful, fading green of the upper Jersey shore, and the many varied craft which respectfully made way before the progress of the mammoth ferryboat.

Afterward, they thrilled deliciously, as the car sturdily made the steep ascent from water-level to the summit of the Palisades. When they had reached the top, and Julian turned to ask for further orders, Doris cried delightedly:

"Oh, somewhere up-stream, where there are woods, and we can touch a real live tree or two."

Various emotions were struggling in her soul, and she wanted an environment unmistakably vital in which to consider them carefully. Lillian's presence would assist, not hinder, the thinking out of things.

Not only had the little trip to Stoddard's studio somewhat helped to make this "thinking-out" a real necessity, but half a dozen other things had happened which demanded revery.

Life was rapidly becoming complicated. As a girl

knows many things—by intuition—she knew precisely what Virginia and her parents had been seriously discussing. It seemed to her incredible that she should really have reached the years when the great things of existence inevitably impend—great things like—well—marriage.

She recoiled before the word as it intruded on her thoughts, although she used it frequently enough in conversation with girl friends; but these conversations were so very different—they meant nothing, while this communing with herself, might possibly mean much.

"I know what you're thinking about!" Pickle-lily said, smiling at Doris's knotted brows, as they skimmed along the hard, smooth New Jersey road.

"I don't believe *I* do! It's all so very muddled."

"Yes, I suppose it must be. With you there are so many."

"So many what, dear?"

"Men, of course. You needn't say you were not thinking about men. I know the meaning of that look of agony when it appears upon a sweet girl's face! Haven't I seen it on my own, when I've been thinking about men and have just happened to look up into a mirror? And I've had just about one-third as many beaux as you have. It must be intensely wearing to keep a tab upon a multitude. You must get all mixed up as to the color of their various eyes."

Doris relaxed against the motor-cushions with a little laugh. She had been leaning forward rather tensely, while, without her knowledge, somewhat quizzically, her friend had studied her expression.

"I know one who thinks about *you* pretty constant-ly," Doris ventured in retort.

"Who?"

"It would be a breach of confidence to tell."

"You don't mind a little thing like that, with an old college chum, do you?"

"Very much indeed. I am most careful about such things."

"Please, please, Doris!" Lillian evidently had fond hopes that she knew whom Doris had in mind, and wished to have her guess confirmed.

But Doris would not gratify her curiosity.

She was thinking about Jack. That energetic youth had lately shown interesting signs of violent love for Lillian; and she hoped earnestly that he might win her; but it did not seem as serious a matter as her own quandary; and, with this reflection her mind returned to a consideration of that problem.

The influence of the increasingly rural aspect of the country soothed her; there was a lulling rhythm in the faint purring of the motor; at her side was the one loyal friend to whom she felt she could reveal with ease the longings of her heart.

At a low speed they entered presently a stretch of real country road. Instead of the hard, smooth macadam of the sophisticated highways, this was of soft, woodsy dirt; trees closely bordered it, not in formal rows, but carelessly, as nature had placed them. It was a friendly road, more like the roads down South, than those with which she had become familiar in the neighborhood of the metropolis. Suddenly, it debouched illogically into a ragged grove, and beyond a rugged sweep of rocky ground, she could see the sharp edge of the serried Palisades, commanding a clear, inspiring view of the great river.

She had lost track of distance and direction; the glorious prospect came upon her, therefore, with all the force of a surprise. She made Julian stop, and dragged the less, energetic Lillian from the motor.

Far, far, dimmed by shifting, rising, settling, weaving veils of thin blue mist, lay the less imposing New York shore, stretching beyond into a gray-blue, full of neutral shadings; the river gleamed before it, smooth as a mirror, its polished surface broken only where desultory shipping loafed along, so far below that the progress of the craft seemed merely casual—the turmoil of their creamy wakes not foam born of commotion, but white fans of peaceful cream, inlaid in the darker waters of the river.

"Oh, Lillian!" she cried, "did you ever see anything so lovely?" In an ecstasy she threw her arm about her friend and drew close to her side. "See those gulls! Isn't the sun upon that schooner's sails too marvelous for words? There are some things which cannot be painted. They may be painted at—but no artist ever will be able to transfer the soul of them to canvas."

"It *is* beautiful," said Lillian, almost awed by the scene's grandeur.

"We will stay, a little while," Doris said to Julian; and almost instantly he disappeared beneath the great machine to investigate and tinker. In these days motors exercised over Julian a fascination little less absorbing than that of drugs for their unhappy victims.

The influence of the balmy, perfect day, with just

a touch of autumn crispness in the air; of the wondrous view which stretched before them; of the friend beside her who had proved trustworthy through four years of troublous college-life; and, reaching out of the near past, the memory of that call at Stoddard's studio, which seemed to be continually with her, clinging like a faint perfume, all tended to make Doris yearn to settle there upon the rocks, *en face* of the tremendous beauty of the scene, and pour out the troubles of her heart, asking counsel of herself far more than of any other, but certain that the speaking of the words to sympathetic ears would help to make that counsel wise.

"Oh, Lillian," she cried, "I am so troubled!"

"What is it, dear?"

"What shall I do? I don't know my own mind!"

"Can I help you?"

The recital which ensued was a little tearful toward the end—comfortably, confidentially, not tragically tearful. Doris gave Lillian a glimpse of the bewildering maze of her emotions. There were those which stirred her when she was with Arthur—comradely, congenial, happy with pure merriment; there were those George Chapman roused—comfortable, admiring, eminently satisfactory; and there were those which she had felt when she had been in Stoddard's studio—dreamy, yearning, almost tragically sympathetic.

"Because his struggle has been so heroic; because I have the feeling in my heart that when he made that little, living statuette, there was far more in his soul than the desire to transform marble into a sweet image of a picturesque and happy girl. Somehow, as I looked at it, it seemed to me that nothing but a yearning heart could have transmuted me—*me*—unthinking me—into such loveliness. I——"

"You don't have to be transmuted into loveliness. You're loveliness personified. And you're not unthinking!" came the fervent protest. "You're the most extraordinary girl I ever knew and we're all—men, women, girls and boys, dogs and cats and little birdies in their cages—half-crazy over you. If people like you were commonplace this world would be a dizzying whirlpool of emotion. If you were unthinking, you wouldn't be worrying this way now. Go on, please. Tell me more."

But Doris would not, for it suddenly occurred to her that what she knew of Stoddard's lofty struggles toward achievement was not her property to tell—even to her dear Lillian.

"I can't tell you about him," she explained. "I have not the right. But I can say this: that his life has been one long, unceasing sacrifice to an ideal; that his courage has not faltered in the face of odds which would have bowed another to the earth; and that—oh, Lillian, I am sure he loved me when he made that statuette! And I —and I——"

"Do you love him?"

"I don't know, and I can't find out."

"Well, then, and Arthur?"

"Sometimes, when I'm with him, I am sure I love him. Then again, all I can say is that I do not know. I really do not know."

"I understand," said Lillian. "I've not had in all my life more than one one-hundredth as many admiring looks as you have—but I know exactly how you feel about it. And as to Mr. Chapman—in a burst of confidence the Wild Goose told me that his sister Jane was sure you were in love with him, and, furthermore, that she was as certain he loved you."

"Sometimes, he seems so—so comfortable, so thoroughly dependable," said Doris, "that I feel as if life with him would be lovely. Sometimes, I am afraid he is too grave. I wonder if he'd sympathize with all my foolish girlishness; I wonder if he would be happy with a—with anyone so young and—fond of life as I am."

"I fancy that is what would make him happiest," said Lillian judicially. "But I don't know whether he could make *you* happy."

From the abyss below them, where, at the foot of the great cliffs, irreverent quarrymen were tearing down the marvelous foundations of nature's pillared, rocky edifice, came the wheezing of a whistle.

"Oh, it's noon!" said Doris, worried. "We must hurry. They're to be there, this afternoon, with a new gown! I must be certain it is right."

It broke the tension of emotion. "Lucky girl!" exclaimed Lillian. "I can regard one who's surrounded, as you are, with walls of love, parapets of devotion and a moat full of the milk of human kindness, without wicked envy, but, without fear of successful contradiction, as Prexy used to say, I can also state that you've not the least idea what a fortunate girl you are!"

"I know it. But come on; that gown will *be* there, and they'll go—a—way!"

The long smooth journey homeward again stimulated thought, and Doris, considering Jack and Lillian, suddenly thrust her arm about her friend and drew her to her in a quick embrace, which was so violent that it almost cost Lillian her hat.

"You've let me maunder on about my own assorted troubles of the heart," said Doris, delivering new hugs with every word and with a fervor which made the astonished Lillian gasp, as she endeavored to refix her hat pins, "but you've not said a word about your own."

"I haven't any," Lillian replied, as carelessly as possible, but with flaming cheeks belying her denial.

"You have one," said Doris, with some emphasis, "and if you go and get another, it will break Jack's heart."

"Don't, you——"

The violence of the embrace ceased. But, taking her friend's face in both hands, Doris turned it toward her and looked earnestly into her eyes.

"He loves you very dearly, Lillian. You won't make him unhappy, will you?"

"Does he?" Lillian asked solemnly, almost beneath her breath.

"You *know* he does!"

"It seems—almost—too good to be true!"

Doris again threw her arms about her. "I'd rather have him marry you than anyone else in all the world! Honey, we'll be sisters, then!"

Within ten minutes after their arrival, the house was in a turmoil of strewn furbelows which scarcely ceased at all until what Jack termed "the lull before the storm" came on Tuesday morning.

.   .   .   .   .   .

The great width of the famous Drive was crowded by carriages and motors, and the sparkling sun of a brilliant autumn day, showing New York at its best, did what it could to make inanimate surroundings as brilliant as the faces of the swarm of pretty girls who gathered to accentuate with their own charm the radiance of the loveliest among them.

In the drawing-room, from which all natural light had been excluded, the soft glow of lamps, subdued by opalescent shades, fell caressingly upon the flushing face of the slim debutante in delicate blue chiffon-cloth, as she stood beside her stately mother, in a shimmering creation of pearl-gray satin.

It was not until all but belated comers had paid their respects to society's new entrant that she had an opportunity to more than casually glance at the massed flowers which had been sent to her, and which, with those already scattered everywhere in the elaborate decorations, turned the drawing-room and even the great dining-room into veritable bowers.

She was exclaiming in delight as she stooped over a box of marvelous orchids, when she heard Jane Chapman's name announced, and, on the impulse of the moment, hurried toward the coming guest, with, still in her hand, the card which had accompanied the orchids and which she had not yet had an opportunity to examine.

Jane Chapman made a somewhat bizarre figure in this dazzling setting. She wore a queer little bonnet set on the tip-top of her head, with an intoxicated tilt, and little ribbons were knotted tightly underneath her chin. Her gown was of elegant material, but out of fashion, and her voice was cracked and squeaky. Time had played havoc with her youth, but in no wise had retarded her extraordinary fluency of speech. After the most perfunctory congratulations, she launched at once into a description of a meeting of striking laundry-girls which she had just addressed upon the subject of woman suffrage.

Doris, trying to be cordial and seem interested, bore up rather bravely under the tremendous verbal onslaught, but, behind her back, with the hand which did not hold the card taken from the box of orchids, she made her sorority's sign of distress, in the hope that Lillian might see it, and come quickly to her rescue.

But Lillian was not in range, so Doris bore Miss Chapman on to the massed flowers which she had left to greet her.

"I had just opened this box of exquisite orchids," she explained. "Aren't they lovely?"

"Who sent them?" was Miss Chapman's only comment.

"Why, I haven't even looked. I've the card here in my hand." She glanced at it, and read George Chapman's name.

For a reason which she did not stop to classify, it seemed to her unfortunate that the examination of these flowers and the reception of Miss Chapman had been simultaneous. She disliked answering her guest's question, but, when it was repeated, she could not well avoid replying.

"Why—er—your brother." Doris was confused by her own confusion, annoyed by her own annoyance. "Aren't they the most beautiful things?"

"Humph! Yes!" said Jane, and, with set lips, and a brow suddenly grown stern and forbidding, passed along to Mrs. Marquis. The latter had seen who was with Doris, and even then, was hastening to the rescue.

A moment later, resisting the desire to run, but careful to keep on the far side of a group of girls, Doris went toward the dining-room. There, where hundreds of pink roses and soft ferns, with many electric lights glittering among them, produced a fairy-scene of beauty, and sweet inoffensive college-maidens were pouring tea, she felt measurably safe.

"Oh-h-h!" she sighed to Lillian. "I know just how a soldier feels when he's a coward, and flies madly from the gory field!"

"You poor, dear child! She surely did look voracious —and although you're *sweet* enough to eat, undoubtedly this party never'd be the same again if its young hostess should mysteriously disappear into the midst of Miss Jane Chapman."

"She *hates* me!" Doris whispered, almost fearfully.

"Why in the world do you care if she does?"

"I don't want anyone to hate me."

In another instant she was borne away, laughing, and thrust into such a whirl of gay excitement that she forgot even the grim ogress of the gray and plastered coiffure.

When the news spread to the dining-room that Judge Marston had arrived, Doris turned with a radiant face. As she ran to greet him, he was standing almost where Jane had stood when the disaster had occurred, and, strangely enough, was looking at the very card, which Jane scornfully had let fall into the box in which it had arrived.

"Ah, Doris! Doris!" he cried gayly. "I suppose I've broken all the rules by coming—not even grandfathers were invited, were they?—only lovely woman; but I couldn't keep away! My brightest jewel takes on an added luster as she steps into the world. My desire to see the transformation was too great to be resisted."

With his hands upon her wrists, he held her off, so that his genial eyes might joy in the crisp beauty of her youth.

"And George Chapman has been sending you those lovely orchids! I've been spying at the cards. Like his father. Exactly like his father. Always gallant."

He smiled as the color rushed into her cheeks.

"Oh, everyone has sent me flowers," she countered. "Isn't the world kind to me? And his were not the loveliest."

"No?" The Judge made a gesture of astonishment. "Those gorgeous orchids not the loveliest? Which were?"

"You know very well, dear grand-daddy—your flowers were loveliest of all." She reached a hand caressingly to a waist-high vase of bronze, and pulled down an American Beauty, which had been nodding gracefully at head level. As she touched her lips to it, he slipped his hand through her arm, and explained that she must take him on the rounds, let him see the whole delightful gathering, and—then send him home.

"I've taken a grandfather's privilege," said he, "but I don't mean to keep you long."

"I shall set the loveliest of all the girls to guard you, and see that you don't run away," she cried; and this she did, much to his delight.

"Well, dear," said Virginia, after it was over, "are you very tired? Was it a happy afternoon? Is the world begining to do homage to you properly?"

"It has all been perfect—absolutely perfect! Miss Chapman was the only false note in it all, and she was not so very *false,* I think. I'm sure her hair is all her own. But she nearly stabbed me to the heart, with piercing glances, when she saw her brother had sent flowers."

"Why shouldn't he send flowers?"

"I don't know, but she was furious."

"Well, she's not been invited to the dance to-morrow night."

"You are a dear—to give that dance! Everyone is so very good to me."

"We want you to be happy!"

Understanding better with each passing day Virginia's own colorless existence, Doris caught her in her arms and kissed her, trying to keep the pity from her eyes and voice.

"Now tell me whom you have invited," she urged, quickly.

"You shall see whom you shall see," was the reply.

In the glittering affair which Virginia had prepared as her part of the celebration of her niece's entrance to the social world, Arthur escorted Doris to the dining-room, Chapman sat at her left; black coats and white waistcoats were impartially distributed among the gay gowns of her chattering girl friends. Lillian smiled at her across a mammoth bowl of ox-eyed daisies from a chair next Jack's, and only her mother, father, aunt and grandfather of all those present, were sober-minded and mature, unless George Chapman must be included in that category. The moment she first met Arthur's eyes Doris felt that danger signals flew in them, and laughed, when in a stolen confidence, Lillian also warned her of it.

"He doesn't look a bit more dangerous than Jack," Doris answered gayly. "My brother is progressing rapidly——"

"But we are brave," said Lillian. "We court danger, do we not, Mike?"

"We devour it," Doris answered. "It's much nicer than mere fudge. That is, if boys are danger, we love it to court us."

Arthur was not talkative, at first. It was evident that Lillian was right in thinking serious ideas were revolving in his brain.

"Why are you so serious?"

"How strangely things have come about!" he answered, refusing to be frivolous "I wonder if you can remember as vividly as I can, that dim moment in the woods, down south, when you——"

Like a flash the scene came back to her; Northrop's tense face and glittering revolver; the fierce words thrusting incongruously through the softly fragrant night.

"You saved my life, you know!"

"Nonsense: it was probably not as serious as it seemed then."

"Yes; quite . . . . And here we are, again together!"

"You mustn't think about unpleasant things."

"Unpleasant? To me it's not unpleasant. I shall never forget one detail of your——"

"You must remember me in more agreeable surroundings. This for example." She turned to Chapman. "Aren't they too good to me—all of them?"

"Too good to *you?* Who could be!"

She turned back to Arthur smiling.

"It is splendid to be part of so much happiness," he exclaimed.

"Aren't you always a part of happiness? I am."

"You have more than everything—you have every*one*—your family, and all—while I——"

From an older and a different man, it might have seemed a definite bid for sympathy: from him it did not.

"I have everything that doesn't count," said he, and emptied his champagne-glass. "See? There is my life—now! I wonder with what nectar or what bitter draught the glass will be refilled."

"It shall be refilled with champagne, at once," she gayly answered; but despite her gayety of manner, her heart really thrilled with sympathy.

"Let me give you a little toast!" said he, and raised his glass again when it had been refilled, looking straight into her eyes.

She tried not to flush, tried not to drop her eyes. "A toast!"

"May the sentiment I kindle in your heart, to-night, last as long as my life, or, rather, may my life last no longer than your——"

He looked keenly, almost imploringly at her, and for the last word "love," which he had almost uttered, substituted "friendship."

"What a charming toast!" said Doris, confused because she had heard the toast before and had expected the word "love."

None the less, it was with a little worry that she saw

his glass filled more than once again, and noted that his cheeks were flushed.

While coffee was being served in the drawing-room, came the announcement of Miss Chapman's name.

Virginia and her sister exchanged astonished glances, each wondering if the other had invited this unlisted guest, each sure from the first glimpse of the other's face that such was not the case. And the caller's brother, too, who, at the moment, sat by Doris, seemed somewhat startled. Lillian sidled over to her friend before the visitor came in.

"The shillain still pursues us!" she said, darkly.

" 'Shillain? Shillain?' "

"Feminine of 'Villain,' child. Did you not take English when you were in Welleslar? Yes? Do you feel like taking poison, now? Brace up, strong soul; have heart! The elevator may yet fall with her, and crush her to a pulp."

" 'No such luck,' I want to say; but it would be too wicked."

Miss Chapman entered.

"No; no such luck," said Lillian, in a last aside, as they went forward. "Why do they make machinery so perfect?"

"I am flying from the enemy," Miss Chapman, with an extremely honeyed smile, was explaining to Virginia and Mrs. Marquis, as Doris joined them. "Reporters! I have been down at a suffrage meeting, and they've been trying for an interview. When I eluded them, they took a taxi and gave chase."

Doris irreverently wondered why.

"My chauffeur could not shake them off, so I ran in

here, hoping you would be at home, but never dreaming that—why, how absurd of me! I knew, of course, that you, Miss Marston, were giving your niece a party, and I have no doubt I am intruding."

"Oh, no indeed," Virginia assured her with gracious smile.

"I must run away at once."

"Why not join our little group of the comparatively aged, and watch youth disport itself?" Virginia asked.

"Is my brother here?"

"Yes, somewhere."

"Well, I mustn't stay long, but I'll have just a word with him."

"Hear how she says that, Doris?" Lillian whispered. "How thirsty her voice sounds."

"Thirsty! What do you mean, now, dear?"

"Bloodthirsty—your blood, you know."

"Hush!" Doris went forward. "So nice of you to come in, Miss Chapman."

(Lillian nudged a friend and smiled. "There are times when it is only decent to lie a little," she whispered.)

"It is a privilege, I'm sure," said Jane. (There was something, Lillian later said, about the way in which she spoke these words, which would have made the Puritans arrest her for profanity, in the good old Roger Williams days.) "Ah, there is George! I must have one word with him, and then I shall be going."

The word took but a moment. "Short, but sharp, not sweet," said Lillian, who was watching from the corner of her eye. "Brother George has erred. I assume that he was booked to suffer at the suffrage meeting, this fine evening, rather than to hop here in the midst of happiness. I——"

"Hush, Pickles!"

"I pity you, if you by chance accumulate Miss Chapman as a sister!"

"I'm getting used to having her come in and try to cast a chill on my affairs," said Doris. "After this, we'll always count on her."

"It would be a new idea—to send the skeleton an invitation to the feast!"

"Pickles!"

When Chapman came up, after his sister had departed, a little flush blazed on each cheek, and he showed Doris even more than his customary devotion for the remainder of the evening, to Arthur's intense dissatisfaction.

"The race is on; the gun has gone bang-bang; the flag has dropped; the starter's gate has risen to the skies!" said Lillian, sportingly, the next afternoon when, running in on Doris, she found flowers there from both men. "One would think you were to have a party every day, for an indefinite period, the way they carry on."

"Must no one send flowers to me except when I have parties?"

"They ought not, but they will. Undoubtedly you will be smothered in pink rose-buds till someone rescues you from the sweet but prickly mass by marriage—and it may not stop with that."

"Yesterday, I helped buy flowers for you."

"Isn't Jack the dearest thing? If he were not your brother, he too, would be pursuing you, no doubt."

"Do you mean the members of my family don't love me?"

"Love you! They're your slaves; but they can't marry you, and they're the only ones—your father and your brother—who aren't trying to at the present moment, I guess."

"Pickle-lily, you are too absurd. I shall have to put you out if you are not less noisy."

"You couldn't do it," Lillian answered nonchalantly. "You're 'way off your training. All this gayety since you've left college has softened you. A game of basket ball would make you puff like the first motor car. Ker-chug-chug-chug-poof-poof!"

Doris, blushing, smiling, trying to suppress her friend, sat beside her on a sofa, and they were submerged in laughing gossip when Judge Marston entered.

"Are you busy for an hour, dear?" he asked Doris.

"Busy? No. Why, grandfather?"

"Can you come down-town with me?"

She went to him with sparkling eyes. "You darling grandfather!" She turned to Lillian. "He promised me the most beautiful ring! It's down at Tiffany's. He said he'd buy it in a week or so. Oh, grandfather, I am wild to see it!"

"Won't you come with us, Lillian?" he asked. "We'll start presently."

"I can't," she answered. "I'm so sorry. There are some other things which I must do; but may I join you there?"

Judge Marston nodded. "Yes; meet us at Tiffany's." Watch in hand he looked at Doris. "It's half-after-two. Shall we say we'll meet her at half-after-four?"

"Can you be there at four-thirty, Lillian?"

"Oh, easily."

The judge was rather glad to make the down-town journey alone with his grand-daughter, although he had grown fond of Lillian, as they all had. But he had planned that this occasion should afford him opportunity to discuss some very serious matters with Doris.

"Doris," he said, slowly, gravely, after they had started, "we who have passed the middle milestone, and are marching toward the sunset, watch you, who have not reached life's zenith, with a good deal of curiosity."

"That's very pretty; I am glad you do, grandfather."

But she was a little startled. The beginning of the conversation seemed too solemn to lead up merely to the purchase of a ring.

"With curiosity, and, sometimes, a wee bit of anxiety," he went on.

"Have I done things to make you anxious? Have I——"

"Nothing, dear; it is not you, but the long road which stretches out before you, which, naturally, makes those who love you anxious. You see, we know its Hills of Difficulty, and its Valleys of Despair. No traveler on Life's road can entirely escape them."

"Difficulty? Yes; I expect it. But I do not expect despair."

"God grant, my child, that you may never know it! It will depend to such a large extent, on the decisions which you make at crucial times."

She was disappointed in her grandfather. He was usually so nicely comfortable to talk to. At times he showed what really amounted to a genius for entering into her small personal interests, and now he plainly was intending to be prosy—or—or—— She had a shrinking sense of fear that he was about to force an issue for which she was unprepared.

"The choosing of one's partners for the long life-journey is one of them," he said softly.

He was not without appreciation of the fact that he might shock her by discussing these things, now; but he had been wondering acutely. He had watched her growing interest in Arthur Armsby. It worried him. He did not agree with Colonel Marquis that the son of a defaulter could wipe out his father's sin, and Virginia had told him of their visit to Stoddard Thornton's studio. Each of these men constituted a problem. He had an enormous admiration for established things—and George Chapman was established beyond the shadow of a doubt. He glanced quickly at his grand-daughter, almost furtively, indeed, to see what the expression of her face might be.

Had she fully understood him, doubtless it would have been a look of shocked surprise; but she did not: she merely guessed and feared a little.

"Choosing of one's partners?" she said, vaguely troubled.

"Dear, you are coming to the years, now, when that will be the greatest problem you will have to meet, and a great deal for you and for those who love you will depend upon your choice."

"Why, grandfather," she exclaimed incredulously. "I'm just out of college! I'm—why, I haven't thought about such things." She caught herself, remembering her talks with Lillian. "That is, I haven't thought about them seriously."

He scarcely had the heart to reveal, baldly, the problems he was pondering, so he became strategic.

"I saw George Chapman, this morning," he said, trying to be casual.

"So early in the day?"

"At a board-meeting. Prompt to the minute, as he always is and as his father was before him. Bright, energetic, wide-awake. No one could take advantage of him."

"I'm sure of that."

"Splendid fellow. Cultivated, handsome and rich."

"Yes. He *is* a splendid fellow."

"I am glad to hear you say that."

"Why; does anyone think otherwise?"

"No. No one could. I wish, my dear, that you——"

But at this moment, the motor swung up to the curb in front of Tiffany's.

"Well, here we are—I hope I haven't bored you with my prosing!"

"Bored me, grandfather!" She spoke reproachfully, as if the mere suggestion were to be decried; but it was with a feeling of gladness and intense relief that she stepped from the motor.

She had not failed to catch his meaning; but she was not ready to receive it; she was inexpressibly glad to go into the brilliant, fascinating store and lose herself in thoughts of sparkling jewels and gay trinkets—to lose herself, that is, as nearly as was possible; she could not entirely escape from the depression which the conversation in the motor had produced. Why should these things be forced upon her—yet? Why, there should be years of care-free gayety before her ere she should have to meet the mighty problem at which he had hinted. When Lillian came, presently, she greeted her with a sigh of actual gratitude.

Then the selection of the ring began in earnest and occupied a delightful hour. Long before it was completed she had quite forgotten matrimony, George Chapman, problems of all sorts, except the fascinating one of choosing precious baubles.

When they left Tiffany's she was still intoxicated with the glory of massed gems, vibrant with delight over the possession of the very thing she most had wished.

"Come and have tea with me children," the Judge suggested gayly. He was in the highest spirits. He had been giving pleasure to the being he loved most on earth, next to Virginia, and he also thought that he had paved the way along which, he devoutly hoped, his partner's son could march to victory.

"What fun! Where shall we go?" They were standing at the entrance of the store.

"Sherry's? It's not far. Is it too far to walk?"

"No; it's only a step."

The Judge gave the chauffeur his instructions about meeting them, and they started up the sun-lit, animated avenue.

"You're almost as much fun," Lillian said, smiling up at him as they started carefully across the roadway, "as if you'd been in college with us."

"I consider that the highest of compliments," said he gravely.

And then——

Doris never could remember how it occurred. There was the frightened blaring of a Claxton horn; startled spectators screamed shrilly; a policeman cast himself toward them and pushed her and Lillian back toward the sidewalk. The next instant, she saw her grandfather prone on the pavement, disheveled, his face appearing ghastly by contrast to the wet asphalt, and beginning to be ominously marked by slow and spreading red.

Neither she nor Lillian really screamed. Before three officers had formed their prompt, efficient cordon about the injured man, and a fourth had sprung to the arrest of the offending taxi-driver, she was kneeling by her grandfather. And she bore up bravely as they took him into the great store upon the corner, where white faced clerks preceded them into a private office, provided with a couch.

But on the arrival of the blue-capped ambulance surgeon, young, energetic, calmly professional, but very kind, and radiating an atmosphere of competence, she weakly sank into a chair and covering her pale face with trembling hands, sobbed in unison with Lillian who remained close at her side.

"I shall have to take him to the hospital," the surgeon decided presently. "It is a bad concussion; I'm not sure but that it may be a fracture."

"Is it—is it very serious?" Doris faltered.

"At his age," said the surgeon, "it may be or may not be. Is he a relative of yours, Miss?"

"He is my grandfather."

There was nothing in the words, but there was something in the voice, which touched the busy, alert interne.

"Would you like to go with him, Miss? In the ambulance, I mean. And is there anyone whom you would care to notify?"

"I'll attend to that," said Lillian competently. "You go with them, dear. I am sure you want to. I'll come to you directly I have telephoned."

And so the morbid crowd upon the sidewalk had the satisfaction of seeing a beautifully gowned young woman pass through the lane which the police kept clear, and step hurriedly into the ambulance followed by the litter bearers with the victim of the accident.

All the way to the red brick hospital, crouched far on the west side, up-town, she sat silent, cramped, making no movement, save to make certain now and then that her grandfather still breathed, and to touch his cheek caressingly.

At the emergency reception door, when they transferred him from the ambulance to the wheeled litter, she bent above him, watchful for the comfort of his attitude, observant of the faint returning tinge of color to his waxen cheeks, anxious to be of service, but never in the attendants' way.

In the room to which they hurried him, and where an older doctor and a white-capped nurse took charge of him, she stayed as long as they would permit, and then, until Lillian came, waited patiently, pathetically, in a small outer room, to which a kind faced head nurse sympathetically guided her.

When her friend, who had been delayed by a street blockade, finally arrived, Doris began to weep quietly. Soon, her father, mother, and Virginia came. Then, as there was nothing more to be done, and as the doctor had reported no immediate danger, the two girls went home in the motor.

What happened afterward at the home upon the Drive,

Doris later remembered, without much more detail than that which marked her recollections of the accident. She found Chapman waiting there, and as he listened to the story of the disaster, putting in occasionally a vibrant word of sympathy, she was glad that he had come.

After he had reluctantly departed, the fact seemed like a dream that at a certain stage of her recital, he had taken her hands tenderly, kissed them affectionately, and then, in a voice thrilling with emotion, begged her to become his wife; and that, reflecting that this was what the injured man had wished above all things, influenced tremendously by this reflection, she had murmured an assent.

When Jack heard at the club about the accident, he hurried to the hospital, only to be sent home promptly, with good news from the patient, to comfort Doris.

She told him very simply what had happened. He tried to offer his good wishes, but found many words impossible. Indeed, he felt this news to be almost as tragic as the news of the catastrophe which so unexpectedly had sprung out of the innocent-eyed afternoon, to strike down his grandfather.

"I must telephone to Armsby," he said glumly. "Poor chap! He'll take it hard!"

CHAPTER XIII

Wearily returning late from the hospital, Colonel and Mrs. Marquis were not surprised when they found Doris waiting for them. As they glanced through the wide door from the hall, she sat at the far end of the library, her figure in its dark dress scarcely visible against the dull elegance of the heavy furnishings and hangings. But the near-by radiance of a lamp revealed almost startlingly the pallor of her weary face.

"*Doris*, dear!" said Mrs. Marquis, hurrying to her. "Dear child, you should not have waited up for us!"

"How is grandfather?" The girl's voice was faint from the weariness following the startling day.

"Oh, better! Very much better. He's quite all right, in fact."

"Then why did you leave him at the hospital?" The horror of the accident was still vivid in her mind.

"He's not quite well enough to come home, dear." Her mother smiled sympathetically, despite her own exhaustion.

"You are sure he's really all right?"

"Absolutely. Come, dear; you must get some sleep."

"Where is Virginia?"

"She waited at the hospital. They made her comfortable in an adjoining room. She felt she must be near him."

Doris drew her mother down upon the chair-arm, and

191

took her father's hand. While she did not realize fully
the importance of the step which she had taken, she
knew her parents must be informed at once.

"I've something I must tell you." Her voice and face
were exceedingly grave.

"You are tired, dear. Won't to-morrow do?"

"No; I must tell you now. I wish grandfather might
have known to-night. It—it would have pleased him, I
am sure."

"What is it, dear?" her mother inquired anxiously,
vague apprehensions stirring in her breast.

The Colonel smiled indulgently. His less acute mind
did not grasp, intuitively, the fact that the information
which his daughter wished to give was likely to be epoch-
making for them all.

"Mr. Chapman came this afternoon," said Doris,
slowly. "I told him of the accident, and he was very
sweet and sympathetic."

"Yes?" said Mrs. Marquis, in a frightened voice. The
muscles of her heart were tightening rapidly.

"And—then—he asked me—to marry him."

"Doris!" The mother's exclamation was the merest
gasp.

Colonel Marquis, at last vividly alive to the importance
of the moment, stepped forward, startled. "Doris,
child!"

"It was just as I was thinking about grandfather. Oh!
I was so worried! The accident never would have happened, had he not gone to buy that ring for me. I was
wishing I might please him, in some way—do something
which would make him happier, and make his pain a
little easier to bear."

The Colonel spoke with more intensity than he intended: "And you told Chapman——"

"He was so dear, and kind, and sympathetic! I . . . said . . . 'yes.' Don't you think it will please grandfather?"

"Doris, Doris! you must think about yourself, not about your grandfather!" her father urged.

"Do you love him, Doris? Do you really love George Chapman?" was her mother's anxious inquiry.

"Yes, mother," Doris answered readily. But she did not hurry on enthusiastically, nor did she hesitate, with radiant blushes, silenced by the shyness of a great happiness. "I suppose I must," she said, with rather striking gravity. "He is so kind, so thoughtful, so—so genuine. Is he not, father? Love him? Love him? Have I not told him I would marry him?"

Her mother went with her to her room, and lingered there anxiously, almost as in Doris's childhood when Mammy's ministrations chanced to be impossible because of rheumatism, or because Doris, swept by love, demanded that her mother wait with her until she went to sleep. All the sensations of the day, save this alone, were for the time forgotten.

"Orlando," she said later, to her husband, "I—wonder! Oh, I wonder! When I think of how I felt just after you had asked, and I had answered, and then think of Doris, as she was to-night——"

"She is worrying about her grandfather," he suggested, advancing an explanation which he had recently devised to calm his own too definite anxieties. It was the instinct of his long and perfect married life to be the comforter when anything distressed her.

"Could it have been that worry—an exaggerated desire to please poor father? No; oh, no; that would be impossible in such a *vital* matter; but—it seems to me that something must be wrong. Something . . . something . . . she does not love him as I loved you, Orlando! Not as I loved you!"

"We cannot see into her heart, my dear; and you are overtired, overwrought. You must get some rest, sweetheart. There is yet time, you must remember."

She sighed wearily. "Her one wish is to please father," she lamented. "She mentioned it a dozen times."

"Well, it *will* please him."

"But if that has influenced her unduly——"

"Go to sleep, dear. We shall see the matter with more understanding in the morning."

Mrs. Marquis knew how deep her husband's disappointment must be. She felt certain he was thinking not alone of George Chapman, and worrying about his fitness to make Doris happy, but was also thinking about Stoddard.

.   .   .   .

The following morning when he sat opposite his sister at breakfast, George Chapman's difficult hour came. Perhaps he was not quite afraid of Jane, but in his earlier years he had been, and even since his arrival at maturity she had exercised over him a dominating and somewhat domineering influence. He had defied it rarely in his youth and never in his later years, perhaps because he shrank from the inevitable discord which would follow such a course; or perhaps because it never seemed worth while. He had not been able to decide exactly how Jane felt toward Doris, but on various occasions he had been promptly informed of her feelings toward any matrimonial tendency upon his part.

For these reasons, he led up hesitantly to the subject of his betrothal. He would have been glad to put it off until a future time; the thought of mentioning it at breakfast was particularly distasteful, for Jane's often trying temper was more likely to be definitely acid then than later in the day. He knew, however, that it would be worse than foolish, besides being inconsiderate, to delay the great announcement. A newspaper lay folded by his sister's plate, and although it was not possible that the engagement could be mentioned in it, the printed sheet suggested to him that should he not reveal it then, she would be almost sure to hear of it from some other source before the day was over. Newspapers are but one means through which the current information of the world is spread.

"Jane, dear," he said, at length, "I have some news for you."

She looked up quickly from her habitual task at the coffee-urn. Puzzled and even slightly worried by the look upon his face, she sent a meaning glance out of the corner of her eye toward the two servants, and he was much abashed to realize that in his abstraction he had not at all remembered them. He acknowledged the hint a little awkwardly.

"Er—certainly," he said hastily. "The greatest news! Judge Marston——"

"I hope he is much better."

To tell the truth, he did not know just how the night had fared with the unfortunate old gentleman; but he nodded, saying somewhat ineffectually: "I hope so, surely."

"Now what is it?" she asked sharply, as soon as they were left alone. Her anxiety had been growing during every moment of delay after his original announcement.

He hesitated. The episode had disconcerted him.

"What is this greatest news of yours?" she asked, looking at him with suspicion.

It took some courage to reply at once, but he managed it. "Jane, dear," he slowly said, "I have—er—asked Doris Marquis to—er—marry me."

His expectation of electrical results was by no means disappointed. Aghast, Jane sat back in her chair. So great was her sharp relaxation of surprise that it almost took disaster to the coffee-urn. "George Chapman, are you crazy?" she demanded. Then: "Well, what did she say when you a—er—first became insane?"

"Jane! Jane!" he soothed.

"Did she accept you?"

"Yes!"

"I've been afraid of it!" Jane snapped the words at him.

"Why," he declared falsely, "I thought you would congratulate me!"

"You know better. It scared you half to death to think of telling me—and heaven knows it should have! You must be mad. Quite mad."

"Isn't she a beautiful and cultivated girl? You can't say she is not."

Her eyes flashed fire. "Was it the work of cultivation —to make me wink at Professor Adzit?" There was no humor, but an acid edge in her voice.

He did not understand. "To make you wink at Professor Adzit! Why, what can you mean?"

"You come with me. Never mind your chop. You'll eat many a cold chop if you leave me and marry any flighty girl. You might as well get used to it."

"But Doris——"

"George, come with me."

Obediently he followed her into the drawing-room, where Doris's rather striking portrait of her held a place of honor. "You see it?" she asked earnestly.

"Yes; but I have seen it many times."

"Examine the left eye."

He did so, but saw no suspicious signs about it. There was certainly more paint around it than elsewhere on the canvas, but——

"She repaired it with the utmost care before she sent it to me," Jane said grimly. "But, for the Exhibition, she cut a slit above that eye and fixed a piece of painted canvas, like an eyelid, with which to make it seem as if I winked. She had a rubber band to pull it back to place, and a long string ran down behind the picture which she could twitch, when—when the devilish thought was in her mind. She twitched it while Professor Adzit was standing looking at the picture."

A turmoil of mixed emotions filled her brother's soul. He was seriously concerned, but also somewhat amused. These warring tendencies left his face entirely without expression. "At Welleslar, was it?" he inquired.

"Of course it was at Welleslar. Where else could it be? And you propose to marry any girl who would make your sister—your own sister—wink at a professor!"

"But, Jane dear, even if she did do it——"

"You doubt me, do you?"

"No; no," he declared hastily. "I was only thinking that you might possibly be mistaken."

"See! At the very start she makes you doubt me!" Jane's face assumed a deeply injured look; such a look upon Jane's face was a danger signal with which he was only too familiar. He went back hastily to the breakfast-table, but did not complete his breakfast. "I must hurry down-town," he declared. "I am leaving for Virginia City Saturday. I'm sure you'll feel quite differently after you have thought the matter over. A girlish prank, Jane, ought not to make a life-long enemy."

"Girlish prank!" said Jane, with an unmistakable sniff. "I *never* shall feel differently."

"Jane—please don't make me unhappy!"

Not without an effort did she control her wrath, substituting for it the appearance of sorrow. "Yet, without a moment's thought, you make me miserable!"

He lingered, touched a little, not very far from anger —thoroughly uncomfortable. His sister looked at him appraisingly. She had not studied him for years without acquiring the ability to read his moods with uncanny accuracy. She now knew his mind to be thoroughly made up and that nothing but a miracle would change it. She knew perfectly that open opposition would not work that miracle and so decided to avoid it. But she made haste to burst into bitter tears, so that he might not be out of range before they had begun to flow, though he departed with as little delay as possible.

At the Marquis home, where, presently, he called to make his adieux before departing for the West, he found the parents of his bride-to-be most hospitable and cordial, and—a little grave. Judge Marston, Colonel Marquis said, was much improved and, as soon as he had learned of the engagement, had asked that Doris and his old friend's son should come to him at once.

Accordingly, alone in Chapman's car, they made the journey to the hospital. The Judge greeted them with a smile.

Doris could not find the words with which to talk to him, at first, and so, in lieu of them, reached for Chapman's hand, and conveyed it with her own, to the old gentleman's. The resulting glow of satisfaction on the pallid face delighted her.

"Doris, I am very glad!" His eyes held her face, a moment, lovingly, and then turned to Chapman's with a strange expression of appraisement and authority in them. "George?"

"It is more good fortune than I merit," Chapman answered humbly.

This pleased the Judge. "No; not that; you are your father's son and there was no unworthiness in him. But —you must never, now, forget your parentage; you must never for an instant lose sight of the fact that we are trusting you with the very greatest of our treasures. Can we trust you, George?"

"Yes, Judge; you can trust me." Chapman's voice was low and solemn.

"Yes; I believe we can trust him, Doris," said the Judge, his earnestness relaxing after a moment's study of the younger man's expression. "The Chapmans always could be trusted."

She gently pressed his hand, which she had not once relinquished. It seemed very solemn to her—all of this.

His head settled in his pillow. Evidently the episode had wearied him.

His face was strangely gray against the spotless linen of the prim hospital bed; its pallor was accentuated by the careful bandage which was bound about his forehead. His hand, now lying loosely in his granddaughter's, was tremulous, pathetic; indeed, there were about him many signs of age which Doris never before had observed. His injuries had proved not very serious, but she was certain that the accident had done him grievous harm, the shock affecting him more deeply than the surface wounds. It suddenly had made of him an old, old man. Her heart went out to him anew. His age and her developing youth had been the closest of companions; an extraordinary sympathetic understanding always existed between them.

She bowed her head upon her hands, as they held his in a tender clasp, and with difficulty fought back the tears.

Presently the nurse came in to tell them that their time was up.

A ruddy-cheeked Canadian girl, attractive in immaculate uniform of blue and white, and comforting, despite the jaunty tilt of her white cap, went with them down the hall. Sympathizing with the keen distress of the young visitor she spoke reassuringly as they waited for the coming of the elevator.

"Is there really any danger?" Doris begged. "You know the doctors wouldn't be as frank with us as they have been with you."

"Oh, no; there is no danger," was the nurse's cheerful answer. "He will be longer getting well than if he were,

say, of your age; one as old as he, has less recuperative
power, you know. But never fear; he will get well."

Doris clung to her appealingly. Afterwards she wondered why it had not been her impulse to turn for comfort to her fiancé, but at the moment the idea did not
occur to her, and, while he evidently sympathized with
her—she could not possibly doubt this—she believed that
he, too, had failed to think of such a thing.

He did not even take her hand; but, instead, with a
distressed face, stood beyond the elevator-shaft door,
while the strange girl offered solace and assurance. And
after they were in the motor, settled for the homeward
trip through the brisk autumn air, he was content with
saying carefully considered words of comfort.

She would have been happier had he put his arm about
her and drawn her protectingly to his side, omitting all
his placid, reassuring phrases, although Doris did not
realize this at the time.

Within a week it was decided that the wedding should
be hastened. Judge Marston wished it very much and
under the circumstances they were anxious to comply
with his desires. Virginia opposed the haste, at first,
but her slight opposition disappeared as her father's condition failed to improve.

"It must be a beautiful church-wedding," Mrs. Marquis declared firmly. "The one thing in her life of
which it seems most cruel to deprive a girl is a
church-wedding. Doris's wedding-day, unfortunately,
may be overshadowed by her grandfather's illness, but
we must make it otherwise the most perfect of all days.
We must do everything to insure this."

Preparations were hurried forward without pause, but

strangely lacked that gayety which should characterize such preparations. In order to arrange his business matters so that he could leave the country later on the wedding-journey—provided Judge Marston's condition should improve sufficiently so that a wedding-journey would be other than a period of worry for the bride—George was obliged to leave the city. Doris was astonished and a little frightened to discover that his going gave her no deep grief, but, rather, an indefinite sense of relief.

At first Jack sulked a little over the whole thing, and spent much time with Arthur Armsby, whom, he thought, had been ill-treated, and was completely crushed, Jack told his mother, by the blow to his own hopes.

Virginia paid a rather trying secret visit to the studio on the quaint street, down-town.

"May I ask you to take something to Miss Doris?" Stoddard asked, as she was leaving.

She found that looking at him was a tragic matter; his face had paled when he had heard the news which she had carried with such reluctance, and the color had not yet returned to it.

"Certainly; I shall be glad to," she replied.

He went to the little niche which Doris had discovered when she had visited the studio, and which she had not mentioned, even to her aunt. Virginia gave a little cry of admiration as he drew back the curtain and revealed the statuette.

He took it from its place and then stood, a second, contemplating the bare space where it had been. Then he placed the exquisite bit of marble in Virginia's hands.

"I should like to send it to her as a wedding-gift,"

said he. "It is not quite a duplicate of the one I gave her mother, for it is done in marble—rather a nice bit of marble, too. Will it please her, do you think?"

"Oh, it is beautiful!" Virginia cried; but her voice quivered strangely. It would have been difficult for her to master a long sentence at that moment.

"I have been—fond of it," he said. "Please give it to her with assurances of—of my highest respect and admiration."

She was half certain of a tremor in his voice, but he soon controlled it.

"I shall guard it very carefully," Virginia answered solemnly, "and I am sure that she will value it far above most wedding-gifts."

"His voice was very near to choking," she said to Mrs. Marquis, later, "but he was superbly brave about it. It all depressed me beyond words."

"Virginia, dear!"

Nor were thoughts of Stoddard entirely absent from the mind of the young bride-elect. She found them not less difficult to evade than reflections on the sorrow which her marriage would give Arthur, although she tried to put all reveries of this sort from her, indefinitely feeling them to be disloyal; but she could not invariably force them to the background.

Soon, however, preparations for the wedding so absorbed her time that she had vitality for little else except her daily visit to the hospital. And Virginia, finding that affairs were moving forward with inevitable swiftness, endeavored to resign herself to what seemed ordained, and joined energetically in the great work of getting ready for the ceremony.

As the enormous boxes holding the trousseau came home, to be emptied by the somewhat careless, always clumsy Desdemona's fingers, Doris longed unaccountably for Mammy Rose; and the fact that her old nurse would not be present when the ceremony was performed was still another cause for sorrow when she allowed herself to dwell upon it in those crowded weeks so strangely blended of elation and depression.

All day the house was filled with flocks of chattering girls; Lillian, especially, was rarely absent; there was a continual flutter of arrival and departure. An almost feverish restlessness kept Doris from any extensive measure of real thought.

A week before the date set for the wedding an imposing array of gifts already rested on the tables which had been reserved for them in the library and drawing-room —an array so gorgeous and so valuable that Colonel Marquis, being warned by experienced New Yorkers, added a new member to the household in the person of a man from a detective agency.

This man startled Virginia, when, after much hesitation, she decided to place the statuette secretly with the display. She had taken it, boxed carefully, to the house, and left it in the hall, where it attracted no attention, during an era of so many packages. It was her wish that it should be a real surprise to Doris; that it should be standing by itself, its loveliness undulled by juxtaposition with any of the other gifts when she should catch her first glimpse of it. The detective, making his rounds of the rooms with a cautious and suspicious tread, encountered her as she was arranging it, and the small fright attendant on this episode revealed to her the wrecked condition of her nerves.

The following morning, when, bearing in her hands new gifts for which to find suitable places, Doris discovered it in all its snowy, airy grace, she paused, spellbound. For a full minute she stood gazing at it wonderingly; then she deposited the packages she carried without knowing where she put them, went closer to the statuette and, to her own amazement, presently bowed her head upon the little silken rug Virginia had placed upon the table before she had arranged the statuette upon it.

Desdemona entered with a mammoth box, staggering behind the size of it, rather than beneath the weight of it. "Why, Miss Dawiss!" she exclaimed, "Heah's yo' pooty bride-dress, honey, an' theah yo' is, a-cryin'!"

Frivolous might Desdemona be and unreliable, but when she saw her loved young mistress in distress her sympathy was instantaneous and keen.

Doris realized the need of quick dissembling. She, herself, did not understand the exact reason for her tears; but she was instinctively aware that it must be concealed from all the world. That consciousness was definite.

"Oh, thank you, Desdemona. Take the box up to my room, please. Don't mind my little fit of weeping. I suppose I'm overtired."

"Sho' 'nuff, wid yo' gran'pa sick, an' all!" said Desdemona, sympathetically.

Then her eyes were caught by the white purity of the statuette and she actually let the precious box slip to the floor.

"Lawd! Sakes! Ef dere ain't dat very little image

Mistuh Tho'nton wuhked on in his room, down Souf! Ah thought he mus' be crazy——"

She stepped closer to it and then recognized its true intent. Her astonishment increased.

"But close by it looks lak—why, Miss Dawiss—why, it's *you!* Jes' ez little—an' so white—cut out o' gravestone—but it's *you!* Well, now! Ah suspicioned 'twus a heathen idol! Yo' ain't changed so ve'y much, Miss Dawiss—mebbe yo' wuz jes' de leas' mite slimmuh."

"It's very perfect, isn't it?" said Doris, struggling for her self-control.

"Puffick! It's ez good ez—ez a tin-type! An' Ah remembuhs when he wuz a-makin' it—kind o' seemed lak he wuz settin' in a pew in chu'ch. Mebbe dat's what made me think it wuz a heathen image—he seemed so kind o' lak he wuz a-wuhshippin'."

"Run on with the gown, now, Desdemona," Doris urged, unable to endure the conversation any longer. "Was any message left with it?"

"Dat madam, she'll be heah to fit at 'leben o'clock." She started from the room, but her eyes wandered back toward the slim purity of the statuette. "Laws, laws! Ain't dat jes' unpossible!"

During this exciting period, Jane Chapman was an occasional visitor. To the best of an ability which was but meager, she was accepting the situation pleasantly and calmly; but Doris now and then caught a glance from her, which may have been unconscious, but which almost made her shudder. The thought that her *menage* should be disturbed by the departure from it of her brother; the thought that, should he die before her, after he had married, his share of the Chapman fortune would not be all hers, but would pass principally to another—these two reflections surely were partially responsible for the animosity which Jane dimly veiled; but more than either of them, the remembrance of that painted, winking eye disturbed her and helped her to achieve what was, unquestionably, a feeling close to hatred of the bride-elect.

Later that morning Jane was present when Desdemona, with excited, reverent fingers, took from its great box the bride's gown, stuffed into a meager counterfeit of shapeliness by tissue-paper, wrapped in soft, protecting fabric. As the rustling charmeuse-satin and the shimmering chiffon-cloth were gradually revealed by the removal of the covering, the maiden-lady suffered an accession of resentment which she found extremely difficult to hide.

The arrival from the jeweler's, at this very moment, of the bridegroom's gift, the gem-studded ornament with which the veil was to be clasped, almost made her ill. Her brother had not told her of this lavish token and she looked at it with keen appraisal, her wrath growing into fierce antagonism as she realized how very valuable it was. With considerable difficulty, she kept herself from giving voice to her displeasure, or from making some unfavorable prediction, based upon the mad extravagance which it was plain had been implanted, simultaneously with love, in her brother's surprising nature.

When, a moment later, as Jane was struggling with this feeling of bitterness, Doris, handling the pin with fumbling fingers due more to her excitement than to carelessness, dropped it, Jane actually opened her set lips to speak sharply. Had she gone further, and really yielded to the impulse, Lillian, who was watching her with bated breath, half-frightened, half-amused, would not have been surprised.

As the glittering thing fell to the floor, Doris did not cry out, alarmed by the mischance, but actually laughed!

"How clumsy!" she said lightly, as she bent over to recover it from the mass of crumpled tissue with which the floor was littered.

She did not find it readily, and stepped slightly forward as she bent to more minute examination of the rubbish.

"Oh," she cried, "I've stepped on it!"

When she raised it, it was evident to Jane's angry eye that Doris had not only stepped on it, but had broken off its clasp.

That Jane refrained from critical exclamation was supreme proof of her self-control. Not only had the girl received a gift which meant a mad expenditure on the part of George, but, immediately, she had treated it so carelessly, so disrespectfully, that it had suffered injury! Disrespect to George's gift was disrespect to George! And the sin was magnified by the fact that George, himself, had sinned in sending her a jewel so superb.

The ornament was to play its large and almost tragic part in subsequent events, which Jane surely did not know, though she gave much bitter thought to the unfortunate jewel. Her own life had been singularly free from romance, and, although she did not realize it, this helped make unpleasant the joyousness of Doris, the mere sight of her wedding-finery.

In all her life her brother had not given Jane a single

jewel (she would have been resentful of his wild extravagance if he had done so) and this doubled her displeasure at the large expenditure, which the beauty of the diamond-studded pin implied. Into what insanities might he not plunge after marriage, if he wasted thousands now, upon a jeweled bauble for a bridal-veil? And if the woman he had chosen for his wife could treat so rich a gift so carelessly, what hope was there that she would later show conservatism in the care of that part of the Chapman fortune which would be unfortunately at her mercy? Jane departed, almost at once, her yeasty anger unexpressed, but bubbling close upon an outbreak.

That afternoon and evening she could think of little else than the insulted pin and the great sum George must have paid for it. She wondered fiercely what that sum had been.

At length the wish to know became a real obsession, and, next day, she went to Tiffany's to make inquiry.

The morning had been dark and lowering, with occasional showers, although the sun had recently burst through the clouds and changed the pavement of the famous Avenue into a jewel-spangled way. An awning had been stretched from the curb across the sidewalk to the door of the great store, to shelter from the rain the favorites of fortune who form the major portion of the throng of visitors to the celebrated jewel-mart.

Short-skirted, thickly-shod, armed with an umbrella which, even when rolled as it was now, was still of formidable proportions, Jane approached the arched opening affording footway through the awning to sidewalk pedestrians. Among the little group of waiting motors, she saw the Marquis chauffeur in his car, and, almost at the same moment, saw Arthur Armsby approaching in another car. Drifting listlessly up the street, at the wheel of his dull-black, high-powered runabout, he looked pale and haggard.

This gave Jane a certain satisfaction. His face was set and moody and dark shadows beneath his eyes might have told of grief alone, or as Jane instantly and uncharitably surmised, might have told of grief, and, also, unwise efforts to find surcease from it in champagne.

She did not like him. That she believed him suffering because of George's triumph where he himself had wished to win, was one of the few comforts which the situation offered her.

Close by the awning she paused, watching him with curiosity, just as Doris, somewhat to Jane's confusion, stepped out of the store, a jewel-box held in her hand. Being far too lightly shod for a wet day, according to Jane's notions, the lovely girl was picking her footsteps daintily along the now somewhat sodden carpet stretched beneath the awning. She did not see the sister of her fiancé, nor glance out to the roadway, where Arthur had been compelled to stop by a halt in the dense stream of traffic, which had just occurred in obedience to the raised hand of an officer upon the crossing.

Jane saw Arthur's uninterested eyes roam along the sidewalk carelessly until they glimpsed the little group there by the awning. To her genuine relief they passed her by, unrecognized, but half to her indignation and half to her curious and ungenerous delight, they lighted wonderfully when they found Doris standing waiting for her car, which, like his own, had been brought to a standstill by the traffic and for the moment could not get to her.

While he could not go forward, it was still possible for him to shoot his car in through a narrow gap, to the entrance of the canvas-covered way, and this he did, after a moment's slight hesitation.

Jane saw Doris move back almost shrinkingly, astonished at his abrupt appearance. Then, recovering, the girl held out her hand in greeting.

There was not the slightest evidence that the meeting had been pre-arranged; there was, indeed, every indication that it had not been; but the sight of it enraged Jane. It would have been difficult to suggest a means by which Doris could have avoided Arthur, had she wished to; there was no reason known to Jane why she should wish to, or feel obligated to. Certainly not even Jane could think a girl who had achieved the honor of betrothal to her brother George should feel it necessary to refuse to speak to other friends; yet there sprang into her heart the bitter thought that Doris was disloyal when she greeted Arthur pleasantly. That the meeting was plainly unexpected and that the girl was evidently embarrassed, did not allay the older woman's wrath, nor her suspicions.

Now the young people were within an arm's length of her, but instinctively, if not too honorably, she slipped behind one of the flaps of canvas which hung on either side of the curb-end of the awning and there waited, listening intently. It is doubtful if she definitely planned eaves-dropping; only the merest chance made it possible for her to overhear a few words of what passed between the two. Indeed she did not hear their greeting and what immediately followed it. Before she caught a word Arthur already had said something, while on his face played a look of yearning, sorrow and reproach that did not escape Jane's keen, suspicious eyes.

Then, she heard:

"But may I not have, for the last time, a few moments' talk with you? For the last time, Doris!"

Jane saw the girl's eyes as she listened. "She is frightened," she reflected. "I should think she would be!"

She noted very carefully the look upon his face. "He's suffering horridly," she mentally commented.

"For the last time, Doris!" the boy pleaded. "The last time before your marriage! . . . Oh, what a lovely bride you'll be!"

Jane observed that Doris was as pale as death. The hand which held the little package was pressed tightly against her breast; the other trembled as it fumbled in the readjustment of the chiffon about her throat.

"Arthur!" Jane heard her say. "Oh . . . Arthur!"

"Let me take you in my car a little way—please, Doris. Just once, and for the last, last time!"

"Would it be wrong?"

"Wrong? No. Why should it be? How could it be? . . . Please, Doris!"

After another second's hesitation Doris stepped into his car, waving her hand toward Julian, as she did so, in a signal to him to fall back and follow.

Just then the stream of traffic started on again and Arthur's car swung out into the moving line. They soon had disappeared, merged indistinguishably into the slowly-moving mass of vehicles. But long after it was impossible for her to identify the car which held them, Jane stood gazing intently after them—so intently that presently a pedestrian collided with her rather sharply. It roused her, and she passed on into the store, more bent than ever on learning just what George had spent upon that ornament.

She gained this information without difficulty, and it added to the fierce resentment against Doris which was burning in her brain.

During every moment of her slow walk home, she dwelt upon the great cost of the ornament and the episode of Doris's meeting with young Armsby. The one filled her with a growing wrath, the other began slowly to suggest to her one last, desperate move which she might make at this, the eleventh hour, to stop the marriage of her brother to the girl whom, now, she definitely hated.

She had reached the entrance to the great, gloomy, brownstone Chapman residence, before she felt a thrill of hope. There she began to wonder if it might not be possible that out of the young folks' meeting she might build a story which would prove his error to her brother?

Entering the house without disturbing any of the servants, she went at once to her own room and there sank into depths of thought. Lowered shades held the room in a half-gloom, but she did not raise them; she did not lay aside her wraps or stoop to remove her rubbers. Even her umbrella remained gripped tightly in her hand as she sat down to make a final, desperate effort to work out the problem.

Slowly and laboriously a plan grew in her mind.

When she rose from her absorption, for the first time conscious of the fact that she still wore her hat, she believed that she had found an angle from which she might approach her brother with some chance of making a definite impression.

It was a strange, weird afternoon she spent there in the gloomy house; such window shades as had been raised she drew down with her own hands, to the amazement of the servants; she declared she did not care for any luncheon. All the afternoon she sat in the drawing-room, immersed in thought, and when the bell of the telephone rang she did not go to the instrument to answer the call. When the aged butler somewhat timidly appeared to speak of this, she motioned him away with an imperious gesture.

She ate very little dinner, and after she had risen from the table went at once to her own room, where, for several hours, she either paced the floor monotonously or sat at a low table, drumming with her fingers on its polished walnut, or, statue-like, remained inert, gazing frowningly at nothing.

To such a tense rigidity of excited readiness for her great effort was she keyed, by midnight, that it was with the greatest difficulty she secured a few hours' sleep. By sunrise she was up again and dressed, waiting with a stony, grimly tolerant patience for the moment of her brother's coming.

When the message which told the exact hour of his arrival reached her, she tore the envelope with fingers, which were strangely tremulous for her, and that afternoon she telephoned for the car not less than a full hour sooner than was necessary, going down the steps and getting into the great limousine the moment it pulled up before the house. She had given but slight thought to her dress; that she had not even paid her hair enough attention to make it lie smoothly upon her forehead was a neglect which so impressed the chauffeur that he inquired cautiously if she were ill.

"No; quite well," said she. "Quite well. Be quick, please. Mr. Chapman will arrive at four o'clock. I wish to meet him at the station."

"But it's not much after two, ma'am."

"Never mind; please get along. We shall very likely be delayed upon the way."

The man looked at her incredulously. "I'll bet she's got bad news for him," he ruminated wisely. "She never would be so anxious to be prompt if she was carrying good tidings."

The chauffeur knew Miss Chapman. He had been with her for years.

When they reached the station she waited in the car while he went in to learn if the train would be on time, and when he returned, telling her that it had been reported somewhat late, but might make up the loss, she amazed him by replying that she would remain where she was, although at the best an hour must pass before her brother could arrive.

Fully fifteen minutes before the train, by any possibility, could reach the train shed, she left the car and disappeared within, openly feeing with a dollar a uniformed porter, on condition that he take her to a point where she surely would get the first glimpse of the alighting passengers.

'A sturdy rope was stretched to separate incoming

travelers from the waiting throng, but when she saw George coming down the platform she completely disregarded the polite protests of the astonished guard, dodged under the frail barrier and approached her brother breathlessly.

Her appearance startled him. In days gone by there had been little in the nature of their family relationship to warrant him in thinking she would meet him at the station. Theirs never had been a demonstrative affection. And her demeanor and attire astonished him. Her habitually elaborate, unfashionable neatness was conspicuously absent; her bonnet was a bit awry; her hair wandered in loose locks; her face was somewhat pale; she raised her hands to catch his arm in a queer, eager gesture.

"Why, Jane! What in the world——"

"Oh, George," she interrupted, "I have such dreadful things to tell you!"

"Dreadful things to tell me?"

They had stopped and were blocking those back of them. An officer, observant of the meeting, and judging by Jane's looks that nothing less than death in her immediate family had stirred her to such a violation of the station rules as dodging underneath the rope, refrained from making any protest, but urged them insistently along, so that the stream would not be further hindered.

"You must not marry Doris Marquis! You must not marry Doris Marquis!" Jane exclaimed, as soon as they were in the motor.

"Jane? Jane?" he said, amazed and frightened. "What do you mean? What can you mean?"

She had, by this time, intensified her deep emotions to the point of tears.

"She doesn't love you," she said brokenly; "I am sure of it."

The man was speechless, staring with frightened eyes out of a pale and startled face.

"I saw her yesterday with Arthur Armsby, and——" Jane's voice broke and she did not complete the sentence.

"Saw her with Armsby? Suppose you did? Why should that make you think——"

Jane had now reached a state bordering on hysteria, a condition so extremely foreign to her that it seriously alarmed her brother. The noticeable graying of his face, apparent to her, even in the dim light of the limousine, added to her excitement, for it was another proof of his strong affection for the girl whom she had learned to hate.

"He loves her!" she thought bitterly. "He loves her far better than he ever has loved me!" Then, with a touch of exultation: "He loves her well enough to give her up if I can once convince him that if he marries her he will be making her unhappy."

Then, making every word count, adding a touch not quite truthful here and there, she told about the meeting by the awning.

At first he could make nothing of this, looking at her curiously as if suspicious that an illness had affected the normal balance of her reason, but, she added, just before they reached the house:

"George, dear, it will mean unhappiness for both of you. It is Arthur Armsby whom she loves, not you. If you could have seen them! And everyone is talking of it. She was forced into accepting you by the Judge's illness. He is crazy to have you in the family."

Had she been able to impute to Doris some unworthy motive she would have been better satisfied. Ah, if only she could have charged her with being mercenary! But the Marquises themselves were rich enough, and young Armsby's fortune was as great as Chapman's own, while socially his family was more distinguished. But she talked on ceaselessly with an impressive earnestness, and finally convincingly.

Once within doors, George sank into a library chair in a stunned silence, having waved away his man, who met them in the hall with broad, congratulatory smiles as befits a valet on his master's wedding-day.

Jane watched her miserable brother with intent but furtive eyes. It was plain that she had shaken him to the foundations of his soul; but would this be effective?

For a long half hour he remained silent, thinking deeply; and Jane did not break in on his silence, although she wept almost constantly, but noiselessly, in a near chair. She could not feel sure of the nature of his thoughts, and the uncertainty was maddening.

At length his valet knocked, and George duliy called to him to enter.

"I. beg your pardon, sir; it's getting late, sir. It is nearly six, sir, and the ceremony is for seven."

"Go away, please!" his master answered, without looking at him.

The man withdrew, so utterly amazed that Jane saw him bump into the door frame as he passed into the hall.

"George!" she said softly, really frightened.

"And you, too, Jane; please go away," he told her gently.

"But, George—why, you've not even taken off your overcoat!" She did not realize that she herself was dressed exactly as she had been at the station.

"No," he replied. Then he looked up at her sharply. "You've not been lying, have you, Jane?"

She shrank, amazed. Never in his life had he said anything like that to her. *"Why, George!"*

"You hate her," he said slowly, and so calmly, judiciously and dispassionately that it frightened her anew. "You are jealous of her. You'd do anything to harm her. I've been thinking it out carefully. You have not been lying, have you, in a sort of desperation?"

This was so near to the exact truth that it filled her with terror. "No . . . no . . . no!" she gasped. "No, George!"

"Well, sit down again, then, while I think. If you have been lying, Jane . . . Don't go away and don't talk, please."

She did exactly as she was ordered, now stirred by a great apprehension. Had she overshot the mark? If he should find her out what would he do? Perhaps he might refuse ever to speak to her again! That was a dreadful thought, for, although Jane really knew little about love, he was all she had—it had been as much as anything her terror of impending solitude which had tempted her to definite wickedness.

Perhaps she had not realized, until that moment, the viciousness of her course; she had merely had an end to gain and gone about attaining it without much thinking of the means which she employed. Would he ever forgive her if he learned how trivial had been the base upon which she had reared her tower of lies? Would be . . . would he . . . ?

As Jane Chapman sat and pondered these things, she suffered as she never had before, in all her life.

And what would happen at the Marquis home? The hour set for the ceremony was almost at hand and he had not even dressed, or spoken to them by telephone. Had she started a procession of events which would involve them all in scandal and newspaper talk? She shrank from thought of this with horror.

"George, dear?" she said timidly.

"Keep quiet, please."

Another half-hour passed, and then, to her inexpressible relief, he rose. "Ring for the car, please, Jane," he said in a dead voice.

"But you've not dressed!"

"Ring for the car, please."

CHAPTER XIV

Before the Marquis home, the motors stood waiting to take the wedding-party to the church; around the place was everywhere the flutter of excitement, of arriving guests and messengers; every window glowed brilliantly; laughter and subdued talk marked a group of young men waiting near the threshold; as yet, there was no evidence that anything had occurred which had not been expected.

A little knot of curious passers-by had gathered at one side of the entrance.

Within half-an-hour Desdemona and a white maid, better trained to such occasions, had finished dressing Doris. Mrs. Marquis and Virginia had arranged the long, shimmering veil; Lillian, somewhat nervous, very much impressed, had aided with countless little services.

When Mrs. Marquis clasped in its place the jeweled ornament which had been broken, it was with very tremulous fingers. She was about to lose her greatest treasure, but she was bearing up with that quiet, accepting bravery, with which mothers must endure.

Observing her sister's struggle with emotions almost stronger than she could control, Virginia tried valiantly to be amusing, to divert the mother's mind from the tragedy of her impending loss, to the pleasanter reflections that her darling was about to step upon a pathway leading to inevitable happiness. She rallied her with tender reminiscences of her own wedding-day; but her voice occasionally broke. Gay talk of weddings and of wedding-days required especial bravery from Virginia. Little sobs, adroitly smothered, formed the punctuations of her laughter.

Below, in the library, Colonel Marquis tried to calm, with a cigar, his own undeniable uneasiness. He had seen Judge Marston an hour before, and the old man's worries had added to his own—to those uncertainties which he had striven steadily to put out of his mind. Recovering slowly, the Judge had given much thought to the step Doris was about to take.

"You don't suppose, Orlando," he had asked anxiously, "that Doris has been unduly influenced in this matter by my wishes and my accident?"

"No; Judge, of course not," he had answered; but the thought had been in his own mind.

"She is so young and joyous, and—George——"

That was it! She was so young and joyous, and Chapman so sedate, so cautious, so entirely her opposite in every way. Could it be possible that of this union could come sympathy and understanding, such as he had known with Doris's beloved mother?

But he put away this thought—not without real effort—and turned to greet Jack, as he entered.

"I'm going to the church, dad," said the boy, looking startlingly mature and very handsome in his formal dress.

"All right, Jack." The Colonel tried to smile at him with his usual frank good-fellowship. They were fine companions, this father and his son.

Impulsively the young man strode toward him and took a firm grip on his hand.

"We're going to be lonely, dad." The Colonel saw the muscles of the lad's throat work convulsively as he spoke.

"Yes; we shall be lonely, but—it's the way of life, Jack; it's the way of life."

"Are you satisfied with things, father? Do you think Chapman really is the man to make her absolutely happy? It's absurd to discuss such things now, it's so close at hand, and——"

"Why, of course!" The Colonel tried to put into his voice real tones of reassurance, but, he feared, did not succeed.

Jack, still pressing his hand closely, looked long and earnestly into his eyes.

"Well, I'm off to the church. You'll all be coming, soon?"

The Colonel glanced nervously at his watch. "Yes; soon, now."

When Jack had gone, his nervousness increased.

Titters and gay talk from the lovely group of bridesmaids floated down the stairs to him. The heavy frarance of many flowers filled the air. He walked to and fro, unconscious of the fact that his cigar no longer was alight. Presently, realizing this, he cast it from him and lighted another. Within five minutes, this, too, had been discarded, and he gave up thought of smoking.

Presently Lillian came up to him, to pin a boutonniere upon his coat. He had grown extremely fond of her, but now found it hard to smile genially, as she appeared. He could not even thank her with his accustomed gallantry

She was to be the maid-of-honor, and was very lovely in blue satin trimmed with duchesse lace. A picture hat, from which sweeping plumes drooped gracefully, crowned her animated face. She carried a great shower boquet of pink roses, and raised them to his face, so that he might catch their fragrance.

"Aren't they *lovely?*"

"Almost, but not quite, as beautiful as you are, Lillian."

He smiled at her for a moment, forgetting his worries in her loveliness. He had not realized, before, what clothes could do to accentuate a girl's beauty. He had never thought of Lillian as being beautiful, but, to-night, dressed to act as maid-of-honor at his daughter's wedding, she was really very lovely.

"I? Beautiful? Pooh! It's plain you haven't seen your daughter!"

"No; they were to call me."

"They will, almost at once. And when you see her —w-e-l-l! Colonel, she monopolizes all the beauty in the world to-night! You'll *gasp.*"

A dainty flower-girl ran into the room. "Is Miss ——" She caught sight of Colonel Marquis, and, embarrassed, hung poised on her tiptoes.

"Yes, she is here," said he, smiling down at her, knowing that she was seeking Lillian. "But suppose she is! I am, too; and aren't you going to stand there in the light and turn around, so that I may have a good look at you?"

Blushing, with all the airs of a coquettish belle, the tot did as he asked, and coyly smiled across her shoulder at him.

"Shame! Shame! You two are flirting!" Lillian said gayly. "Colonel, I shall run, at once, to tell your perfidy to Mrs. Marquis. Come along, dear." She held out her hand to the little one.

He looked after them with smiles, his gaze concentrated on the child.

But as they went through the door his smile dropped from him like a mask.

Somehow, the child reminded him of Doris, years before, in the rose-garden. Like the other flower-girls, she was dressed in white mulle, decked with pale pink ribbons, and had upon her arm a basket filled with white sweet-peas. In the early mornings of the long ago, Doris had gone flower gathering in the garden, guided by old Mammy Rose. How often he had seen her coming toward the veranda along a rose-hedged path, carrying on her tiny, graceful arm a basket full of blossoms, just as this little maid had carried hers! What perfect happiness had then been hers! She had seemed a sprite in which the soul of joy had been embodied. What would this approaching ceremony mean to her?

He turned away with a deep sigh and, with a fresh cigar, settled in deep reflection to pass the few remaining moments before he would be called upon to leave for the church. His face fell into heavy lines of dull anxiety.

At the church, all was in readiness. Palms and American beauty roses softened the fine austerity of the dignified interior; rising high above the altar, spanning it completely, a floral bridal arch gleamed through the half-gloom of preliminary lighting, whitely and triumphantly. Presently, with a quick flash, the lights blazed into full brilliancy and the flowers seemed to spring into a richer blossoming.

Half-an-hour must elapse before the ceremony, but guests already had begun to come. Soon, the stately auditorium was all a-flutter with the wave of languorous fans; a-glitter with the glint of jewels; gay with the soft, luxurious colors of an infinite variety of lovely toilettes.

Grouped in the vestibule, or busy at their appointed tasks throughout the aisles, the slim, smart ushers, in their conventional evening dress, made crisp notes of black and white in the surrounding riot of delightful color.

The place was filled with perfume; there rose in it the murmurous hum of repressed conversation, the rustle of fine silks.

As the time appointed for the arrival of the wedding-party approached, a flutter of anticipatory excitement surged through the great edifice. With each unusual sound from the direction of the vestibule all heads were turned expectantly. The ushers rapidly hurried late-comers to their places.

In the vestry, the celebrated cleric who was to pronounce the momentous words, made a final readjustment of his flowing robes; his assistants looked at him with nerves a-tingle, waiting for their last instructions from his distinguished lips, wondering if, like him, they one day might be famous.

The appointed hour came, and the minutes dragged along, beyond it, fruitless of what everyone expected—what all had gathered for.

Jack was in the vestibule worried. Five, ten, fifteen

minutes slipped away. "What's up, I wonder?" he said, nervously, to an attendant friend.

"There's a telephone back in the vestry."

"Try it, won't you, old man? I ought not to leave the vestibule."

His friend, soft-footed on the padded aisle, hurried to the vestry.

"Funny thing," he said when he returned. "His train got in on time, but he's not reached your house yet. His man probably has lost every shirt-stud he possessed—or stolen them. When Dicky Stone was married, his man had packed and sent down to the station every shoe he owned, while Dicky rushed around in slippers, trying to achieve a dignity of calm. Had to send his valet with the keys in a fast machine to get some shoes, and of course, the valet was arrested for speeding. Looked, for a while, as if Dicky's marriage was all off. Finally he roused wit enough to think that the second man could wear his shoes—he'd often given shoes to him.

" 'If he can wear my shoes,' said he, 'then I can wear *his* shoes.'

"Always was a clever chap—that Dicky Stone. No one else ever would have thought the matter out so. Tried it, and he could, but they pinched horribly, and he limped like a beggar as he marched up to the altar.

"When he was being congratulated, afterwards, one of the Wright boys said to him:

" 'Gad, I wish I were in *your* shoes, Dicky!'

" 'Gad, I wish I were myself!' said Dicky.

"Some silly thing like that has probably caught Chapman. He's so remarkably precise though! Still, you can't tell, Jackie. These prosaic chaps get rattled beyond words when they *do* get upset. He'll be along."

"I wish he'd hurry; it's getting on my nerves."

It was getting upon the nerves of those back at the house, also. The bridesmaids and flower girls had become less vociferous in their laughing gossip. Uncomfortable lulls in conversation continually became more frequent. When the buzz of the telephone in Colonel Marquis's study penetrated to the upper floor, some of the girls jumped from excessive nervousness.

"Oh," one of them cried apprehensively, "I hope it isn't bad news!"

"What bad news could it be?" the competent Lillian inquired.

"I can't imagine, but—a bridegroom late to his own wedding! Something *dreadful* may have happened."

"Nonsense! A punctured tire, perhaps, or it may be he has been arrested for a little too much haste. They're so beastly, these new traffic officers!"

Titters ran about the room. "Imagine the impeccable George Chapman haled before a judge! He'd faint!"

"What if they should lock him up? Would Doris have to go to the police-station and be married in a cell? It——"

"Hush."

"He's not so very late, and you know what a motor is. If you're in a hurry, something's sure to go wrong with it."

"It can't be that anything really has happened."

"Stop talking of it, girls," Lillian begged. "Nothing serious has occurred. Anyone is liable to a slight delay in this New York of ours. When I watch the crowds upon the streets, the wonder is, to me, that any of us get anywhere on time."

"*I* never do!"

"True, dear! How many painful moments have I waited for you in theater-lobbies! You're always just a little later if you chance to know that I am anxious to hear every word of the first act. I'm sorry he is late, though."

"It's bad luck!"

"Hush! Don't say such words on Doris's wedding-night. Let's talk of something pleasant."

And the charming girls made valiant efforts to do so, though without very much success.

Someone who had been downstairs and heard the talk into the telephone appeared. She was very much excited.

"They're telephoning from the church! They're wondering why we do not start."

"I suppose the place is packed."

"Oh certainly, and they must be frightfully worried, or they wouldn't telephone."

And so the anxiety and excitement grew, both at the church and at the house.

Intensely preoccupied, Doris, perhaps, was the only person who had not begun to feel alarmed. Mrs. Marquis, seeing this, made new details to attend to, and remained thoughtful enough to stop, with a finger on her lip, Desdemona's comment on the lateness of the hour, although her own face was slowly whitening with apprehension.

She worked desperately to keep Doris from a realization of the flight of time—pretending to find changes to be made in the adjustment of the veil, exclaiming, as if there had been an error in the hooking of the bridal-bodice, resorting to a dozen little subterfuges to protect her child from the wild worry which an idle instant now would be almost sure to bring.

But, presently, she could do no more, and standing by the dresser, Doris glanced at an open watch which had escaped her mother's careful eyes.

Her face paled instantly. "Why—why, he is late!"

"He'll be here in a moment, dear. Some little thing has happened——"

But the seed of apprehension had been sown in Doris's mind, and almost instantly, seeing the pallor of her mother's face, she began to try to conceal it from her.

Thus, for a few moments, they endeavored unselfishly, each to spare the other; then both suddenly admitted their distress.

The telephone in the library was ringing now, and its tinkle came to them with ominous suggestiveness; the buzz of comment and of speculation from the bridesmaids was unceasing and not so stifled now that some of it did not reach them.

Doris looked into her mother's eyes with a frightened glance.

"Oh, mother, what can be delaying him?"

Mrs. Marquis who, a few minutes earlier had left the room, for a flying trip downstairs to consult with her distracted husband, assured her that she had spoken to her father, and that he thought there was no cause for apprehension.

But this assurance gave neither of them comfort;

they drew close together, their faces troubled and their hands clasped.

"What—oh, mother, dear—I—I——," but Doris could not formulate the question.

"Don't worry, sweetheart!" The voice which tried to reassure, was itself a tragic whisper. "Everything is all right, I am sure. Something has delayed him."

The deep rumble of an electrically tapped gong reached them.

"Someone is at the door," cried Doris, catching her mother's hands in a spasmodic grasp.

"Yes!" said her mother, almost in a whisper.

Even the footman had been affected by the general disquiet. He hurried to the door, forgetful of his habitual dignity. Colonel Marquis, too, stepped out into the hallway at sound of the gong, so that he could see quickly the new arrival.

When he heard the footman greet the visitor as Mr. Chapman, he felt a thrill of deep relief; but, as George stepped into the bright light of the hall-lamps, a feeling of wondering amazement took the place of the relief. Instead of being dressed as would become a bridegroom, the newcomer was in business clothes, disheveled. Colonel Marquis hurried forward. "What is it, Chapman?" he asked anxiously.

George scarcely looked at him. His pale face was set in an expression of determination. His eyes were startling in their look of agony. He did not answer Colonel Marquis, but, without a moment's pause, went straight to the foot of the broad stairway.

"I wish to see—Doris—for a moment," he declared.

"But——"

"Please do not deny me, Colonel Marquis," the distraught man pleaded. "I must see her for a moment."

The worried father stepped aside, to let the strangely mannered bridegroom pass in front of him. "She is upstairs."

"May I go there to her?"

"Why—I suppose so—but——"

Without another word, George hurried up the stairs and into Doris's presence.

His entrance was extraordinary, ominous of some disaster. Doris shrank a little, nearly crying out from nervous shock, as she noted his appearance.

Mrs. Marquis, not less startled, stepped forward as if she would protect her child from some real peril, but almost instantaneously saw there was no peril of a kind from which she might be guarded, even by a mother, and, pale and trembling, merely took her place beside her, looking at Chapman with an inquiry which throbbed with agony. He bowed gravely, but did not address her; even his glance at her was fleeting. He had eyes, as he had thoughts, for Doris only.

If his appearance had been startling, then his words were even more so, not alone because of the extraordinary meaning they conveyed, but because of the strange tone in which they came—a stifled, deathly tone, which told of agony of soul almost too great for endurance.

"Doris" (his enunciation was unusually clear), "I have come to offer you five minutes . . . in which to tell me that you love me."

She stood, speechless, gazing at him in blank dismay.

"If you say you do, there is no power on earth which

could make me believe otherwise . . . but I do not want a loveless bride!"

Ever since the episode with Arthur, in the afternoon, she had been fighting back the very question which the man before her just had asked. Now she saw that she must face it—for some inscrutable reason he demanded it, and he had, beyond a doubt, the right to make demand.

She put the query to herself, as if there might possibly be some doubt about the matter, although her heart kept urging her that there was none. Did she love him? Did she? Did she?

White as the pure white of the bridal costume which she wore, she stood transfixed, and gazed at him with widening frightened eyes. She had been pulling at a glove, and her hands remained fixed in the position in which his words had caught them. It was as if his question brought with it a blight of cold, which had congealed her.

She tried to speak, but could not. Did she love him? Did she? The question multiplied itself in her bewildered, frightened mind.

"Haven't you . . . one . . . word?" he asked unsteadily.

Her voice was low, pathetic, most unusual. "No . . ." she said in tremulous answer.

"Doris . . . Doris, you don't love me? You don't love me?"

She could not lie to him, while his big, anxious eyes were fixed upon her, while the agony of the brief question was still aquiver in the air about, and suddenly she realized that if she made him any answer other than the fatal little monosyllable, she would be violating truth.

"No!" she repeated faintly.

Tragically, as he walked the floor, he moaned: "My . . . God! and this is the end of my dream! . . . The . . . end . . . of . . . my . . . dream!"

Then, passing through the door, he turned to take one last lingering look, with agony unspeakable upon his face, his voice, now a low quivering groan of anguish, repeating: "I don't want a loveless bride." And he was gone.

A moment later weighed down by despair, wrapped in a death-like silence, George Chapman stepped out into the darkness.

CHAPTER XV

In two widely separated sections of the city, two other men also were suffering, as the hour for Doris's marriage neared, and passed.

In his apartment upon upper Broadway, Arthur had dressed, determined at whatever cost of harrowed soul, to be among the guests at the church, but, his courage failing at the final moment, had thrown his coat aside, called his man to bring him a smoking-jacket, and, morose and sorrowful, had sunk into a deeply-hollowed leather chair.

The boy's mental agony was intense. He could not understand what had befallen him. Never in his life had been denied him anything he really wanted: now came the refusal of that which he had wanted more than all. He railed at Fate, he railed at Chapman, hating him intensely; he railed at Doris's family. He believed the marriage had been indirectly forced on her; he assured himself that it never could have occurred if her grandfather had not been injured by that wildly driven taxi.

The bell was at his hand, but he did not use it. "Dean!" he called, instead. "I say, you—Dean!"

His man came in hurriedly.

"Why didn't you bring me a drink?"

"You didn't ask for one, sir."

"Well, I'm asking, now."

Dean hastened out and back, bringing a decanter, upon the cut glass neck of which, a silver label "Whiskey," hung by a looped chain. Arthur looked at it without approval.

"One of the things you must learn, Dean, is to keep things up around here."

"Yes, sir," said the anxious Dean, not knowing what had so displeased his master.

"Take this decanter back and fill it!" Arthur ordered, while he poured the last drop from it into his glass.

As the man departed with the empty flagon, the youth heard the booming of a distant church clock. He shrank, as if the blows had been struck upon his very heart, then rose, and, going to the window, peered out into the night. He took his watch out of his pocket and held it in his hand, counting, meanwhile, the clock's strokes.

"Seven," he muttered. "Seven."

He heavily went back to the big chair, and sank into it dully. Dean brought in the freshly filled decanter and set it on a tabouret beside him. Armsby poured a glassful from it, taking it at a quick gulp.

"My God!" he murmured. "Who would have thought it in the old days in the South!"

He studied the slow hands of his watch, as one might observe the gradual march of some inexorable and inevitable fate.

But it was not the white face of the watch he saw, nor the slow-moving hands. His mind had visualized for him the scene in the old church, and he watched the vision as one might watch the flashing pictures of a cinematograph. So many times had he built up in his brain this visualization, that now it came with magic quickness and clarity of detail.

He could see the carriages and motors pausing at the curb outside the edifice to discharge their freight of handsomely dressed men and women; he could see these cross the narrow space between the sidewalk and the church, and enter; he could see the crowded, perfumed, flower-decked lobby, hear the soft laughter and the subdued hum of well-bred gossip undertoning it; he could see the great, profusely-decorated interior, and the black-coated ushers, guiding newcomers hurriedly, but noiselessly, along the deeply carpeted aisles.

Somewhere below, a street-piano sent into the night the measured cadence of a waltz. He had heard it last at Doris's ball, when they had danced together to it. He rose impatiently, believing that a window must be open. Finding all tightly closed he pulled the heavy curtains snugly across the deep embrasures, hoping thus to shut away a little of the maddening sound. As he sank into his chair again, he poured another glassful of the whiskey, and drank it almost automatically.

As he had risen he had left his watch upon the tabouret, and now, he noted that its hands had traveled almost to the hour. His face contracted. He sat tense and staring as those hands moved on . . . on . . . .

"Boom!" went the bell in some near steeple. "Boom!" . . .

Now she was walking down the aisle beside her father, and at the altar Chapman waited!

The boy's agony was like that of a man into whose breast a knife is thrust. He rose and paced the floor, with swinging arms which, now and then, came together in a wild wringing of the hands.

"God! God!" A dozen times his tense lips formed the word. They trembled, and his footsteps faltered . . . . .

Almost every time he neared the tabouret in his increasingly unsteady march, he paused, poured out and drank more liquor. As if intentionally designed to add to his heart-broken misery, the street-piano shifted from the waltz into the "Wedding March" from "Lohengrin."

. . . .

Down in the studio in the quaint street near Jefferson Market, Stoddard Thornton suffered as intensely, but, unlike Arthur who had dulled his misery with draughts from the decanter, Stoddard arose, shrugged a raglan into place upon his shoulders, and went out, with set face so distinctly revealing his agony, that more than one wayfarer turned to watch him as he strode across town, first through the deserted streets of the lower western island, then through the Broadway district, and thence along the crowded highways of the dense East Side, until, at the end of a long walk, he found himself at the approach to the tremendous spans of the Blackwell's Island Bridge.

There, no one noticed him; misery in that part of the town is common. Faces drawn in mental agony are not infrequent on the teeming sidewalks of these narrow thoroughfares.

But as he started up the incline leading to the bridge, an officer, keen-eyed and watchful for such signs upon a passing face as might indicate the later probability of a quick spring from the footway in the center of the bridge and a mad plunge from the outer girders into the black waters far below, hurried to a sheet-iron telephone-kiosk and notified his mates along the promenade, to be upon the look-out for a desperate looking man wrapped in a raglan overcoat. That officer who let a suicide occur upon the bridge while he was walking his post was liable to criticism.

No thought of suicide was in Stoddard's mind, however, although his agony was great. He was striving mightily, not to find a coward's way of ending his distress, but to find a man's way of enduring it. The officer who had seen him as he had reached the center span, and followed him, became convinced of this and at length abandoned him as one who, though in trouble, would fight his battle out and in God's good time would win.

Half-an-hour later, when he saw Stoddard still upon the bench the policeman, instead of questioning him and telling him to move along, looked at him sympathetically, and touched his hat in a salute.

Stoddard returned his friendly greeting, but scarcely saw him for all that. He was busy with the problem of his own struggling, sorry life. With his eyes raised to the starry vault, against which the bridge cables stretched in somber fret-work, and the thin filigree of the great iron towers stood out fantastically, he had tried to look into the future, but had only looked into the past.

Two mighty spectacles he saw there—one that of his father's downfall, the other that of his own hopeless love. There was no justice in the burden of indebtedness which had been thrust upon his shoulders before they had been stiffened by maturity to bear it; but there was no impulse in his heart to cast it off; that he might do so did not even rank among the possibilities. He felt no resentment, only a regretful love for the dead parent who so foolishly and sinfully had laid the weight upon him; but, for the first time since he had assumed the debt, he wondered if he were not acting foolishly in giving all his life to its repayment.

His face grew hard in its expression of resentment as he remembered that scene in the bank directors' room, when his crude, rich critic, mercilessly and contemptuously, even with a definite enmity, had cast aside his work not because it was not good, but because it had been executed by the lad who was endeavoring, with his every ounce of brain and muscle, to atone for the great wrong his father's hands had wrought.

Surely that man and his associates had shown no understanding or appreciation of well-doing! Was he right in making sacrifice to them of his whole youth? Would he not be building better and more justly if he gave himself a chance? He had planned to pay soon a considerable sum upon the debt. Would it not be better judgment to think now, a little of himself? His art had reached the point where, he knew, it could grow rapidly and splendidly among the right surroundings; and those surroundings were not in New York, but Paris. Ought he to lay it, a tribute upon the green cloth of that director's table? And now his earning was so slow! Would it not be true efficiency first to fit himself to make money, and then make it rapidly and competently? He would pay the debt the quicker for it.

Ah! What might he not do in Paris! Paris, where the atmosphere is all surcharged with art, where waits for the one who struggles an instruction not gauged by money-standards, but by his own capacity to take as it is offered; where helpful criticism is at hand; where recognition does not wait until it is too late to smile on merit.

His art! He had that, alone, to live for, now; the woman he had loved and longed for was another's—he, like Arthur, had listened to the chiming of the church-bells, and the hour was passed!

Sitting on the bridge-bench in the soft air of the night, he visualized her, not as Arthur had, walking slowly down the church-aisle on her father's arm, in time to Wagner's great harmony, approaching at the altar the man she was about to marry, but as he had seen her in the happy days down South—as he had seen her in the dim dawn of that distant morning—as he had pictured her in his white "Goddess of the Garden."

Was not that good? His whole heart lay hidden in it, and art with heart is always good. In the gloom of the soft night, while from the dark river's waters underneath arose to him the soft moan of some far vessels' deep-toned whistle; the jangle, now and then, of a mysterious bell in an unseen, throbbing engine-room; the droning cry of a hoarse bargeman, hailing "along the rope" the captain of the tug which towed his craft, there came forgetfulness of all these things, and grew a vision.

His little "Goddess of the Garden" rose against the velvet of the sky, as white as angels and as graceful as the goddesses of old Olympus, and smiled at him; but she was no longer small. Life-size and thrilling in her purity and charm she glowed, smiling at him gloriously. Ah, would not the Salon bow before her and acclaim her? Ah . . . ah . . .

Dazzled by the thought, he sat there a full hour, and then, with mind made up, hastened to his studio.

Mad hours of hurried packing followed. When dawn came, the place was quite denuded, desolate. When Whilk came over, trunks, bags and boxes were piled near the outer door.

He paused, startled by the disordered room and luggage.

"Great Caesar's ghost, old man!" he cried. "What the deuce——"

"You're just in time to go with me to the steamer," Stoddard answered.

"What steamer? You didn't take that studio up at Fishkill Landing, after all, did you? It's too late in the season for——"

"I'm not bound for Fishkill Landing, man; I'm bound for Paris."

Whilk, failing to find a chair to sink upon, sank cross-legged to the floor.

Not too much time was left in which to catch the boat, and Stoddard made his friend rise quickly and help to get his baggage down the narrow stairway to the side-walk. They had just piled the many pieces into a somewhat imposing heap when the four-wheeler he had sent a butcher's boy to get, came rattling, loose-hubbed, around the corner.

Half-an-hour later, Stoddard was standing at the rail of a small steamer, while, upon the dock, Whilk, who scarce had realized till now that all this unexpected activity could possibly be real, was gazing and shouting at him enviously. A newsboy raced along crying his wares.

Whilk caught the boy's arm. "Here, give me one of everything you have."

At the moment Stoddard's face was turned away, and, when he turned again to wave his hand in final farewell to his friend, it was just in time to catch a bundle of newspapers which Whilk had fashioned with the sheets snatched from the boy and a bit of twine found lying on the planks. Stoddard held the papers clasped against his chest and smiled his thanks, as the ship warped from her dock and out into the stream. When he went below he tossed them into the far corner of his berth.

"I'll not look at them, and I'll not look back," he told himself, as he went out upon the deck. "My business, now, is wholly with the future. I'm going to new places; I'm going to new work; I'm going to find something—something—something to make me forget!"

And, steadfastly, as they ploughed past the Statue of Liberty, he held his firm gaze seaward. He spent the morning upon deck, pacing back and forth and round about until exhaustion drove him to his cabin; and in the afternoon he watched the smooth sea illimitably stretching out, and endeavored to see nothing but white figures of the Goddess of Success in the far cloud-banks—striving, constantly, to check their tendency to shape themselves instead into the likeness of his "Goddess of the Garden."

About the time when his man was rubbing Arthur into some semblance of vitality, late that afternoon, Stoddard went below to freshen up for dinner. In searching for his brushes, he threw a suit-case on his berth, and, as he did so, caught sight of the papers Whilk had tossed to him.

His heart sank leadenly. They would have in them the story of her wedding. Indeed he saw, in heavy headlines upon one of them, the words: "Marquis-Chapman Ceremony——" He caught them carefully in his two hands, made a tight bundle of them and, going to the deck, dropped it gently overboard to the surface of the undulating sea.

And so he did not see the finish of that headline, the short, tragic word "Off," into which some uninterested copy-reader had condensed the startling news of the previous evening's strange events.

.   .   .   .

While Stoddard settled down in Paris to work as even he had never worked before, endeavoring by ceaseless concentration on his art to win forgetfulness of what had cast so black a shadow on his already shadowed life, Doris, in absolute seclusion from everyone but the members of her family and Lillian, strove to recover from the shock of the tremendous episode which, so unexpectedly, had been substituted for a wedding.

Her nights were sleepless and her days were miserable; her soul shrank from the storm of talk which her family tried earnestly to hide from her, but which, she knew, must have arisen because of the abruptly halted wedding-ceremony.

At first, her grief was deepened by the knowledge that her grandfather's recovery undoubtedly had been much retarded by the unfortunate affair, nor was it easy to shut out from her memory the vision of the unhappy Chapman as, reeling with the shock of disappointment, he had left the room that tragic night.

Upon the third day after the occurrence, Desdemona,

foolishly determined that her beloved young mistress should not be denied anything she wanted, smuggled a newspaper to her and, for a week, after that, there was real danger that the horror of the situation might result in serious illness.

But youth has wonderful resilience and sympathy and no criticism reached her ears from the only folk with whom she came in contact. Pleasant messages of all sorts came to her from her young friends; the sweet girls who had garbed themselves as bridesmaids for the wedding were constant in their inquiries; Jack proved himself a brother most adorable; her parents, knowing that the kindest course would be to let her bear her sorrowing in silence until such time as she should cease to brood on it, were tender and loving, nor did they attempt to question her. Virginia was with her almost constantly.

In the dainty room of blue and white there were moments of a grief which was not far from desperate; an exceedingly pale and woeful face it was, that gazed at her when she stood pensively before the mirror; the enameled arms of the slim-legged chairs were scarcely whiter than the hands which rested languidly upon them, as wondering why this horrid episode should have been thrust upon her, she took what little comfort she could find in utter physical relaxation.

A fortnight had elapsed before her mind began to turn from the acuteness of her misery; then she determined to mope no longer in useless worry.

"I'm going down to luncheon, Desdemona," she told her delighted handmaiden.

It was with a glad smile of welcome that her mother

met her in the morning room. The girl slipped an arm about her.

"I've been so depressed, dear mother! But I will not mope any more. I'm sure I have made you all as miserable as I have been."

"We all sympathize with you, sweetheart."

Doris gave her arm a little squeeze of gratitude. "Who has been to see me?"

"Nearly everyone," said Mrs. Marquis, smiling happily, for the first time since the dreadful evening. Then, a little hesitantly, but too well pleased by the great change in Doris's manner and appearance to deny her the small pleasure which might result from the announcement: "Arthur Armsby, more particularly. He has called at least once daily. He and Jack have been inseparable."

Almost as if it had been a stage trick, a tap upon the door preceded Desdemona's entrance with a splendid cluster of chrysanthemums that bore Arthur's card.

Her mother's observant eyes saw that Doris flushed as she gazed at the beautiful flowers. Doris, herself, was conscious of it, and the consciousness annoyed her. But Virginia appeared just at that moment, brimming with good news from the Judge, and broke the tenseness of the situation.

She made the welcome announcement that the doctors said he could be moved almost immediately to the Newport cottage they had taken for the season.

It was decided, largely through consideration for the invalid, that the journey should be made by boat.

.   .   .   .

Moonlight on the water always had held a particular

fascination for Doris, and, after her long seclusion, the Sound seemed more than usually beautiful. Virginia scarcely left the Judge's side, and Mrs. Marquis retired early, but Doris and her father sat in a quiet, sheltered nook on deck, long after most of the vessel's passengers had disappeared.

The great boat's wake, shining like molten silver; the twinkling lights ashore, and upon passing craft; the stars in the black velvet canopy of night above; the soft swish of the waters, thrust aside by the advancing ship, calmed Doris's soul with a peaceful sense of rest and serenity.

"Ah, father, it is lovely! The sky—all spangles, and see the flicker of our lights upon the water! It makes me think of . . . the old home."

The Colonel had been wondering of late, with an intense anxiety, just what course would be the wisest to take. His training in the world of men outside the home, had enabled him to take a broader and less painful view of the unfortunate affair than had been possible for Mrs. Marquis or Virginia; he never had been as strong as the Judge in Chapman partisanship.

That evening his thoughts also had turned longingly toward the old southern home. The beauty of the night upon the water had brought him vivid memories of that brilliant evening when Stoddard had declared himself to him, by the fountain in the wonderful rose-garden. What Virginia had told him of the young man in New York, added to what he, himself, had learned of his progress, had made his mind dwell frequently on the artist of late.

Like his wife, he felt somewhat uneasy when he considered Arthur Armsby. Now, he wondered if there might not come from that far episode in the rose-garden a solution of the tangle in which his daughter's life had become suddenly involved. With every fresh report concerning Stoddard, which had come to him, his admiration for the struggling sculptor had increased, and he decided to sound Doris, cautiously, and to be guided, later, by what the talk revealed.

"Doris," he said slowly, "I have been wondering if I ought not to tell you something. Dear little girl!"

He took her hand in his, there, in the seclusion of the deserted deck, and slipped his arm protectingly about her. She nestled comfortably against his side.

"Life has gone rather badly with you lately. Life has a way of doing that, dear, with the best of us; but it has torn my heart to know of your unhappiness."

"Dear father!" Her voice was solemn, but there was no catch of sobs in it.

"We have been so worried about you—you are our 'little girl' you know, even if you have grown up. We want you to be happy. And, Doris, happiness—real happiness—for a woman can come through marriage only. I am sure of that, and my belief has been accentuated by the weary tragedy of your Aunt Virginia's sad experience. I should be heart-broken, dear, if you let the horror of this—er—unpleasant episode—set you all wrong with the future, as her misfortune set her wrong with hers."

Doris did not answer him in words, but crept a little closer to him, moving her chair a trifle, so that its arm pressed closely against that of his.

"She let the bitter disappointment of her first love-affair destroy the possibilities of the highest joy in life," he went on, slowly.

He gazed reflectively upon the passing waters, wondering just how to say the things which troubled him for utterance.

"You must not do that," he went on at length. "We—have been greatly distressed about it all."

He waited for the vibrant clamor of a near-by bell-buoy to recede into the distance.

"Now that you have suffered so intensely, we have been thinking of the great necessity of guarding you, if we can do so, from the likelihood of other pain."

"I know—you are always thinking of me, daddy; always trying to be helpful."

"Yes, dear."

He wondered if it would be safe to tell her in what way he thought he might help most; he wondered if it would be safe to warn her about Arthur Armsby. In dealing with impetuous young hearts such action is not always wisest.

He finally determined to say nothing in disparagement of anyone, but to remind her of the man whom, in his heart, he favored most—the young sculptor whose undoubtedly strong character, he felt certain, was being woven by the agonies of struggle and denial, into a close-knit fabric, fine, dependably genuine.

"I have been wondering if I ought not to tell you something—about Stoddard Thornton."

Doris quickly showed her astonishment. "About Mr. Thornton?"

"Yes. I think it must have been the brilliance of the night which brought him to my mind so vividly. It was on another such a night as this, down South, that he explained to me the dreadful handicap he had accepted without murmuring; the laudable ambition he had formed to wipe it out completely—his unalterable determination to repair another's wrongs and set right the memory of his own father."

With bated breath she listened to the story of the horror which had shadowed Thornton's youth; with kindling eyes she heard her father tell how firmly the young man's soul had held to its determination of vicarious atonement.

"Ah, that is splendid!" she said softly.

"Isn't it? Well, he told me of this great resolve, the evening before he went to New Orleans to get the last word from the bank directors as to the drawings he had made for the stone figures that were to be placed on the façade of the new building. And he also intimated, Doris, that, if he won the contract and was thus assured of a reasonable expectation of success in his great undertaking, he should try, later, to win your hand."

"Father!"

"Even then he loved you, Doris. I do not mention this to you because I am his advocate. There has been enough of advocacy of suitors. In the future, you, yourself, shall choose as you will. We do not fail to realize that, had you not been influenced, you would have saved yourself, through your own right instincts, the sorrow which lately has lain so heavily upon you.

"I only want to tell you that this man—this fine, strong man, filled with an ambition to do right, of which I scarcely know the parallel—was thinking even then, of you, as the one complete reward which life could offer for his ceaseless struggle."

"I don't know what to say," Doris exclaimed softly.

"Say nothing, my dear; but, by and by, when others may present themselves for favor, remember that splendid fellow, whose every moment now is proving him. He has not let his burden crush him; he has fought and fought and still is fighting. Perhaps he may not win, but I feel sure he will; and if he does, his fighting will have hardened him in moral muscle as few men are hardened. And when I look at that delightful little figure of you, that little 'Goddess of the Garden,' I feel convinced of the truth and the exquisite charm of his ability. I thoroughly believe in him."

When they had parted for the night, he wondered if he had done wisely. He had said no word of warning to her about Arthur, which he firmly had intended to accomplish in some way; but he knew he had impressed her with his story of the sculptor's real superiorities. His position had been difficult; he could but hope that he had acted well.

Long after she sought her state-room, Doris sat, with arms resting on its window-sill, gazing thoughtfully at the thin strip of sky which showed between the cross-roped rail and the sharp line of the deck above. Her heart was in a tumult. She knew that her father had been thinking not only of the sculptor, but of Arthur; she had guessed his fine reserve in saying nothing of the rich, impulsive southern boy who, next to Chapman, had most won her favor since she had left college.

But in her mind a film of romance had always surrounded Stoddard, and now this impression had been intensified, making him a fascinating figure. She tried to force her recollections of him into a clearly limned distinctness, but could not; •he had hazed into a blurred memory like that of a book read years before. Her remembrance of his studio, however, was vivid; her heart throbbed with delight as she recalled the statuette enshrined there in that evidently sacred niche. Thornton, himself, was like a hero read of in romance; not really indefinite, but impersonal. Try as she might, she could not visualize him as a living, breathing, ardent suitor for her hand. While Arthur! . . .

It was after twelve, and the memory of her father's talk was still absorbing, but she suddenly realized that she was chilled. She left the window and soon forgot her manifold perplexities in slumber, to which the soft rush of the waves against the vessel's side supplied a soothing lullaby.

Next day she found herself still bewildered with the complexities of newly suggested thoughts. Of course, she knew that she was beautiful, for, since her earliest recollections, everyone had told her that; she knew that she attracted; but to know that around her, as a center, still whirled the hopes and fears of two men, even though George Chapman now had been eliminated from the contest, was a little overwhelming. And of these two? Ah, there could be one answer only! Stoddard was but a memory, a vision of the past. He could mean little to her now, though her heart twined wreaths of romance all about him.

One mid-afternoon, not long afterward, Doris stole quietly away to the small stream, winding deep and placid from far farm-lands and beautifying the place

Virginia had taken, by cleaving its magnificent garden and then curving tortuously onward, to the sea. She was skilled with oars and paddle, and a canoe was lying idle on the little dock. She righted the small craft, carefully, slipped it into the water, and went slowly upstream.

She had started peacefully on the homeward journey, letting the canoe drift, save as an occasional paddle-stroke was necessary to keep it centered in the stream, when a sharp curve brought her close upon the highway, just as a depot-wagon carrying a single passenger came into sight. Her thoughts had been of Arthur, and she was scarcely surprised to recognize him. She waved her hand to him, and as she did so, ran her little boat against the shore.

Arthur, his face brightening at sight of her, sprang from the wagon and, sending the man on with his luggage, quickly joined her in the canoe.

The sun was westering. The haze of a warm autumn day was concentrating, making distances deep and mysterious, ashore and out at sea. Leaving the roadway, the stream wound through pleasant fields, musical with chirping insects bidding farewell to the dying summer.

"I—I couldn't wait; I—had to follow you," he said, almost as soon as the canoe had once more started on its lazy drift with the slow current.

She smiled at him.

They were underneath an overhanging tree on which a riotously luxuriant crimson-rambler had gaudily festooned itself. A great peace crept through her soul, as, unafraid, she answered the long, steady signals of his eyes. She raised her hand to stay his paddling, and lightly looped her fingers first upon one rose, then on another.

"Do you know all of these roses look as though they had little faces in them?"

"The face of love," he murmured.

She was not startled. As she glanced at him, the thought flashed through her mind that those who disapproved of him, did so because they did not understand him. Her heart built for him the same argument which women's hearts have built for erring and weak men since love and life began. Her smile, more shy, gained radiance.

The sun had started its slow dip into the brief oblivion of night; the evening was unusually placid. The spotless white of her soft outing-flannel emphasized the glory of the lovely flush upon her cheeks. As she looked at him, she was sure that, this time, there could be no error. This was true love at last! The others were all wrong in their vague criticisms of the man who sat before her, plying the long paddle automatically. If he had erred, then she could set him right; if he was weak, then she could give him strength.

When he put the old, sweet question to her, she did not reply in words. She only held out her hand, clasping his, and nodded, smiling. She looked into his eyes, which steadily returned her gaze with an expression that aroused in her emotions which she strove in vain to combat: it was so tender, so caressing that she seemed to feel its touch upon her lips.

Slowly, after they had reached the landing, they walked up the flower-bordered path together; slowly they climbed the terrace, just before the house, and the broad steps that led to the wide piazza. Jack was lounging in a wicker-chair, with a magazine held loosely in his hands. He turned his head, and, the next instant, sprang up and went to them with hands outstretched.

"Don't speak," he cried. "Don't spoil my chance. I'm a mind-reader. I know just what has happened. It is written in your smiles."

Doris threw her arms around him. He, at least, was fond of Arthur—and he knew him—they were friends. She gave them a quick glance of farewell, and sped indoors.

Mrs. Marquis and her husband, dazed by the unexpected suddenness with which this episode, which they had feared, had come upon them, were, for a moment, unable to express themselves. But the Colonel, determined that no further agony should come to Doris through meddling, pulled himself together quickly. While her mother held her to her breast and wept, as women will, he took her hand with trembling fingers. As her head was bowed, in turn, upon his breast, he cast one inquiring look toward his wife, and it was as if, in that brief interchange of glances, they signed and sealed a solemn compact to say nothing which could mar the brilliant joy of their loved one.

"May your life be bright with sunshine, dear; your joy grow with the passage of your days," he softly said; and Doris thought that in his voice was more of prayer than benediction, although she did not understand the reason of his prayer or the doubts which lay back of it.

After dinner, she was left alone with Arthur, Jack going to visit friends in town; Virginia remaining with her father in an upper room; the Colonel and Mrs. Marquis starting for a somewhat solemn stroll.

The lovers stood before a spacious window which looked out upon the sea, hands clasped, gazing dreamily into the night. A soft land breeze was blowing, interrupted, now and then, by brief, sharp gusts from the sea, mingling the rich fragrance of far autumn bonfires with the salt, Atlantic tang. Far away, upon an anchored yacht, an orchestra was playing the "Wedding March" from "Lohengrin." It startled Arthur, bringing vividly to his mind that other night, when he had sat in agony in his own rooms, and heard those same strains rising from the street-piano at the curb below.

"How near I came to losing you, dear heart!" he murmured. "When I heard of your engagement, I thought I could not live. I was so miserably unhappy! Until then, I did not know how much I loved you. Those weeks—how terrible they are to look back upon! I was at the breakfast table at the club when I heard the startling news that the engagement had been broken. I could have shouted for joy. The two chaps with me must have thought I suddenly had lost my mind."

"You poor boy!" she said sympathetically.

"My precious Doris! I always felt you did not love that man and that you did not realize what you were doing. You were not meant for him—you're mine! Mine forever!"

"Yes, Arthur, I love you with all my heart; I think I always have loved you."

"Precious girl, we shall be so happy! My friends shall be your friends, and I shall be so proud of you! We will go to Paris for our honeymoon—there are charming villas at Versailles. You shall have another garden there—a rose-garden with winding paths and fountains, like those of the sweet garden in the South, where I first met you. What evenings we shall spend together there! Think of the sunsets, and the white moon rising over the wonderful old trees! What a setting for you! Endlessly we shall pour out our heart's love to each other. Ah, adorable one; my heart is bursting with the joy of it! I could not live without you, darling girl! I cannot believe; I cannot realize that all this wondrous happiness has come to me."

Doris listened with an overflowing heart. His expressions of endearment made her soul throb with delight. He spoke with exquisite tenderness, every word vibrating with life, permeated with love. They were such words as women love to listen to.

"I thought I loved you to the ultimate of my capacity, but I find I love you more and more each day," the ardent southern boy went on, "I am beginning to learn what love really means. It must be as great as the universe, or it is not love at all."

"Nothing is so sweet as love," she murmured.

"Nothing, dear. I am constantly thinking of you (what wonderful eyes!) and your sweetness . . . I never want to see you weep. Your tears would break my heart, which has been filled with such deep grief and turbulence. It is now calm, peaceful, very, very happy. And it is to you I owe all this new serenity of soul! What strange power you have over me! You know that, dear heart, do you not!"

Then with her hand held tightly in his, against his heart, the fervent and adoring boy recited:

"I believe if I should die,
And you should kiss my eyelids where I lie
   Cold, dead and dumb to all the world contains,
The folded orbs would open at thy breath,
And from its exile in the aisles of Death,
   Life would come gladly back along my veins.

"I believe if I were dead,
And you upon my lifeless heart should tread,—
   Not knowing what the poor clod chanced to be,—
It would find sudden pulse beneath the touch
Of her it ever loved in life so much,
   And throb again, warm, tender, true to thee.

"I believe if in my grave,
Hidden in woody deeps all by the wave,
   Your eyes should drop some warm tears of regret,
From every salty seed of your deep grief,
Some fair, sweet blossom would leap into leaf,
   To prove that death could not make my love forget."

CHAPTER XVI

The wedding preparations were not elaborate. Doris felt that she could not endure a repetition of the bustle and excitement which had crowded those gay weeks of the past—that gayety which had so suddenly changed into an atmosphere of tragedy, as wreathed and gowned to journey to the altar with George Chapman, she had instead responded to his imperious questioning and her heart's insistent promptings and confessed to him that she did not and could not love him.

The ceremony was set for an unusually early hour, as the bride and groom were to go from it directly to the steamer which would carry them abroad upon their wedding journey. It was quiet, modest, simply elegant—not secret in the least, but most unostentatious. Enough friends had been invited, to supply a goodly rain of rice and flowers, as the bridal couple entered the big limousine, which was waiting to take them to the dock.

As they ascended the gang-plank of the steamer, Doris charmingly attractive in a tailor-made suit, with hat, gloves and shoes to match, Arthur perfectly groomed and handsome, they were a striking couple. They felt convinced, however, that the myriad eyes turned on them with frank admiration did not suspect them to be bride and groom. They did not hear the buzz of whispering which followed them from smiling lips, and proclaimed this very fact.

Friends were grouped upon the promenade; flowers in boxes and bouquets, addressed to Mrs. Arthur Armsby, filled an entire table in the saloon. A dozen of the Kaiser-Wilhelm's nimble stewards, smiling with amusement, were burdened before the ship had sailed, with generous cases of champagne addressed to the young bridegroom.

The voyage was a revelation of joy to Doris. Arthur, tender, thoughtful, gallant, scarcely left her side. Invigorated by the fresh salt breezes, which never became unduly boisterous; stimulated, not depressed, by the long, steady swing of the great vessel; fascinated by the clever, interesting passengers she met, the bride found each day of the quick journey on the sea a novel joy.

After a month spent in London, they went on to Paris, Arthur full of eagerness to show his lovely bride the gay French capital, with which he was so familiar. There, as had been planned, they settled down, taking upon lease an old and roomy house upon the Faubourg.

It was late in August before they were comfortably settled, and Doris had begun to know and love her Paris. It is said that every woman finds a different Paris waiting for her when she explores the city, and that which Doris found was not the Paris of Dumas and Hugo, Zola, Balzac, Prosper Mérimée, nor yet the Paris of the milliners and modistes, but the artist's Paris—not the sordid Quartier life which was so gayly gilded by Du Maurier, but the hard-thinking, continually striving, earnestly-at-work Paris where live the men and women who accomplish things with canvas and with brushes, with clay, chisel, marble and bronze. London had not much appealed to her: this Paris caught her to its heart and held her throbbing there, exquisitely happy in the ideally congenial life and folk.

She selected as her own particular studio a great room in the gabled roof, already fitted with good skylights, and, much to Arthur's unexpressed amusement, began to search out stretchers, canvases, innumerable brushes and a multitude of little color-tubes. Then came the long discussions over schools, instructors and the many conflicting methods, each of which found advocates among the people they consulted. The big group of expatriate Americans who find the fascinations of the great French city far too alluring to let them even think of going back to the United States save for the briefest of brief visits, and who are ever on the look-out for recruits among the more desirable of visiting Americans, seized them with delight and offered entertainment lavishly.

It was at an ambassadorial dinner that she had her first real heart-ache. As it proceeded Arthur's glass had been filled often, and when she passed him in the ball-room, later, she noticed that his cheeks were highly flushed, his eyes a bit too brilliant, and his laugh a little loud and strained.

That dinner gave her the first vaguely uncomfortable moment she had known in her short married life.

In the motor, as they glided rapidly toward home, she timidly referred to this. His arm was loosely around her, as it generally was when they were riding thus, together, safe in the seclusion of the darkness of the limousine.

"Arthur, dear, don't you think so very much champagne might injure one?"

He pressed her to his side and held his cheek against her own.

"Nonsense, darling: this is Paris!"

His voice was still a trifle higher than usual in its pitch; as they passed near a street-light, she saw that, since they had entered the car, his face had taken on an even deeper flush than it had shown immediately after dinner.

That night, she went to sleep with a vague unrest gnawing at her heart.

As the days passed, this feeling became more strongly defined. Arthur undoubtedly was drinking far more than he should.

It changed him unconsciously, as it always changes men. He was less constant in attendance on her; he went out without her, and, one night, did not return for dinner, nor send any word.

After her lonely meal, during which she shrank from the keen and sympathetic eyes of old Marie, the maid, and François, the grave butler, she sat hour after hour in the dim and shadowy library. Nine, ten, eleven o'clock and midnight passed, each knelled mournfully by the dull boom of belfry clocks, some near, some far.

Then her tortured mind turned from the effort not to feel too resentful and from the dull quest for good excuses for him, to the possibility, that after all, he might not be at fault. She began to search her mind for accidents which might have happened, and of which, in the natural course of things, she would not be notified quickly. The recklessness of *cochers* and *chauffeurs* in Paris is proverbial. There, the vehicle, not the pedestrian has the right of way; the man on foot must look out for himself. It was scarcely possible that Arthur could have met with a mishap of this kind, and because of it be lying in some hospital in pain, without her knowledge—she would have heard within the hour, surely and probably, within the half-hour; but some other mishap might have occurred without attracting such attention. She thought about the broad stone parapets of the Pont St. Michel, and how Arthur, as they had walked across, sometimes had swung himself up to a seat on one of them, and rested there for a while, with his interested eyes upon the water underneath, the busy little steamers or slow barges navigating it, or the unclad, reckless gamins who disported in it. Might he not have done this, this night, as he was coming home, and, leaning too far over, might he not have fallen?

Impulsively she started toward the telephone to make an inquiry as to what official she should ask for such information, but stopped half way. If it should not be that, but be—the other—then neither he nor she would wish to have officials making inquiries.

For the first time she yielded to the crowding tears. Oh, what a situation! To be unable to ask questions when, possibly, the case demanded quick investigation! Yet she knew—she knew that there was danger of the very thing she feared—real danger.

And then the lurid fear of those wild, lithe, desperately cruel Parisian thieves and murderers, named after our most cruel Indians, "les Apaches," flashed through her mind. She thrilled with nameless horror. Arthur always carried a good deal of money with him, and was not in the least cautious about showing it when he paid cab-fares on the street. She had warned him more than once about this and had worried over it.

This horrid thought forced her again to the telephone, but, having reached it, she paused dully, her hand raised to make the call. If it should be the other!

She went slowly to her chair again, to think.

Then she descended to the lower story of the house, establishing herself miserably in the little, chill reception-room. In case it should be—that which she feared. she wished to be there, near the door, to meet him and protect him from contact with the servants, which would humiliate them both.

As she kept vigil there, she bitterly reproached herself many times for feeling such suspicions; she told herself that should it prove that he had met with an accident and she had not set wheels in motion to discover this, she never would forgive herself. But something—woman's intuition—still forbade her starting the official inquiries.

Hours passed before she heard a sound which seemed significant. For a long time the house had been awesomely impressive in its stillness; for half-an-hour she had not heard a single motor-car's exhaust upon the nearby streets. A boy had passed an hour before with his weird cry: *"V'la le Soir! V'la le Soir!"*, vending the world's only midnight newspaper; but after he had departed, it had seemed to her that she, alone, of all the city, was awake and waiting.

The noise at the door thrilled her as though she might have touched a live electric wire. Was it a housebreaker? Or would it prove to be her husband, worried into half distraction because he knew that he had given her anxiety, hurrying to her with some reasonable explanation of his long delay? Would it be some messenger from the police *depôt* or a hospital to tell her that disaster had befallen him, and take her quickly to his side?

These questions stirred her with less horror than might have been expected, for again intuition, dreadful and insistent, told her that the noise was not made by police messenger, hospital *commissionaire* or housebreaker. Her soul shrank at the thought of another possibility. Was it really Arthur—after he had filled and emptied too many crystal glasses? Such a thing had not occurred before: she had not thought it possible that such a thing could be; but she felt a growing certainty of it now.

Pale and trembling, but no longer thrilled with terror by the thought of burglars, but only with the terror that her heart might break, she staggered to the door. As she approached it, a key upon the other side was working patiently, but stupidly, to find its orifice. There could be no doubt! She turned the catch, unlocked the door, opened it and let it swing in toward her.

The man upon the threshold did not even see her. It was plain that he believed the door had opened to his key. Glancing neither to the right nor to the left, but advancing with such steadiness as he could manage, he walked into the big reception hall, and there poised, swaying.

His appearance, as she stood back of him, horror-stricken, was a dreadful blow to Doris. His frock coat was open untidily and showed dusty signs that he had leaned upon the coping of the bridge as she had thought he might; his top hat was sadly roughened and his hair hung on his forehead in limp locks; his necktie was awry; his bloodshot eyes were dull and stupid-looking.

"Arthur!" she exclaimed.

But he did not answer her. Heavily, he staggered toward the wide staircase across the polished, rug-strewn floor, while, with trembling lips and tightly clenched hands, she stood observing his uncertain progress, but afraid to speak again.

At the foot of the stairs he fell, having caught a limp and dragging foot beneath a rug.

She sprang to help him, but he had dropped into an instantaneous slumber, whether of intoxication or because his head had struck with force against a newel-post, she could not tell. She knelt beside him.

"Arthur, dear!" she cried, in a frenzy of distress fruit-lessly endeavoring to arouse him.

He was breathing heavily, his eyes were closed; his face was darkly flushed and swollen.

All that dear boyishness which she so loved had gone from his expression. Upon him was a sad maturity—ah, more than sad—the tragic age of youth degraded!

.   .   .   .

She awoke at ten, unrefreshed by the few hours of half-forgetfulness. When she arose and looked into a mirror, her drawn face startled her. With difficulty she kept the tears back. Subconsciously she had decided on a definite course of action. There should be no re-proaches, no complaints, only a short and very serious talk, quite practical and so very earnest that Arthur could not fail to realize at once the honesty, the deep, heart-felt intensity of her desire to help him.

It was mid-afternoon when he appeared, and as he

came to her his face showed horrid in its puffy palor. His eyes, which she had learned to love as bright and fine, flashing with good humor and veiled merriment, were red and dull. His hand was tremulous, although he evidently tried to steady it with a desperate effort. In the middle of the room, a few feet from her, he paused uncertainly, shamed by her forbearance, for she only sadly smiled, making no comment.

"Shall I order coffee?" she asked.

After a pause which held a long look into her eyes, he took her hand. His face was full of agonized regret, self-loathing.

"Would . . . promises . . . have any value?" he asked slowly, ignoring her inquiry.

His remorse was plainly so sincere that instead of answering him in words, she held out her arms to him, as she sank helplessly to a *fauteuil*.

"From now on——" he began.

"From now on——" she interrupted, "this—mistake —shall be forgotten."

"Ah, my dear . . . my dear . . . I do not deserve it!" He let his head sink to her shoulder, while he knelt beside her.

She stroked his hair with comforting fingers.

.   .   .   .   .

For weeks he held to his praiseworthy determination to abstain absolutely, and, after the agony of fear that he might yield again had died away, Doris was measurably happy, although something very real to her and very dear had gone out of her life forever. Then once more he yielded, much less dreadfully, and again repented and was steadfast for a space.

By the time six months had passed, fear so possessed her that she found little pleasure in any details of the foreign-flavored life which, at the start, had seemed so fascinating. She kept her sorrow tightly locked in her own heart, however, although it seemed to her that she would gladly barter everything she had—except him, for in what seemed to be his helpless weakness he made a strong appeal to her: she knew he tried—for one glimpse of her mother's sweet, consoling face.

Sometimes, for weeks, he would be quite himself; but such cheering periods became less frequent with the passing of the days. It became impossible for Doris to go out with him; some untoward incident was certain to occur whenever she attempted it. At balls, dinners and receptions where wine was served—and where and when, in Paris, is it not?—he proved irresponsible a dozen times. She even came to dread a dinner at a restaurant with him. Stimulants made him sharp-tongued and critical of the attendants, and a glance of protest from her when he ordered them about would arouse his irritation.

One evening, after a day in which he had made all sorts of solemn promises, he disappeared to stay away until she was frantic with wild fears. She heard him, when he staggered to his room two hours before sunrise, and not long afterward was worried by his stumbling pacing back and forth. Then he began to talk, sometimes muttering, sometimes raising an unnatural, harsh voice almost to a shout. The words which reached her were not good to hear.

She sat listening in fear and trembling, but his marching did not for a moment cease. His excitation seemed to have made him tireless.

It was just as dawn thrust up pink fingers to roll away the curtain of the night, that she heard him stagger to his bed, heard the sodden impact of his body as he threw himself upon it, and a moment later heard the stertorous breathing of his deep, intoxicated slumber.

When she awoke, near noon, she had formed a great resolve. The life which she had lived, these later months, had been intolerable. In her letters to those at home she had not given the slightest hint which might lead them to suspect the truth, but the time had come when she must make the revelation. Unsupported, she no longer could bear the burden of this sorrow.

Listless and distraught, she was sitting in her boudoir when he entered just after she had reached this great decision. For the first time, she did not smile in greeting. Hitherto, no matter what had happened, even though her heart seemed breaking, she had smiled a welcome when she first saw him for the day.

He understood the gravity of her expression. How much he had slept he did not know; his memories of the night were blurred; he had no recollection of meeting anyone when he came home, but, as he gazed at her, a vague remembrance came into his mind of a white figure which had stood and watched him as he staggered through an upper corridor. Possibly, for the first time, he fully realized the intolerable tragedy, which such events must be to her.

His own soul rose in stern revolt, and bowed him low in horror of himself. He did not venture any explanation or excuse, but, with hands and lips swept by weak tremors, partly from the nervous shock of the debauch and partly born of the strong resolution which was growing in him, he went to her and knelt, taking one of her white, listless hands and pressing it against his fevered face.

"Doris! Doris!" His voice was almost as weak and tremulous as were his hands.

She answered slowly and after a long hesitation: "Arthur, there must be some change. Things cannot drift as they are drifting. To remain here will but wreck our lives completely. I must go home to those who love me."

"Love you!" he said brokenly. "Love you!"

"In your love, there is a flaw," she answered dully. "I must go where I once more will be surrounded by a love which has none."

For a long time she paused, her breast heaving with her agony.

"You will go with me," she said, at length, making the words more an assertion than a query. "I cannot go without you."

The agonized look upon his upturned face went to her heart with knife-like penetration. His weakness, his great need of her, had never been so evident before.

"You *will* come with me, Arthur, dear?" she said again. Then, with newly tender touches of her light, cool fingers on his forehead and his cheeks: "I shall stand by you to the very end, dear, if you will only help me—help me a very little. I am your wife, dear."

There came into her face a fleeting show of hope, arisen from her yearning heart; it battled with the depression of cold hopelessness which emanated from her reason, and, for an instant, won.

"I still believe in you," she told him, and, for the

moment she did. "I still believe in you and feel certain that in time my supplications will be answered and the folly of the course which you have taken will be plain to you. My loyalty and love will surely win, dear—but not here; not here. We must go home. Will you go with me and try?"

His soul was stirred to its depths. Above all things a sentimentalist, to which fact could be charged some of his weakness, he yielded utterly to the strong emotional appeal of the tremendous moment. With her hand held tightly to his lips, he recited tremulously:

" 'I kiss the tips of thy fingers; they are my rosary . . . The palms of thy hands are the leaves of my Prayer-book . . . thy goodness my creed . . . Thy God is my God . . . Thou art slender and fair as the angels of Mary.' "

His voice broke continually. He was in a miserable state of mind, of body and of soul.

" 'Thy hair' " he went on falteringly, " 'is a crown of gold . . . like a flame in a vase of alabaster is thy soul in thy body . . . Through thee it shines . . . goodness . . . tenderness . . . truth.' "

Choking, unable to speak another word, he rose.

The last trace of resentment faded from her heart. As he stood there, with bowed head and hands clasped before him, she realized that he felt a greater horror of himself than she could ever feel of him in his most degraded moments.

Pity welled up from her heart until it flooded her whole soul. She smoothed his forehead with a slow, compassionate hand.

"But Arthur, if you really love me, how *can* you treat me as you do?"

The wretched boy swore faithfully that he would reform and, she felt, with a deeper impulse of resolve than he ever had known before.

Next morning he was definitely ill, and so departure was necessarily postponed, but in the moments she could spare from her attendance at his bedside, Doris went forward resolutely with the work of closing up their affairs in Paris, and of making the final preparations for their journey across the ocean. Home, home! There would be help and comfort there!

It was the day before departure, when, assured that every detail of arrangement was complete, she left him in a nurse's charge, and went out to say good-by to Paris. Many tendrils of the wonder-city had wound themselves about her heart, and her breath caught in a sob at thought of leaving them. She spent the morning in the Luxembourg, and after lunching in a quaint English tea-room, set down incongruously in the midst of French cafés upon the old Boul' Miche, motored to the Salon to view the exhibition for that year. Arthur's illness had prevented her from visiting it before; she had not even read of it—her brain had been too full of her own problems to let her feel much interest in the defeats and triumphs of others.

It was an especially good year in the great galleries, and she lingered long among the paintings. It was not until late in the afternoon that she began to study the year's marbles.

There, a tremendous shock awaited her. In the place of honor, in the very center of the largest room, she faced herself as she had been—Ah, how many years ago? As she had been that morning in the southern garden, when life held naught but joy, when hope was certainty, when only tenderest love surrounded her and she was ignorant that in the world beyond the confines of the graveled walks could lurk sorrow, weakness, disappointment.

"Goddess of the Garden," she read upon the pedestal of the image of her youth.

Underneath the titular inscription was the sculptor's name. She did not need to read it to make sure that it was: "Stoddard Thornton, Etats Unis d'Amerique." That on the silken rope in front of it hung the placard proclaiming that the work had won the highest honors of the year, impressed her very little, save that she noted with keen interest the fact that it announced the sculptor as a resident of Paris.

She had been transported to the scenes of childhood, not distant by the mere counting of the months and years, but inconceivably remote when she computed their division from the present by the span of the experiences which had whelmed upon her since she had unquestioningly joyed in them.

With bowed head, after a long absorption, she went from the building, unconscious of the fact that as she had been standing by the statue, the sculptor who had carved it had gazed at her from a slight distance, at first inclined to hurry to her, and then dissuaded from it by the war of the emotions which disturbed his heart, and by the shocking change in her appearance, which the white, searching light of the great room revealed.

CHAPTER XVII

Snow swirled madly as they approached New York.
When an operator of the wireless went to Doris's state-
room on the upper deck, he stood laughing at the doorway, shaking the dry, white powder from his broad
young shoulders, as he swayed, bracing to meet the ship's
long roll, after she had opened to his knock.

"And we're not even to have fair weather to-morrow,
for the last day at sea," he volunteered. "I've had the
'probabilities' from Washington."

She smiled somewhat wanly as she thanked him and
took the message he had brought to the sheltered nook
on deck where Arthur, wrapped in rugs, was reclining in
a steamer-chair.

"You're looking so much better this morning, Arthur,"
she said with careful optimism, although, really, he
looked very badly. "Read this message. I'm so glad
you had a good night's rest, dear."

"So the operator found you with the wireless," he answered rather weakly. "From home, is it?" He did not
raise his hand to take it.

"It is from mother. She and father will not be in
New York to meet us, but Virginia will be; and, what
do you think? She is to have dear old Mammy with
her!"

"I am sorry your mother could not come. You are disappointed."

"Yes, but I shall be so glad to see Virginia and Mammy Rose!"

The storm still raged when the great ship passed up the Bay. As they steamed slowly in, Staten Island was a vast mound of white, dotted only by such roofs as had been too steep for snow to cling upon; the statue of Liberty was almost hidden from them by the swirling storm. The busy tugs which fought through floating ice to reach the ship, and guide her to her berth, were icicled until they looked like little bergs with smoke-stacks.

But even ice-fringed tugs seemed beautiful to Doris. The keen crisp air exhilarated her as she leaned upon the rail and strained her eyes in hungry effort to see the familiar details of the vast, murky pile of the metropolis. New York! New York was at the threshold of America and America was home! And somewhere in the wilderness of buildings were two who loved her with a perfect love!

As the puffing tugs began to nose the ship in toward her dock, the storm, as if angered by the vessel's safe escape from its fierce onslaughts, attacked it with such force, sent over it such blinding, biting flurries, that she could not hold her place on deck. And so her first glimpse of Virginia was deferred until she started down the gang-plank, with Arthur, following, bearing heavily on his valet's arm.

Virginia sprang forward with a glad little cry, and eyes for Doris only. After the first embrace, she turned to Arthur. Her smile of greeting faded in amazement and it was with an effort that she kept herself from shrinking back, horrified by the great change in him. In her letters Doris had not even hinted that he was not well.

"Arthur!" Virginia exclaimed. "Have you been ill?"

"Not very well," he answered, somewhat stumblingly.

"And the voyage," Doris hastened to explain, to help him, "has been frightful."

Virginia was somewhat reassured. "I'm very sorry," she said sympathetically. "But never mind! A day and night or two on land——"

Arthur tried to answer gayly: "Yes; that's what I need. I'll be all right in a few days."

When Virginia turned from him to study more closely Doris's face, she realized that she, too, was much in need of rest—or something.

The tears of joy were still upon the poor girl's cheeks, and tears of joy were quite to be expected; but there were other signs Virginia had not expected, or, with her first glance, observed. Clearly Doris was no longer the happy girl who had departed on her wedding journey, light-hearted and care-free.

But Virginia was tactful and did not comment or ask questions, although her heart was throbbing with a startled, wondering sympathy, as she hurried them into the waiting motor.

Doris was conscious of the quick restraint which fell between them.

"I thought the wireless said that Mammy would be with you, dear," said she, anxious to do what she could to cover her involuntary surrender to emotion.

Virginia responded instantly. "The dear old thing! She had never seen the snow nor felt such intense cold before, and is sitting at the hotel, wrapped in shawls, hugging a radiator. In spite of the chills which made her shiver continually, she begged to be allowed to come with me; but, dear, you know how the rheumatism troubles her. I was afraid to let her venture out.

"I am so sorry there are no rooms for you at the Holland, where I am staying," Virginia continued. "I tried to engage a suite for you, but the storm has blocked the railways, and the town is full of snow-bound travelers."

"I know," said Arthur, making a great effort to speak steadily. "I tried by wireless and they said they hadn't anything. I've engaged rooms at the Plaza for a day or two."

"And we'll all go south almost at once, will we not?" said Doris, wistfully. That her parents had not met her in New York had made her landing on her native shores seem very lonely, almost unwelcomed, despite the cheering presence of her beloved aunt.

On the slow trip to the hotel, a dozen times delayed by traffic jams and skidding, futile wheels, Arthur, too wearied by exertion and excitement to feel anything very keenly, sat huddled in a corner of the cab, his eyes closed, trying to withdraw his mind from the remorse and self-reproach that this home-coming—every bright look and word of which was forced—seemed to compel. Not in the least recovered from the shock of Doris's changed appearance, Virginia endeavored to keep the conversation gay, filled with gossip of the family, hopeful comment on Judge Marston's health, stories of poor Mammy's wonder at the snow and cold and anecdotes of Desdemona; but the task was difficult. Tears trembled on her lashes each time she glanced at Doris.

It was a relief to all when they arrived at the hotel.

Once there, Virginia could not bring herself to leave Doris, for some hours, at least, and so telephoned to her hotel to have a message taken up to Mammy. This explained her own delay, and assured Mammy that Doris had arrived in safety, although Mr. Armsby's illness would prevent her, that day, from going to her. Virginia explained that the old nurse must be assured that she could certainly see Doris the next day.

The message did little to reassure the aged colored woman, who was filled with sorrow, and the hours which followed its reception seemed to her interminable. She did not touch the luncheon which was taken up to her. Hour after hour she huddled, shivering in the soulless heat from gilt steam-pipes—a very different sort of heat from that which she had known when chill evenings made a crackling fire of pine-knots welcome in the South.

With the passage of each moment, the conviction was growing in Mammy Rose's mind that Doris, whom she worshiped, was unhappy, although nothing had been said to make her think so. Not for a moment were her thoughts at rest. Her busy, puzzled brain devised ten thousand disturbing explanations of the untoward fact that her "Miss Beautiful" had not hurried to her immediately. It did not once occur to her that Virginia's message could have told the whole truth about the situation; she was increasingly possessed by terror for her darling. The unwonted elemental scene which greeted her when she looked from her window increased her fright; the window's very height above the surface of the earth made her head swim. Now and then she rose and feverishly paced the room on limbs trembling from the agitation which possessed her soul.

In the meantime Doris and Virginia were observing

Arthur with a growing apprehension. The excitement of returning to New York seemed to affect him with unexpected emphasis. His face was white, his hands more tremulous than usual (although he had lost all steadiness of nerve, long since), and his eyes were deeply sunken.

Both women were solicitous and worried, and, although he urged her not to do so, Doris sent for a physician, who came without delay, and diagnosed the case. The patient's heart, especially, had been affected by absinthe, he said, making it difficult for him to endure what plainly amounted to an intense nervous strain. Of this, of course, the doctor did not guess the nature; thus he failed to understand how serious was the man's real condition. He merely ventured the opinion that the journey had affected him somewhat unfavorably, and advised a month of rest, after sending out for bromides, and promising an early morning call.

It was after he had gone, and Arthur had been made as comfortable as possible in his own room, that the two women had their first opportunity to talk freely, but when it came they found themselves constrained and ill at ease, neither knowing how to start upon a conversation which both felt would prove intensely painful. For a time, Doris busied herself with the arrangement of small things which might as well have been left to her maid or neglected till the morrow. Virginia offered to assist, but found it impossible to concentrate her thoughts on anything except the sad face of the girl she loved. She was certain Doris was repressing the outpourings of an over-burdened soul, but was unwilling to say anything which might be thought an effort to induce reluctant confidences.

Doris, naturally, was solicitous about the dear ones at home.

"Everyone except father is quite well," Virginia answered, "and he is really better than he has been for six months."

"Oh, I have thought about you all so often!"

"I am sure of it, and you have been a dear to write so faithfully."

"I have tried to write regularly, no matter what—er —what occurred to take my time." As she said this, Doris reflected, sadly, on the many things her letters had not told.

"Your letters have been a comfort to us."

"I am so sorry I could not see Mammy to-night."

"You shall see her in the morning. Poor old Mammy! How cold weather troubles her!"

"She is worrying about me, too, I am sure."

"We have all—worried—Doris."

It was the word. Doris no longer could endure the strain of the repression, so, covering her face with her hands, she burst into tears.

Virginia, who had been leaning forward in her chair, gazing at the girl with anxious, sympathetic eyes, sprang up and caught her in her arms. Impulsively she pressed her to her breast, and, as Doris gave way utterly to a convulsive storm of weeping, Virginia sank beside her, comforting her and petting her as she had often done in bygone years; the tears gushing from her own eyes in quick sympathy, her heart beating high with keen anxiety concerning the nature of the forthcoming revelation.

"Poor dear girl!" she murmured.

There was the tremor of heart-breaking sorrow in her

voice. The great change in Doris since she last had seen her, a happy bride, was so tremendous, so significant of agonies endured, that her heart yearned toward her, as a mother's toward a suffering child. Pale, wan, listless and weary was this new Doris; when she had departed she had been so bright, so beautiful, so full of buoyant youth! And now every saddened line of her face told of agonized despair; her large eyes were shadowed and pathetic.

"What—what can have happened?" Virginia asked at length. "Doris, what has happened?"

"I must tell someone," Doris answered. "Yes—I must tell someone."

Virginia again put her arms about her comfortingly. "If it will help you, dear, but it may be that I am not the one. Perhaps you would prefer to wait and tell your mother."

"No; dear Virginia," Doris answered, struggling to keep back the tears. "For months I've longed for you, yearning for your sweet sympathy, and your advice. I —I've been so miserable!"

"Dear heart! And we all supposed you were so happy."

"I know; I know; I couldn't write—but Arthur—oh, my dear, my dear!—it is so good to feel your arms about me, to know that at last there is someone in whom I can confide!"

"My dear little Doris!"

"At first we were so happy! He was very gentle, very thoughtful. He anticipated my every wish." She buried her sad face in her hands. "Oh, Aunt Virginia! Why should this trouble have come to me?"

"Poor child!"

"And then—and then——"

"What dear?"

"And then came nights when he was cross and sharp with me . . . or . . . did not come . . . when I expected him. . . . How cruelly long those hours seemed . . . when I sat waiting, waiting with some book which we had planned to read together; some sketch which I had done and thought would please him; some queer story to tell him, of the strange folk I had met, thinking he would want to see, to hear, and laugh with me! But—but—so often he did not come home!

"One night I waited hours and hours, sleepless and terrified. Finally I heard him fumbling at the lock. The servants had long been asleep, and I was glad of that, for he could not manage with his key. I went to the door and opened it and he came in, and—did not even see me. He—he——"

"Did not see you?" Virginia was puzzled.

"No; he did not see me. He was——"

"Oh," cried Virginia, horrified. "You don't mean he had been——"

"Yes he had been drinking."

"My dear!" Virginia cried. "So that is the reason for the letters which have puzzled us—the letters which told nothing, which seemed so strangely forced."

"I didn't wish to worry you."

"And you were suffering there alone! Oh, my dear! My dear!"

"It was hard . . . oh, it was very hard!" said Doris, sobbing. "I tried to save him! His own, real self was never bad. It has been a tragedy unspeakable, to stand by, helpless, and see a naturally fine fellow go to pieces—down to ruin—through one fault. I—I had given up so much for him . . . mother . . . father . . . you, dear . . . everyone . . . for him.

"I hid it. I tried to keep the miserable secret locked in my own breast! I . . . tried to keep the world from knowing! But now . . . my enthusiasm is gone, my strength is gone and my heart is . . . broken!

"There is so much good in him; but he lacks sufficient will power to allow the good to dominate . . . I shall never turn against him. I shall try to help him all I can. I am—so sorry for him. In his way he loves me; I know that. For a long time, he has been quite— he has not touched liquor, and I have hopes that here, in America, he will——"

"I know, dear heart, I know; we shall all help."

"He loves me when he is himself. I have seen him writhe in agony at realization of some terrible humiliation he had put upon me; but——"

"Poor child!"

"Oh, Aunt Virginia, the loneliness! The loneliness of one who sits and waits, night after night, expecting, with each instant, to hear the step of him she loves and waits for—longing for it, though she dreads it—only to shrink in fear when it approaches; the spiritual loneliness of one bound irrevocably to another whose love for her has not been strong enough to keep him in the better ways of life, who seldom is entirely himself! It is so inconceivably a tragedy to see a man who might have filled a lofty place among his fellows, lose mastery of himself, and rave, a madman, or sink into a stupor. If he had been less lovable and dear when in his normal state, I could have borne it better; but when—oh, when he had been drinking, then he did not have a thought or aspiration I could share! You remember, dear, the talks we had? What dreams I had of comradeship with my husband! In what an ideal and beautiful way were we to live together, work together, climb together—oh—oh——"

For a few moments the two women sat in close and sympathetic silence.

Neither heard the slight noise in the little dressing-room which separated theirs from Arthur's room; but, unable to find sleep, despite the draught the doctor had administered, he had risen, and wishing to divert his mind from the gloomy thoughts of grim discouragement which thronged it, had gone into the dressing-room, searching for a book or newspaper to read. His head swam with the strong but ineffectual drug, his hand was tremulous, his footsteps weak, uncertain. He still seemed to feel the measured movements of the rolling ship.

He had thrust his feet into soft slippers and they made no noise; his presence near the thin door was not suspected by the two in the adjoining room. The mention of his name caught his attention, and he listened.

"He changed so! He was no longer my dear Arthur," he heard his wife say, tremulously, and he knew that as she spoke she sobbed.

When he had heard that much inadvertently, he could not tear himself away. As he had lain, sleepless, suffering, his conscience had tormented him. His wife's gentle, tearful voice, seemed but a continuation of the fierce

self-arraignment which had been so many times reiterated in his own distracted mind.

"I—I think I died that first year, auntie! How my
ideals crumbled, one after another! Oh, the tragedy of
it, the tragedy of it!" Her words were slow and evidently painful. "That life which we had planned to
lead together vanished as a dream of loveliness, to be
succeeded by a grim reality of horror. He almost
never was his own sweet self. He had changed completely."

The man shuddered as he listened to this indictment
from the loved lips he once had felt sure never would
speak of him save in endearment and admiration.

"That first year of loneliness!" he heard her moan.
"I longed a thousand times to die. Away from all my
loved ones—alone—alone!"

The eavesdropper longed to escape, but could not move.

After a moment's pause the suffering girl-wife continued, abandoning herself to her intense desire for sympathy and comfort from someone whom she knew she
could surely trust with her unhappy secret. "As I sat in
silence while my sorrow ate my heart out, I asked myself
again and again why it should be—when I had always
tried to be kind and good to everyone."

"Dear heart!" he heard Virginia say, "Sometimes life
is very terrible, I know."

" 'Why? Why?' I asked myself a thousand times."

Arthur choked with his own crowding sobs. He raised
his hand and pressed it to his lips to stifle them, so that
no sound should penetrate into the room beyond. He no
longer felt that he was doing wrong in listening. A
true and proper sense of the terrific wrong that he had

wrought was rising in his heart for the first time. Moments of remorse had come to him before, but until now he had not fully realized. An understanding knowledge was sweeping over him. And suddenly his heart was breaking, as, he now realized, the heart of her he loved had broken in its dreadful agony.

"How I wept—oh, how I wept for all the faith and trust and happiness which he had taken from me!" Doris went on. "I had always been so happy. It is natural for me to be light-hearted. I was born with the joy of living coursing through my veins. I could have been supremely happy—I had been supremely happy—and then to be deprived of it so terribly, so wholly, seemed worse, I think, because I once had known it so completely. What bitter tears I wept for the sweet love which he had killed! I had considered him the soul of honor, manliness, strength and devotion, but, now . . . ah!

"I had loved him so dearly, that my love died slowly, and that made the agony more terrible to bear. When I think of the death struggles of my love, I still writhe in dreadful suffering! It died so hard, my beautiful, tenacious love! It endured selfishness and neglect so long, but inch by inch it perished.

"And when a woman's love is taken from her, there is nothing left in life for her to hope for, live for! It is the end!"

"Yes, dear—it—is the—end!"

Slowly, silently, in aject misery, the listener stole back into his room, to contemplate the grim pictures of his own shortcomings which in agony his mind flashed before him, as a cinematograph throws pictures on a screen in swift succession.

A little later he heard Virginia, after having done all she could to comfort the sobbing girl, steal softly from the other room, and down the outer hallway.

CHAPTER XVIII

Virginia was but indefinitely conscious of the drive to her hotel. She heard nothing but the tremulous cadences of Doris's voice, saw nothing but her memory pictures of the sorrowing girl. Miserable to the depths of her sympathetic soul, she sat silently in a corner of the taxi as it toiled slowly, lurchingly, through the snow-blocked and deserted streets. That its laborious progress was halted frequently while its racing motor spun its wheels upon the sheet-ice blanketing of the asphalt where the wind had swept the snow away, or by some drift which proved too deep for it to master without unusual effort, did not impress her sufficiently to make her consciously impatient of the delays in the sharp cold. Her soul was crushed beneath the borrowed weight of Doris's heavy burden.

It seemed incredible to her that the unhappy girl from whom she had just separated could be that Doris who had gone from them, bright, light-hearted, lovely with the bloom of an untroubled youth; confident with the courage of a nature which had never known an actual sorrow, and looking forward at the world with the unfrightened eyes of one who has not realized that men can sin. When she had seen her dedicate her life to the tall, handsome youth who now was but a pitiable wreck of moral nerve and physical fiber, who could have dreamed of such a denouement?

In dumb distress her mind reverted to the sentimental tragedy of her own youth. How much better would it have been for Doris if some seemingly untoward event had come to wreck her romance also! Romance! The thought of all the dreadful changes which this romance had wrought in the dear child, forced from Virginia's lips a groan of anguish.

With great difficulty she suppressed the starting tears, as amidst a veritable blizzard, and with a final, desperate lurch into the gutter, the cab at last drew up in front of the hotel.

Despite the lateness of the hour, poor Mammy Rose was still awake upstairs—awake and worrying. Possessed of that mysterious clairvoyance which is the gift, or curse, of many of the aged of her race, as will be attested by most of those who have lived long among the southern negroes, she was indefinitely conscious that Virginia's long delay in returning had been due to some untoward condition or event affecting Doris. Her whole soul yearned for a speedy glimpse of Doris's face; the hours of waiting had been hard to bear.

Regardless of her rheumatism, she sprang to her feet and hurried toward her, when weary and distraught, Virginia tried to enter her own room noiselessly so that the aged negress would not hear her. The poor old creature's hands were clasped in desperate anxiety, and her excitement made her inarticulate, although she tried to speak. The tear-traces on Virginia's face increased her apprehension. She went weak and helpless, and, before even half-coherent speech became a possibility, Virginia, for the first time in her life, had removed her hat and wraps without assistance, when Mammy Rose had been at hand.

"Wheah's Miss Dawiss, Miss Fahginny? Wheah's Miss Dawiss?" she implored, as soon as she could speak, in a voice which thrilled with anxiety.

"Why, at her hotel," Virginia answered, recovering self-control with a great effort, suddenly realizing the agony in Mammy's voice, and striving to make her words seem matter of fact. "You know it's such a bad night, Mammy."

But Mammy was not reassured. With that accuracy with which a master knows the tones of his beloved violin, she knew the hidden meaning in each inflection of the voice of every member of her "white folks' fambly."

"Dere's mo' dan de bad night a-keepin' huh fum me!" she cried. "Mo' dan de bad night, honey! Bad night? Dat wouldn't evah stop mah own Miss Dawiss fum comin' to huh ol' brack Mammy!"

"No, no, Mammy," Virginia said, soothingly. "Only the bad night and Mr. Armsby's illness. He's not at all well."

Mammy stood with her hands clasped and her body bent a little forward, her eyes fraught with a tremendous earnestness. "Has—has sumpin' happened to dat precious baby, Miss Fahginny?"

"Oh, no, Mammy." Virginia saw that she must now forget sufficiently the suffering child whom she had left, to give some comfort to this child of older growth who stood before her with imploring eyes fixed on her face.

"An'—an' she ain't sick, nor nothin'?"

"No, Mammy."

Reared to the habit of accepting without question any statement from a member of the "fambly," but very far from satisfied, Mammy went to the small desk which occupied a corner of the room, and took from it a packet of mail-matter sent up after Virginia had gone out that morning.

"Heah's yo' lettuhs, honey," she said dully.

Virginia did not heed her, although Mammy knew that in the packet must be letters from the South which, ordinarily, she would have been eager to read. This was a further cause for worry.

Strange impulses were stirring in the aged woman's mind. Virginia, sympathetically understanding though she was, did not fully appreciate the strength of the almost maternal love for Doris which possessed the breast of the devoted nurse. If she had stopped to organize her thoughts she might have told her frankly what had happened, or at least have made it clear that, at this time, there was nothing to be done to comfort the unhappy girl whom they both adored. But she was weary, and instead of making any explanation, admitted her exhaustion and said she must retire at once.

Without another word Mammy assisted her in making preparations for the night, threw back the covers, and, when Virginia was ready, tucked her in, with quite as much solicitude as any mother could have shown a weary child. This done Mammy patted her upon the shoulder, saying soothingly: "Now, honey, yo' mus' go to sleep like a real da'lin'."

"Perhaps I'd better. Good-night, Mammy. I kept you waiting for me longer than I should. You, yourself, must get a good night's rest, so that you will be feeling bright and well when you see Miss Doris in the morning."

"I'll be rested, honey. I sho' longs to see huh."

But sleep eluded Virginia. The multitude of worries which the talk with Doris had inflicted her would not give her mind a moment's peace. Before half-an-hour had passed she had thrown back the covers impatiently; wrapped a dressing gown around her, and gone to a window, to sit looking from its dizzy height into the snow-swept mystery of the great city. Her heart was in a turmoil of distress.

An hour passed while, unseeing, she peered into the storm. The whistling of the fierce wind about the lofty casement recalled to her the low, half-stifled moans of Doris's anguish; she heard the booming of a near-by steeple clock and imagined that the girl was also listening to it, sleepless and worrying; she reproached herself for having left her; she searched the bygone years for contrasts—bitter, bitter contrasts of Doris's youthful happiness with the deep sorrow of the period she had described, with the acute misery of her present. Her distress of mind became an agony, and, at length, she rose to pace the room.

As she walked, she began to moan her thoughts aloud in an access of misery; she was probably unconscious of the fact that she was speaking.

But Mammy's keen ears heard the first sound of her murmuring and, hurrying to the door, stood there listening intently. "Miss Fahginny's worryin'!" she told herself with bated breath. "She's worryin' about Miss Dawiss!" With her every nerve a-tingle with anxiety to catch each word, she crouched close by the door.

"Oh, I hardly knew her! Hardly knew her!" Virginia was murmuring. "That beautiful girl! And now ——"

Mammy's heart throbbed with excitement. Here was confirmation of her dreadful fears! Virginia *had* been hiding something from her! Doris surely must be threatened by some dreadful danger.

The door was slightly ajar, but covered by a heavy portiere, which Mammy drew back a trifle so that she could look in cautiously. As she peered Virginia was standing by the dresser, holding Doris's portrait in her hand and gazing at it earnestly.

"Her beauty was like the Springtime," she was murmuring sadly, "all tenderness, and gold, and pink, and sunshine. Now——"

Unable to restrain herself the old woman stepped excitedly into the room.

"Why, Mammy!" said Virginia, in astonishment. "I thought you were asleep!"

"No; Ah ain't asleep. Ah been listenin'." The old woman wrung her hands; her voice was half a cry. "An' Miss Fahginny—Miss Fahginny, Ah's gwine git dat chil'! Ah heared yo', honey, 'bout what's happenin' to huh! Dat man gwine kill huh! He gwine kill huh!"

"No, no, Mammy; Doris is in no danger. She has been unhappy, and Mr. Armsby isn't well; but——"

"Ah knows! Ah knows! Don't yo' s'pose Ah knows?" The aged, trembling creature was like a lioness who had heard something making her believe that distant cubs are threatened. "Ah's gwine go an' git dat chil'!"

Alarmed, Virginia went to her and put her arms about

her. "Mammy, dear, don't worry so! You don't understand. Doris is quite safe—quite safe, I assure you! Mr. Armsby is not well; but he—why, Mammy, he would not harm Doris!"

"Ah's gwine go git huh! Right dis minute Ah's gwine staht!" And she hobbled toward the door.

"Mammy! Mammy! Why, you don't even know where to find her! And she doesn't need you. If she needed either of us, do you suppose I would not be with her, have you with her? No, no; do be good and patient, dear, and go to sleep. We'll see her in the morning."

For the moment the old nurse was crushed. It was true—she did not know how to find Doris; and she was sure that urging Virginia to tell her would be of no avail. But a great resolve grew in her soul. She became tactful, cunning.

"All right, honey," she said, slowly, with seeming acquiescence, "ef Ah don't go su'chin' fo' huh, den will you go straight to sleep?"

Virginia bitterly reproached herself for having worried the old woman, and now was glad to see a sign that she was becoming more composed. "Yes, dear Mammy," she agreed. "I'm so sorry I alarmed you! To-morrow you shall see her. Now we both must try to sleep."

Mammy led her to the bed, and, after she had tucked her in once more, smoothed her brow with tender hand. "Take a little powduh, will yo'?" she asked gently. When troubled by insomnia Virginia sometimes took a harmless sleeping-powder.

"Yes; I believe I will."

The thought of certainty of sleep especially attracted her, for she would need the utmost of her strength next day, in order to help Doris.

There was a look of grim determination upon Mammy's face as she mixed that sleeping powder. She knew perfectly how much of it comprised a safe, how much a perilous dosage. In the South the negro nurses are the family doctors' most efficient and trustworthy aides, and the old physician who, for years, had attended to the Marquis and the Marston families, had entrusted her with managing these powders for Virginia during many sleepless periods. The dose she mixed, that night, was of full strength, but not in the least dangerous. She knew of no other plan which would enable her to fly to her beloved Doris without delay, and on that course she was determined. She could find her somehow.

"Dere, now, honey; yo' take dis, out o' dis gol'-lined silber cup Ah brought f'um home," she urged. "Hit sho' will make yo' sleep. . . . Drink it all, now, honey." Then, very slowly: "B'leeve Ah bettuh take one fo' mahse'f."

"Yes; do. Don't worry. Everything will be all right for Doris."

"Ob co'se it will; ob co'se it will. Now jes yo' go to sleep an' git all rested fo' de mo'nin'."

"Good-night, Mammy."

"Good-night, honey."

But Mammy's manner changed entirely as soon as she was sure Virginia slept. She tiptoed around the room, getting wraps together to protect her in her venture out into the dreadful cold. She did not know just how best to prepare for it, but she tied a scarf over her bandanna and underneath her chin, wrapped her shoulders in a great gray shawl, found a pair of fur-lined gloves and softly went into the hall.

She had no confidence in elevators. She had been in one—upon the day of her arrival—so she laboriously descended the interminable stairs, occasionally meeting a watchman or a night chambermaid who questioned her, but, smiling, let her pass unhindered when she told them she was the servant of a guest, going out to get a "mos' partic'lar med'cine."

In the hotel office she again was challenged and again her statement that she was on an errand for her mistress gave her passage. A negro night-porter regarded her with sympathy, and offered to go with her to a drug-store; but as she really was not going to a drug-store, she thanked him rather curtly—to make sure that he would not insist. And she listened to elaborate directions, which she did not care to hear.

She was delighted by her cleverness in passing him and hurried through the long, wide corridor, now dimly lighted by the after-midnight allowance of electricity, pushed through whirling storm-doors with some difficulty and bewilderment, but with a grim determination not to permit hindrance by any devilish contraption of the North, no matter how unusual or how vicious, and thus finally gained the street in safety. Indefinitely fearing that she might become the object of pursuit, she made haste off into the night.

Possessed by the idea of eluding capture, should anyone attempt it, she half-ran to a corner, turned it, hurried up that block and turned another angle and another and another before she stopped to think.

She had left the brightly lighted district which surrounded the hotel, and she had also left the section where the fallen snow had been disturbed by traffic. Dimly, through the storm, she could see upon each side brown houses of cut-stone, alike, monotonous, unfriendly, dark. She knew how hotels looked, for, as she had clambered from the cab to enter that in which they lodged she had had a terrifying view of its tremendous, towering front. Doris's, of course, would be of similar general appearance; but there was nothing in this neighborhood which was, and she knew therefore that she was off the track which she should follow. She tried retracing her own footsteps, but could not. Instead she reached a sidewalk which had been more traveled, and, although she did not know it, leading to Broadway.

Now she stopped to make some note of the terrors of the mysterious night in the great city—and was frightened. Although she had watched the snow-storm from the hotel-windows, and thus had become, in a way, familiar with it, as she now looked into the air above her, whence the flakes were falling steadily, unceasingly, by millions—coming down, down out of the dark into the glow of the city lights—the sensation grew that she was underneath some vast, impending peril, which might at any time descend on her and crush her. It seemed as if the very sky, gray and yellow-black and dismal, must also fall. Down, down, came the myriad snowflakes, threatening to overwhelm her, smother her, obliterate her. On the sidewalk they made walking slippery, puzzling her; they caught upon her spectacles and dimmed her sight. Although she had wrapped her upper body warmly she had not thought to protect her feet, and they were clad only in light-soled, cloth shoes. They began to ache excruciatingly from cold.

She realized with horror that she did not in the least know where to go. She had not thought New York could be so vast. Why, it was plainly more tremendous than New Orleans! And it was so aloof, unfriendly! If she had thought of it at all, she had supposed that, living in one hotel, themselves, "Miss Dawiss" must be staying at "the other one," which would be as easy to discover as the second hotel in any of the small southern towns which she had visited. But in half-an-hour she saw at least a dozen ornate entrances, all, to her confused and unaccustomed eyes, looking enough like that from which she had fled to be, each one, a hotel portal.

She became excited, feeling that she was wasting precious time in wandering; and this thought was terrible, because of her conviction that Doris's need of her was instant. She stopped upon a corner, beside a post which bore twin electric-lights, and stood there in a daze, lifting her old feet, one after the other, to relieve them for an instant from the agony of direct pressure on the freezing snow, her hands trembling, her eyes dim with terror, her whole frame shivering, half from cold and half from fright.

"Lord, Ah's los'!" she muttered. "Los'!"

Then occurred what seemed to her to be a thing entirely past comprehension. Although she did not know it, she was on the edge of the great negro quarter, southwest of Central Park, and from a side street a young colored girl, wearing a close-fitting tan-cloth jacket, came into the glow of the next light. Size, walk, skirt, jacket, hat—all seemed familiar.

"Desdemona! Desdemona Snowball!" Mammy called wildly.

The girl passed on, unheeding save for a disdainful turning of her head. Insulted, Mammy turned and asked a brown-skinned, liveried chauffeur, who stood near, slapping his cold hands while waiting for his passengers who were reveling in an all-night restaurant: "Say, ain't dat Desdemona Snowball?"

Save for laughter he ignored her; plainly he thought her mad.

In an instant she perceived the wild absurdity of her supposition; in a great city like New York a strange chauffeur would know nothing about Desdemona; and how could Desdemona, possibly, be there? "Mus' think Ah'm a ol' fool!" she muttered. "An' Ah guess Ah is."

But, none the less, anger rose at the young chauffeur, and after a scornful glance at his fur-cape, long coat and trim, leather puttees, she gave verbal vent to it. "Yo' thinks yo's mighty fine, don't yo', struttin' 'roun' de streets, heah, wid yo' toes tuhned out!"

Doubtless he was convinced more than ever of her insanity, for he paid not the least attention to her.

Help finally came to her unexpectedly from the very heart of the dull gloom which so oppressed her. An old cab was standing near. Between its shafts an aged and decrepit horse drooped, muzzling without much enthusiasm in an all but empty nose-bag. Hunched in a loose overcoat with a worn fur-collar held about his neck by a brass clasp, the cabman shuffled stiffly back and forth on the sidewalk to keep the frost out of his feet. The whole formed a combination often seen in New York's all-night section a few years ago, but, in these days of taxis, rare indeed. As Mammy stood, nonplussed, still very much hurt and worried by the young girl's disdainful attitude and the chauffeur's snub, this man looked up and saw her. He was an aged negro, white-haired, white-whiskered. He rubbed his eyes, as he caught sight of her, as if she might have been some dream-figure, risen from the past to mock him. Deciding she was real he slowly made his way to her.

"You f'um de Souf, ma'am, ain't you?" he inquired respectfully.

"Yassuh," she replied, taking comfort. Perhaps, at last, she had found someone who would help her. She had never needed friendship more. "Ah, sho' is f'um de Souf. Is you?"

"Good many yeahs ago. What's de mattuh, anyhow, ol' lady?"

She was delighted by his pleasant voice and his familiar accent.

"Ah's habbin' plenty troubles, dis night," she replied, her voice breaking. "Ah's sho' habbin' troubles. Ah jus' nachelly done los' mahse'f, Ah guess. Jus' nachelly done los' mahse'f."

"Wheah yo' want to go at?"

"Ah wants to go to mah Miss Dawiss."

He smiled sympathetically. "Wheah does she all lib, ol' lady?"

"Dat's de trouble. Ah ain't sho'. Mah Miss Fahginny, huh an' me, we're libbin' at de big hotel, an' ouah Miss Dawiss, she stops at de uddah one."

"Dey is a lot o' big hotels in New Yo'k city."

Mammy sighed. "Lawd, lawd—Ah knows it, now! Ain't Ah seed a million ob 'em sence Ah stahted out?"

"Don't yo' know de name?"

"Ah heered it, but Ah done furgit. 'Blasted'? Is dey one called dat?"

He laughed, but not unkindly. "Dey's a lot ob 'em desuhves dat name, but Ah ain't knowin' any one dat owns to it. 'Blasted'? 'Blasted'? You got me!"

Mammy Rose was fumbling in her pocket. That very day Virginia had given her some money, and she had brought a few long-hoarded dollars from the South with her. She would offer this old man one-half of all she had, or all of it, if he would help her find her dear Miss Doris.

But she discovered that there was no money in her pocket; then, she remembered that early in the evening, when Virginia failed to come, she had hidden her old pocket-book (string-wound and worn) beneath the mattress of her bed at the hotel. This filled her with dismay.

"Fo' de Lawd!" she cried. "Ah ain't got a single cent! Not one! Back at de hotel, wheah Miss Fahginny is, Ah got enough to make me halfway rich, but Ah ain't got nary penny wid me, now."

"Yo' got money back at de hotel, yo' say?"

"Ah is; fo' Gawd Ah is!"

The kind old negro did not doubt her. He remembered with a thrill of sentiment the old mammies of his far youth in that Southland and recognized her as quite genuine.

But she did not sense his growing friendship. She was overwhelmed by an unreasoning terror of the situation. Here she was, out in the night and storm, without money and without knowledge of the place she came from or of the place she wished to find! While she was delayed, perhaps, some dreadful thing was happening to Doris—something from which, if she could get to her, she might preserve her. Mammy wrung her hands and stood appalled and half-hysterical.

"Oh, mah po' Miss Dawiss," she cried pitifully. "Oh, mah po' Miss Dawiss!"

"What's de mattuh wid huh? Don't yo' git excited. Nobody ain't said dey wouldn't trus' yo' for a couple dollahs cab-hiah."

In this emergency Mammy did what she could not have been induced to do by any other conceivable set of happenings. Briefly and in broken accents she told the old man what was nearly driving her distracted.

The story touched him. "Yo' hop in, ol' lady," he said reassuringly. "Hop in an' git yo' feet out dish yere freezin' snow. Ah's gwine help yo', Ah is. When yo' gits yo' money yo' kin pay me. Ah ain't afeared to trus' you none. We'll jus' staht out an try an' find yo' Missy dat yo's worrittin' about."

Mammy tried to thank him, but was inarticulate.

"Fust," he said, as he began to tuck the horse's nose-bag into a safe place beneath the seat to which, at length, she had ascended, laboriously, "we gotta git a little bettuh line on dat hotel yo' say yo' missy is a-stoppin' at."

"'Blasted,' 'Blasted,'" Mammy said. "Dat sho's de name, er somethin' like it."

"No; dat ain't de name. Ah knows de hotels ob dis town by heaht an' dey ain't any ob dem called 'Blasted.'"

"Well, den, what we gwine do, anyhow?" Mammy was unutterably miserable.

"We might find huh by suhchin' till we struck huh," he suggested. "What yo' say huh name is?"

"Huh name is Mrs. Ahmsby—Mrs. Ahthuh Ahmsby," Mammy answered. "Dat's huh name, an' we-all calls huh jus' 'Miss Beautiful.' She married Mistuh Ahthuh Ahmsby an' not one ob us was wantin' huh to marry him."

The cabman listened closely. "Well," he said, after very careful thought, "we mought take a long chance an' be lucky. Mebbe we mought fin' huh ef we su'ched."

"An' she's jus' home f'um Eu'ope," Mammy went on, eagerly, responding quickly to the hope he offered. "Yessuh, she jus' come f'um Eu'ope, jus' to-day; an' she's about de same as mah own chil'. Ah nussed huh at dis ol' brack breas'. Ah been in de fambly fifty yeahs—Ah reckon, mo'n dat mebbe."

"Well, we gwine fin' huh. Now you listen close while I'm namin' de hotels yo' Missy, ef she's rich an' pros-p'ous, would be likely to be stoppin' at."

When he came to "Plaza" in his list, Mammy stopped him with a cry of recognition. "Dat's it!" she exclaimed excitedly. "Didn't Ah tell yo' it wuz 'Blasted' or close to it."

Without another word the cabman cracked his whip to wake his sleepy horse, climbed to the box and started off as briskly as the icy, snowbound way permitted. "Ah'll git yo' dere in fifteen minutes," he said across his shoulder to his passenger, who was huddling in the cold, beneath the hood of the one-horse victoria.

In half-an-hour, despite the terrible condition of the streets, he had drawn up before the Plaza and jumped down to offer Mammy what further help she might find useful.

"An Ah's gwine to tell yo' somethin' else, ol' lady," the good-hearted darkey said, as he assisted her to pull her stiffened limbs out of the cab, "an' dat is, yo' ain't owin' me a cent. It's been wuth twice de money fo' to heah yo' good ol' S'uth'n talk. Kinda thought Ah nevuh wusn't gwine heah no mo' *real* talk like dat—not 'fo' Ah died!"

"Yo' write yo' name down on a piece ob papuh," Mammy answered with as much of a smile as her increasing worries would permit, "an' yo's gwine fin' dis night's been jus' about de luckies' yo' evuh knowed. Ain't ev'y man 'ud trust a po' ol' nigguh woman—los' an' plumb nigh crazy."

Only because of her insistence the old man fumbled in a greasy pocket and presently drew out a broken card. "But Ah ain't a-givin' it because Ah wants de money f'um yo'," he explained. "Hit's jus' because Ah'd like to heah yo' good ol' S'uth'n talk ag'in."

"Yo' gwine hab de money an' yo' gwine heah de talk, both," she assured him; and, unable to wait any longer, hurried into the hotel.

As best she could upon her chilled and aching legs and feet, she hobbled to the desk.

"Ah wants to see Miss Dawiss," she said to the clerk, pleadingly. "Ah wants to see Miss Dawiss, Mistuh. Ah jus' got to see huh, right away."

"Miss Dawiss?" said the astonished clerk, inquiringly.

Mammy realized her error. "P'raps yo' don't know just who Ah means," she hurried to explain. "Who Ah means is ouah Miss Dawiss Marquis—no, Mrs.

Ahmsby, 'cause she's married to dat Mistuh Ahthuh Ahmsby, an' dey got heah dis very day, f'um Eu'ope."

At this the clerk showed an instant and active interest. During the last hour there had been a quick succession of exciting events connected with guests named Armsby, in the hotel.

"Why do you want to see her?" he inquired. "She's —very busy."

"Oh, Mistuh, Mistuh," Mammy pleaded, "she ain't nevuh gwine be busy 'nough to not to want to see huh ol' brack Mammy!"

"Oh, you are a servant of the family?"

"Ain't Ah been a suhvant ob de fambly fo' full fifty yeahs?"

"Front!" said the clerk, without further parley, "take this old woman up to five-fourteen."

She had scarcely started across the office in the bellboy's wake when the clerk called after her:

"Do you know of a Miss Marston? She's at the Holland. We've been trying to connect with her, by telephone, for Mrs. Armsby."

"Yassuh, yassuh," Mammy answered. "She's asleep, theah. Tell 'em to keep on rappin'. They'll wake huh if it's real impohtant, and dey keeps on a rappin'. But don't yo' be distuhbin' huh fo' no fool mattuhs. Ah can look aftuh Miss Dawiss. Miss Fahginny's tiahd out an' Ah give huh a sleepin'-powduh."

The clerk looked quizzically after her, as she limped hurriedly away.

Five-fourteen had kept him busy through the last halfhour. First had come the frenzied call of Mrs. Armsby for a doctor, then a constant scurrying of servants sent on errands of one kind or another by the half-distracted, but beautiful young wife of the suite's tenant; then the physician's coming and more telephoning; finally the news brought by a frightened bellboy rushing to a drug store, that the ailing man was near to death.

Mammy Rose found Doris kneeling by the bedside of her husband and advanced toward her, frightened into silence despite her great delight at seeing her again. Something very near to mother-love, if not that actual emotion, stirred the old black woman's heart as she drew near, and it was not lessened in intensity by the tremendous shock she felt when the poor girl's face was raised to hers.

Doris, too distraught to be surprised by seeing her, motioned her to kneel beside her, and, as she knelt, put her arm about her. Both heads then bowed in silent prayer.

Mammy, as she raised her face again, scarcely recognized the unconscious man whose head was on the pillow, as the handsome youth whom she had known in the old home.

Beyond the bed stood the physician.

"Mrs. Armsby," he whispered solemnly, "Mr. Armsby is regaining consciousness. He has something to say to you, I think."

Doris bent her head close to her husband's pallid face and pressed the nerveless hand she held. "Arthur! Arthur! What is it, dear heart?"

"For-give," he murmured and lapsed into eternal silence.

CHAPTER XIX

Stoddard Thornton's studio in Paris bore across its face the utterly deceptive legend, *"Voitures et Cheveaux."* No horse or carriage had been in it for a score of years; young sculptor after young sculptor there had pressed his clay between uncertain fingers, or with the firm touch of the inspired, as happened; there had chipped with cautious touches, a little at a time, the precious marble which, mayhap, he had gone hungry to procure, or, swayed by a fine frenzy of conviction, had hammered at it with great strokes, certain of its grain and eager to remove the husk which hid and would reveal to him, and to none other, the kernel of his heart's imaginings.

The floor was of uneven brick. One horse-stall remained in a far corner, now convenient for the staging-timbers which the sculptor had found necessary when he had been hammering out a monument, strong, war-like, so crudely beautiful that it had been rejected by a regiment which wished to mark its place upon the field of Gettysburg. No other large commission had yet come to him, despite the victory of his "Goddess of the Garden" at the Salon, and times were very hard, although he had had some success in selling statuettes of Fisher Girls and Soldiers of the Legion.

He still found the small problem of existence very puzzling, and the greater problem of his payments to the bank almost, but never quite, beyond solution.

His puzzles had been greatly complicated after his glimpse of Doris that day at the Salon. The episode had thrown him into deep depression, as such episodes are likely to affect young persons of high-keyed emotional temperament. Unfortunately this period of despondency lasted so long that it influenced his work unfavorably. He could no longer think of jaunty soldiers or of pretty fisher-girls. His mind, instead, produced but morbid fancies, sometimes terrible imaginings, and when he finished the big model of a crouching, straining figure which he called the "Burden Bearer," Whilk, who had come over from the States and shared his studio, protested warmly. He believed this to be an era with his friend when his very art was threatened, although he did not know the reason, and decided to do what he could to remedy the situation.

It had been Whilk who had informed him that the expected marriage between Doris and George Chapman never had occurred, and had borne to him the news that she had married Arthur. Now he constantly encouraged him and cheered him.

"Go back to the simplicity and sweetness of your 'Goddess of the Garden,' " he adjured him earnestly. "Quit sculpting figures full of woe. Suppose I should draw gamins only when they're fighting or have stubbed their toes! My vogue as a kid-painter would go down and out, too quick. That painful 'Burden Bearer' which" (he waved his hand toward a dim recess in the studio) "is straining in the corner to lift too much for his bent back, is good, old man, but it is the sort of thing that makes the public think you get your fancies from the pit! It gives me the Willies."

Stoddard looked at the weird figure curiously. He knew the tortured thing was true; he sometimes felt that it was a faithful portrait of his own laborious soul, engaged upon its continual and terrific effort. Even if Whilk should be right, he found himself at this time unable to see beauty in the world to mold in clay and afterwards preserve in plaster, bronze, or marble.

An episode confirming Whilk's observations came shortly after, and made that wide-awake young artist wonder what could be the matter with his friend. He had decided once that there was a fleeting likeness between Stoddard's "Goddess of the Garden" and the beautiful young girl whom he had seen that day upon the sidewalk before the New York studio, but he was not sure of it, and, of course, would not ask. Stoddard was a great puzzle to him. A dealer, entering without formality of knocking, found both men gazing at the formidable "Burden Bearer," but, himself, refused even to look at it. Instead, he turned to look with admiration at the delicate figure which had won the honors at the Salon. He insisted that it far surpassed the "Burden Bearer," both in artistic merit and in possibilities of popularity and sale.

"*Eh bien, mon brav!*" he said. "There, you did really accomplish something! Ah, but it is of the art!" He turned and glanced with definite dislike at the grim "Burden Bearer," and then, with quickly altering expression, whirled to face the "Goddess of the Garden." "Why not sell this to me, eh? How much?"

Whilk was delighted. He had urged Stoddard to exhibit the charming figure in a shop which offered it position, and had wondered why he did not take the offer. Of course, however, he would sell, and this man might pay a really good price. His eyes showed that he wanted it. Imagine the amazement of the man who painted "kiddies," when Stoddard glared fiercely at the prospective buyer, and replied shortly:

"It is not for sale, *mon ami.*"

The dealer was not much impressed. Some artists know the value of their wares, and even stoop to haggling; perhaps this young American might be trying to insure a good bid at the start. The dealer was actually enthusiastic, and inclined to name a pleasant figure, for he knew a lady, an emotional American, to whom he thought he might dispose of the "Goddess" at a handsome profit over almost any reasonable price. He continued his appreciative gazing at the spirited and mystic marble.

"All things have their price," he murmured philosophically. Then, after a moment's pause, during which he did not notice how the sculptor's evident displeasure was increasing: "Whom could you have found, here in the *Quartier,* so pure, so lovely, and so—ah, so spirituelle —to pose for you?"

Stoddard looked at him with definite enmity. Without answering the question, he stood studying the dealer's thick red lips, his heavy-lidded, coarse and greedy eyes, with a degree of scorn which would have burned a finer fibered person.

"I have said I would not sell that," he replied. Then he quickly threw across it a large silken drape—the only bit of luxury the room contained, just as the surroundings of the little niche had been the only things of luxury his New York studio had held. "It is not even to be looked upon by such eyes as yours," he added.

Whilk placed his hand upon Stoddard's arm protestingly. There was no sense in angering a man who came to buy one's wares.

Incensed into spluttering wrath, the dealer tried to argue, but with one hand firm upon his arm, the sculptor took him to the door, urged him through it and closed it after him.

When he returned Whilk took one look at his face, said nothing, and speedily absorbed himself in his own work; the dealer, who had meant no harm whatever, but, instead, an honest compliment, with a shrewd bit of bargaining beyond it, passed up the street, his shaking head busy with the reflection that the artist tribe is full of whims, and that these big Americans look very dangerous, at times.

But the "Goddess of the Garden," pure, beautiful, unusual, hung a tempting vision in the mercenary's shrewd, commercial mind, and, a few weeks afterward he decided on another trial. It was late afternoon; indeed, the dusk was falling slowly, when he went again to the studio. The sculptor might be in better temper now, or in poorer funds, and more willing to talk business. If he should throw him out—even such things had happened to this dealer—oh, well, the studio had been a stable and was on ground level; at least, there were no stairs; it might not break any bones. He very much desired to buy that figure.

But Whilk was there alone, and would not even take the great drape from the marble. Instead, he very solemnly advised the Frenchman never to come there again with offers for it, and, if he came upon other business, to keep his eyes turned from it.

"When Mr. Thornton told you it was not for sale," said he, "he meant that it was not for *sale.*"

"But surely——"

"I'm not altogether joking. He didn't like to see you even look at it. You'd better keep away from him. Take my advice, and cross the street when you come near this magic number."

"But——"

"Don't be here when he comes!" Whilk urged with a gesture full of eloquent description of what might occur to him, should Stoddard find him within reach.

"But——"

"There he comes, *now!*"

The man fled, and, from that time forward, crossed the street whenever he approached that number, precisely as Whilk had suggested.

But Stoddard, really, was nowhere near. He had gone to feast his eyes upon the treasures of an ancient mansion of the Faubourg, which, now fallen into sad, impoverished days, was the scene of a great auction sale. He was shocked out of his purely casual interest when he heard the auctioneer declare that a buhl-cabinet he offered was not from the collection which had graced the house in which the sale was being held, but, with a few other articles of really great value, had been brought from an adjoining house, which had been vacated some months before by an American millionaire, named Armsby.

"Armsby?" Stoddard asked. "Armsby? What Armsby, if you please? Do you know the first name?"

The auctioneer smiled down at him from his low stand, and suspended action with his gavel for a moment.

Seeing that his questioner was himself an American, he was exceedingly gracious, for Americans were often customers who bought with charming lack of care and startling generosity.

He gave Arthur's name with a French accent, and volunteered the information that the gentleman had gone from Paris because his wife was ill; that she had died immediately after reaching New York city; and that the gentleman was, therefore, selling out the furnishings which had been left, although the lease had still a year to run. Having achieved this strikingly complete confusion of the facts, the auctioneer went on selling curios and rugs and old buhl-cabinets—some of them quite freshly ancient from the Montmartre shops and smuggled into the old house at night, for this particular occasion.

But Stoddard made no bids; he did not even hear the salesman's marvelously imaginative statements concerning the goods he offered. For a few moments, he stood, leaning on a quaint, carved table, and then departed without much knowledge of just how he threaded the dense, ill-mannered French crowd of buyers and curiosity seekers. Once outside, he paused dumbly by the curb to gaze at the house next door. The man was right. The building bore the number she had written on the order book, in the Salon. Now it was dismantled, its windows boarded up, its steps still strewn with straw, fallen from packed cases as they had been removed.

Appalled, he stood looking at the quaint old building, still impessive in its architecture, even though it so plainly showed signs of its desertion. Upon one window-boarding glared the sign *"A louer,"* in fresh white paint. Vacated, it was again for rent.

The sun was setting when Stoddard reached his studio, and Whilk had gone to dinner, leaving a note telling where to find and join him. The sculptor glanced at it, but did not sense the meaning of the written words.

Dead! Dead! How clearly had been etched upon his memory the changes he had noted in the beautiful young face that day when he had seen her at the Salon! They had been but the precursors of advancing fate— and he had failed to read them rightly! The thought of death and Doris—how could they be linked in anybody's mind? Even now they seemed so utterly incongruous that he could not consider such a possibility.

From the corner gleamed the white, slim loveliness of the "Goddess of the Garden." A dozen times he went to it so that he might study it in the tragic light of his new understanding; but as many times sank back into his chair, nerveless, crushed and stricken. There, for half-an-hour, he sat in misery.

An agony seized him, presently, so dreadful that he could not brook the dusk indoors. He rushed out of the place. After wandering about in misery so great that he could scarcely avoid pedestrians upon the sidewalks, he took a train to Versailles. There was always something to distract and soothe him in its old palaces, its lovely grounds, its fountains.

It was while he was resting there, upon a bench, with eyes held by the soft glow of the sparkling, lighted, spraying fountains, that a strange comfort came to him.

He knew that she was dead; yet knew she lived, vital and immortal, in his heart. He knew his love had not been in vain. He had won while he had lost. What other than the irresistible incentive which his love had given him could have so held his courage, as to make possible the mighty struggle of the recent years?

Dead! He would not think her as dead; rather would he think of her as one thinks of the creations of the master fancies of the word. She could not die! Pure, beautiful, inspiring, she would ever live, to him, and, while companionship with her had been denied in actual life, he now need never yield the sweet companionship of recollection of her, nor permit it to degenerate into such memories as one knows of the dead. She would still be his inspiration, his ideal. Quite unconscious of the fact that he was even thinking of her, she had led him to the doing of the best work he had ever done; she would still lead him, and he felt sure that she would wish to, if she knew, to better, finer, greater things than he had ever known before.

She should lead him from the gloom of his unhappy present to the dawn of a great day of effort and achievement. He remembered her not only as she stood pictured in his marble, the sweet and gentle spirit of the garden, but as he had seen her that same morning with her arms stretched to the rising sun, inspired, beatified, welcoming the dawn. That was as he wished to think of her, henceforth. His memory should no longer picture her as girlish, lovely and alluring, but as inspiring, wonderful—his Goddess of the Garden had been metamorphosed, and was now his Goddess of the Dawn.

As he sat dreaming thus, a picture built itself above the dusky bulking of the Trianon, beyond the fountains, drawn, as it were, by the firm, unfaltering fingers of his artist's soul. He knew the fingers of his material hands, had they been gifted with ability beyond all other hands, would never cut from marble any adequate realization of the vision; but they would do their best, and from that best he hoped might come to others, as had come to him, true inspiration, hopefulness, incentive. Doris would be reincarnated in this other, greater goddess— this marble stimulant to hope, unwavering aspiration, ambition for the high! Thus would she live again in marble, although none but he would know the secret of her origin.

In that high daze of the inspired which only artists know, he made his way back to the studio, and, until the glare of day beat dully brilliant through the shaded skylight, sat tracing with unfaltering certainty the stirring, vivid lines of a superb young girl with arms outstretched, welcoming the day.

He scarcely ate or slept until the plaster model was completed; then came the purchase of the marble, and he gave weeks to the selection, finally traveling, third-class, straight to the Italian quarry for a block which in highest measure should combine grain, purity of tone and flawlessness. It was a joke among his fellow workers that he returned beside that marble on the freight train, as it journeyed up to Paris. This was not in reality the fact, but he did personally supervise its transportation from the freight-depot across the city to his studio.

He gave no artisan sufficient confidence to let him block the marble out for him into the rough measurements which would be required, but did this strenuous task himself, studying the stone with every chip which fell before his chisel.

When he began the nine months' task of taking off

" . . . he let the sunshine flood the studio, illuminating
brilliantly the figure of his dream."

the outer husk which hid the glories of his inspiration, he grew to be, Whilk said, impertinently non-communicative, and there is little doubt that Stoddard felt a real relief when his friend left, bound on a six months' visit to America.

For the inspired man who remained to work alone in the old studio, these months were the finest he had ever known. His life was sublimated, lifted high above the petty details of an everyday existence, as the life of each true artist is once, and rarely more than once. He saw few men, and scarcely talked to those he saw; he read practically nothing, not even newspapers from America; he had not many correspondents, and most of the infrequent letters reaching him were thrust aside, unopened.

When, in good time for the judgment of the great committee, the statue was completed, he knew his work had been the best which ever had developed in him, and probably was better than anything which would develop later. There was no relaxation of despair following the final touches on the marble; he was certain of it, quite without doubt, when one morning, after his first full night's sleep in weeks, he drew back the skylight's shades and let the sunshine flood the studio, illuminating brilliantly the figure of his dream.

"Goddess of the Dawn" had been cut upon its pedestal; the task was finished.

When came the great square envelope containing the acceptance from the Salon, he felt an exhilarating shock, although his friends stood around him, wondering why his joy did not at all seem that of surprise.

Whilk had just returned. "Confound you!" he cried in good natured envy. "You act as if the unexpected had not happened! You act as if this glory were your due!"

"Well, isn't it his due?" asked Goodrich, friend of both.

"Suppose it is," said Whilk. "He might show some astonishment at least. I don't believe he's even glad!"

But he did believe it; he was certain of it; although it was a kind of gladness which much puzzled him; a kind which in his previous experience had never marked a young sculptor's reception from the Salon of a notice of acceptance.

.   .   .   .

When, as he had seen his "Goddess of the Garden," Stoddard now saw his greater "Goddess of the Dawn" shown in the Salon; when he heard admiring groups about it, exclaiming at its truth and beauty with as much enthusiasm as the crowds had shown the year before, for the more modest work, and with a touch of awe besides, in the occasional voice of one who possessed understanding, his heart glowed warmly, but still he felt no exultation.

He felt that days of such emotions must have passed for him. He had achieved success, but only when it brought but a small part of its great gift to him—for she was dead. The sharp edge of the grief which had so long possessed him was now dulled into something kin to resignation, although it never could be quite that; but life had little zest for him.

Even when the aged Frenchwoman who now cared for his studio, and whose presence was a proof of his increased prosperity, one morning took to him a card which bore the name of the New Orleans bank director whose words had done so much to crush him and defeat him long ago in the far southern city, he felt no sense of triumph, although he knew that the man's errand must be peaceable, not hostile, for the celebrity his success had brought him had sold such other work as he had had on hand—had even sold "The Burden Bearer"— to the same dealers who but recently had unanimously rejected it, at prices which, a few months since, they would have thought quite mad. Two years of growing fame had let him make all except the final payment on his father's debt.

The bank director came in with an apology—straightforward, manly, satisfying.

"Mr. Thornton," he said frankly, "we wronged you. You've made good. I'm wondering if you will overlook, forget the course we took."

"Why, I suppose so," Stoddard answered, after a long hesitation. The moment was a very satisfying one.

"Well, will you make the figures for the bank?"

"Why? Haven't they been made?"

"No; we didn't build that year. The panic came, you know. The bottom dropped completely out of cotton. But we are building now, for certain, and we want your work—at your own price. We're proud of you—we are, New Orleans is, Louisiana is, the nation is. I've come all the way to France to tell you so."

The sculptor knew that if he accepted this commission, it would, of course, be necessary for him to go to America, and the thought of that was disconcerting; but he yielded. Being human, he found the sense of triumph rather fine; being sensible, he found the money which was offered most alluring. It would wholly wipe away the burden, leaving much with which to start an independent and unhampered life.

With his designs in duplicate in the mail and in his baggage, he set sail from Havre, six months later, wondering what effect the sight of the old city in the South would have on him; finding it difficult to keep the mist out of his eyes as he remembered that no matter at what early hour he went among the roses, no matter how exquisitely the wild canary might sing, no matter how divine the rising sun might be in its effulgence, no "Goddess of the Garden," no "Goddess of the Dawn" would await their homage—or his own.

CHAPTER XX

Scent of roses weighed upon the air almost too heavily; her old friend, the wild canary, again held Doris's eyes as he soared up, up, up, dropping to her notes of song which seemed as golden as the sun-dust in the languorous air. She was at peace once more.

Two years of quiet in the old home had dimmed the vivid memories of those dreadful months in Paris; dulled the horror of the tragedy in New York city which had ended Arthur's struggle with a Fate too strong for him.

The home-coming had been sad enough, but there had been and was great comfort in the presence of her loved ones; in the familiar, dear surroundings; in the reflection, now calm and undisturbed by the turmoil of first grief for all that might have been, that in Arthur's life she had left naught undone which she might possibly have done to save him.

Through the first year she had worn deep mourning; but now there was a bit of white about her neck and a white camelia was pinned loosely at her breast. Her strength had gathered wonderfully, and the sweet sympathy of old friends and neighbors, evidencing that sense almost of kinship peculiar to the South, had done much to brighten her dulled spirits.

Mammy came hobbling toward her down the veranda steps, carrying a filmy wrap.

"Yo' bettuh wrop dis heah aroun' yo', honey," she advised. "Yo' all well now, an' Ah wants yo' to *stay* well. Miss Lily, she's a-comin' out—mebbe—anyhow she *said* she wuz." The aged nurse laughed almost noiselessly, folding her old face into a thousand wrinkles.

"Tell me the joke, Mammy."

Mammy went close, and bent above her with an air of mystery. "Mistuh Jack, he done growed up, fo' suah," she said confidentially.

"But you were speaking about Lillian."

"Same t'ing, honey; jes' perzackly de same t'ing, Ah reckon, f'um now on."

"You don't mean——"

"Uh-huh. Will Ah go an' call huh—er call him—er ——"

"Not for the world."

Mammy chuckled happily. "Dey sho' is ockerpied, Miss Dawiss. Oh, Ah done fergot yo' sketchin' pad yo' tol' me to fetch out."

"Can you get it without disturbing them?"

"Right on de table in de hall. An' Ah don't reckon dey'd be much disturbed ef Ah should go an' take it off deir laps. Dey ain't a-seein' or a-hearin' much but jes' deir selfs."

"I'd like to have it, out-of-doors, here. Aren't these warm days delightful—in February! Think!"

"Ain't much like New Yo'k, wid all its blizzards an' its whizzards." Mammy shivered. "Ah'll go fetch it."

With the utmost malice Mammy dropped a little tray as she removed the sketching-pad from the hall-table; but she did not glance through the open door to see what havoc this might have wrought in the composure of the two young people in the drawing-room.

Returning, she did not find Doris where she had left her in the rose-garden: she had gone through it, into the well cleared grove beyond.

"Thank you, Mammy. Will you stay here with me?"

"Spec's Ah couldn't keep 'way f'um de house, jes' now."

Doris smiled. "Well, don't spy. It might annoy them."

Left alone, Doris basked in the beauty of the scene about her. The sun was bright; the green of foliage shaded from an emerald almost into black; near her the low palmettos tufted the sand with green, and one of them, with an enormous root of brown, furnished her a seat, its fronds swaying softly just above her head in the fragrant, gentle breeze.

She let herself relax in drowsy comfort, entirely forgetful, of sketching-pad and pencil. But presently the sound of near footsteps disturbed her reveries, and, turning, she saw a man approaching.

At first she did not recognize him. In his maturity Northrop Reese was very different from the uncontrolled and startling youth who had clutched dreadful fingers upon Arthur's throat in that fierce struggle in the woods; much of the stolid wilfulness had left his face; his eyes seemed larger, as if, perhaps, they might be taking broader, better views of life. He had not been in the neighborhood since her return to it. The years had wonderfully softened and refined him, but they had not wholly wiped away that unusual crudeness of the physical, which had so frightened her in the old days before she had gone away to college. There was still in his expression an uncomfortable intensity; the corners of his strong, large mouth twitched nervously as in the old days when she had known him as a boy.

When he had answered her somewhat constrained greetings, she noticed, with a thrill of nervous reminiscence, that his fingers which, after she had seen them clasp so mercilessly on Arthur's throat, had seemed horrible to her whenever her eyes rested on them, were as notable as ever in their expression of abnormal strength.

She did not dislike him in the least, but his coming distressed her. Instinctively she felt that pain for him would be the outcome of the meeting, and the thought unnerved her. Could she have devised one, she would have made some quick excuse for hurrying to the house; but she realized that she was settled far too comfortably, too permanently, with books and sketching-implements about her, to make such a course seem other than a plain announcement that she did not wish to talk to him.

He sat down beside her.

With his every hesitant and nervous word, it became plainer to her that it was no casual wish to offer his respects to an old friend which brought him there; but for half-an-hour she managed to retain the conversation in purely impersonal channels. Then, with startling suddenness, he broke bounds and began upon the declaration which, from the beginning, she had felt to be inevitable.

"Miss Doris," he said slowly, "I must say something to you. Will you listen to me, please?"

"Why, surely, Northrop," but her heart sank as she acquiesced.

"I can't tell you how we all have missed you. Life was unutterably dreary while you were away." He swept a hand about, so that the gesture included the surrounding landscape. "There was—nothing here! The sky was far less blue . . . the sunshine colder . . . the flowers bloomed less brightly . . . the world was without beauty."

She could not fail to note the nervous twitchings of his lips between the carefully chosen words, and, far more distinctly, because she could not keep her eyes away from them, she saw those powerful fingers tearing into bits a tuft of grass which sprang out of the ground close by his side. The poor grass blades! Ruthlessly, if quite unconsciously, he crushed, and tore, and ruined them. A shell lay near; and automatically, evidently without knowledge of the little act, he ground it into fragments in his hands. The crunch of it was dreadful to her, but he did not seem to hear it. Then, without looking at them, he released some of the fragments from his fingers and she noted that the shell had been thick, thoroughly matured. No other hand which she had ever seen could have so crushed it.

"Miss Doris," he began slowly, plainly with a great effort at repression, "is there—any hope for me?"

"Oh, Northrop," she replied unhappily, "please say no more! I do not wish to pain you, but——"

She stopped, unable to find words.

He waited a few seconds. His voice had been harsh and hoarse. It was now soft with weakness and despair; but the long fingers closed tightly on a fragment of the shell.

"You have not—forgotten," he said slowly, and his great frame tautened as if bracing in defense of her against himself. "Well, why should you have forgotten?" He looked down with a sort of loathing at his hand. "It is natural that you should remember the dreadful thing which you prevented this great hand from doing. I was a fool . . . to think you ever could forget . . . But, Miss Doris, I have kept the temper down; the hands have harmed no one."

His breath caught in a quickly stifled sob. "Of course, you cannot understand." In his voice as he went on there was the quality of a cry repressed. "But, oh, it seems as if my love must be as much, much stronger than that of other men as are my hands—my dreadful hands—than those of other men!"

She looked at him in startled pity. "I am sorry, Northrop!"

He rose, and, towering in his physical massiveness, stood for a moment looking out across the landscape. "I know," he said, at length, while she gazed up at him, almost in fright and yet with a feling of overmastering pity. "And you are wise." He made a motion as if about to fling his great arms heavenward, but stopped them midway. Then, letting them fall limply to his side: "Oh, what is there in life for me! What can there be in life?"

She would have risen, going to him, striving in some way to comfort him, but without another word he strode rapidly away. Nor did he turn a single farewell look upon her.

The episode was inexpressibly depressing to her. Long after he had disappeared she still saw those massive heaving shoulders and heard the heavy crunch of his departing feet. Above, the sky still glowed serenely blue in the warm sunshine, the greenery of the foliage was as bright as ever in its beauty. But, now, to her, everything was dimmed by a thickening haze of tears. Was all life a tragedy?

She sighed, and starting toward the house, discovered that it surely was not. The Comedy Divine enwrapped Lillian and Jack. She came upon them in the rose-garden at a moment when they were oblivious of all save one another. They did not see her, and she was glad they did not. She could not fail to hear their words, although she tried not to listen.

"It can't be true that you love me," Jack was saying.

"It can be, very easily," said Lillian. "That's not the thing which is, but can't be."

"What is . . . dear?"

"That you love me!"

"That I could not help."

Lillian laughed softly. "We're getting into something which reminds me of the Wild Goose and Ibsen-lecture-day at Welleslar—the things which can't be are, and those which can be are not. It sounds very metaphysical."

"It sounds lovely to me."

"Yes; it's rather nice I think."

With a smile of satisfaction Doris hurried on.

She paused beyond the shelter of the roses, just as her father motored up the drive after a half-day in New Orleans. She almost told him about Jack and Lillian, but decided it was Jack's secret and would not rob him of the joy of its confession.

"Well, daddy, what did you do in town to-day?" she asked, when she had come to this conclusion.

"Went to the Southern National to get some money, tried to see a man or two but found them busy with the Carnival Committee, bought you a box of candy and a bundle of new novels."

"Nothing else is really important. Dear old daddy! You are always thinking of me. But the Southern National? I thought the Planters' was your bank?"

"Not for some years, dear. Once, long ago, I learned how the Planters' Bank had treated—er—a friend of mine. It was not a pretty story. I stopped banking with them, then."

She grew grave instantly. "You mean Stoddard Thornton, do you not? I remember."

"Yes, dear. It came back to me to-day—the rank injustice of it! They did not build then, as they had planned to do. The price of cotton fell, that year, and made money more than usually valuable, I think. But they are building, now, and to-day I saw the accepted drawings for their new façade. It is to be ornate with sculpture. Much of it, as indicated, reminds me strongly of the drawings Stoddard made, which they rejected. I do not know who made them, and I would not ask. It fills me with resentment. Perhaps I am unjust—but that commission, at that time, would have meant so much to him!"

She sighed. Then: "Did you bring the mail, dear?"

"Julian has it."

They walked in silence toward the house, and saw

Julian as he was about to enter. He was in the highest spirits; he always was, of late, whenever he was likely to see Desdemona.

"Both pockets fit to bust," they heard him call to that now handsomely maturing colored maiden, as he approached the veranda. "Ah guess ouah folks is suahly gwine to *move* down to New Awlyans at *dis* Mardi Graw!"

Desdemona's smile was wide, resplendent with white teeth. She would go with the family, for there were traditions that she was dependable—and few servants are during the carnival.

"Gimme de mail," she offered. "Ah'll fetch it in." Her eyes dilated as she saw the growing pile of letters which he brought from pocket after pocket.

"What loads of letters!" Doris cried, arriving. "Mail, children!"

Looking somewhat startled, Jack and Lillian appeared, followed presently by Mrs. Marquis and Virginia from within doors. The judge was not long behind them.

So, gathered on the veranda was the group of the old days, save for the absence of the sculptor.

"This will be your first Mardi Gras, Lillian," said Doris, as she began to open letters.

An instant later, a little cry of joy escaped her. She held a white card in her hand.

"A call-out!" she cried merrily. "How lovely!"

Now "call-outs" at King Comus' Court at Mardi Gras time in New Orleans, be it understood, are desired by every lovely woman, and but very few receive them. That Doris should have one, indicated that society had not forgotten her; that she would make re-entrance to it with unusual distinction. None but herself had doubted the cordiality of welcome which would greet her; that in fact it would be ardent, was indicated, a few moments later, when a second little cry followed her examination of the second small, white envelope.

"Another!" she exclaimed. *"Another!"*

Here, the custom must be made quite clear. A "call-out" at any of the great balls of Mardi Gras entitles its possessor to a place in certain boxes in the famous old French Opera House, from which such unfortunates as have not received the magic bits of cardboard are rigidly excluded. Many a lovely girl has lived her whole life in the old city and never known the honor. Such must sit in upper boxes, or the gallery stalls, and watch the highly-favored ones as they are led upon the stage to be presented to the king and queen. And Doris had two "call-outs," two days before the ball!

"Lillian, dear," said she, "you shall have one of these."

"But that's against the rule, dear, isn't it?"

"Nothing ever is against the rule for Doris," Jack replied.

Next day came the departure for New Orleans, where the gayety would be so constant for a week that there would be no thought of a return, even over the short distance which separated the house among the roses from the city.

In town, many old friends rallied to bid welcome to the charming girl who had been so long absent from the unique carnival. Still another "call-out" awaited her at the hotel.

"I never heard of *any* girl receiving three," Jack said with pride to Lillian.

.   .   .   .

GODDESS OF THE DAWN 331

New Orleans at the time of Mardi Gras! The streets swarm with delighted strangers come on crowded railway trains from every part of the United States; the residents are quite content to have the ordinary routine of their lives upset; even the old French quarter, usually so sedately calm, feels the pulsating thrill of the excitement and wakes up a little, at the eleventh hour; among the colored folk, the merriment is such an absolute abandon, and such is the tolerated unreliability of servants at the time, that many families despair of even having cooking done at home, and depend entirely upon hotels and restaurants.

The world does not present another city-festival like Mardi Gras. The old town thrills and throbs to it. The balmy air of the late winter is full of perfume softly wafted by warm, caressing breezes from the delta; the days are brilliant with a sunshine quite as perfect as the Mediterranean's; the streets swarm with all sorts —all gay. The days are full of smiles and pageantry and music, and after night has fallen . . .

Imagine a great city gone shouting mad with joy! Everywhere are maskers, everywhere are song and gayety untrammeled. If a youth goes to a maiden and throws handfuls of confetti at her rosy cheeks and laughing eyes, she does not yield to wrath; she smiles and winds the same material, in strips, about his neck, with gay words of good-fellowship. She does not know the youth; she does not wish to know the youth—and never will—but life is merry and is free, at Mardi Gras!

The youthful spirit of ebullient joy is rampant in the ancient town—and this year, Doris was its perfect exponent.

It was at the Comus ball that, with other thousands, she reached the zenith of delight. Entering the French Opera House, she might have been a fairy queen, so light her step, so dazzling her bright face. Before the curtain rose upon the tableaux, while the lights still glowed in the auditorium, there was a constant buzz of exclamation as the crowds caught sight of her. So persistent was the admiration that at first it almost drove her from her front place in the box; but without the slightest vanity, she soon felt a fine exhilaration in the acclamation which she heard on every side. The constant stream of maskers which slowly made the rounds through the cramped floor-space lingered, as they passed, to gaze; there was a steady stare from scores of opera glasses leveled at her from other boxes and the galleries. The wondrous tableaux of "King Comus in Arcady" scarcely kept attention from her after the curtain had gone up, and each time it fell, and lights again flashed bright in the great auditorium, the battery of eyes and opera glasses opened a fire of glances which knew no interruption.

The building was crowded to the roof, and when her name was heard, as a courier in mediæval costume announced the first "call-out," there was a sigh from all parts of the house, so many who had had no means of finding out had wondered who the beautiful young woman could be. As she rose, blushing charmingly, and, stepping forward, gave her hand to her elaborately costumed guide, a spatter of applause began which deepened presently into a veritable roar.

None but the queen herself had an ovation which approached it. But all through the long, delightful hour which followed, it curiously seemed to Doris that some portion of the moment's joy was missing, although she did not in the least know what it was. She felt her sense of triumph to be less keen than it once would have been; the lights, the pulsing music, and the gayety, all seemed impersonal.

She had reached the point which every woman of real worth must reach, when mere surface joy does not entirely satisfy. Even the applause her beauty won seemed less worth while than it had seemed in bygone days, although it never had amounted to such wild acclaim.

. . . .

A traveler from afar, who long had lost track of carnivals and many of life's other pleasantries, arrived, entirely by chance, in New Orleans, the night of that same ball. The mad hilarity of the old town at first attracted him and pleased him; but it soon began to pall, and then almost to offend. When a friend, costumed gorgeously and passing in a carriage, saw him as he stood beneath an arc-light, and bade his coachman stop and call to him, the traveler was not quite sure whether he was glad or sorry to be drawn into the vortex of this merriment; he had not been certain he enjoyed it, even as a spectator.

A little knot of somewhat awed bystanders gathered on the sidewalk to observe the meeting, for the man who sprang out of the carriage when it stopped was none other than the King.

"Well, old man," exclaimed the traveler, "you are much more gorgeous than anything I ever saw in Paris —and some Indian rajahs came visiting there, last year."

"And you're queerer than anything I've seen at home, and I have watched the maskers of the carnival," exclaimed the King. "Mardi Gras quite at its climax, and you in a gray business-suit!"

"I'm just off the train, and I had quite forgotten Mardi Gras."

"What a state of mind! Come, get yourself together. You must go with me to-night."

The traveler smiled, shaking his head in a firm negative. "But I've nothing in the world to wear."

The King drew from a fold in his white satin trunks a watch which was not a mediæval timepiece, despite the costume of the man who carried it.

"That can be arranged," he said decisively. "Get in. There's time enough, and there's not a costumer in all New Orleans who wouldn't do anything on earth to please me. I am the King, you know, and, during Mardi Gras, the King is very real to costumers."

.   .   .   .

The Opera House was ablaze with light, pulsating with music, fragrant with perfume, glittering with jewels, blooming with flowers and dazzling with bright smiles on countless lovely faces, doubly brilliant because not alone the women but the men who thronged it wore richly colored silks and velvets of rare dyes. The hum of blended voices formed a steady undertone beneath the joyous, leaping music of stringed instruments, the blare of brass, the mellow richness of the chorded clarinets and murmuring 'cellos.

As striking in his way as Doris was in hers; the cyno-

sure of fair women's eyes as she was of gallant gentlemen's, the traveler, now graceful in the blue and buff of
a Continental soldier, his finely chiseled, somewhat pallid
features partly hidden by the black velvet of his mask,
looked at the marvels of the fairy-scene before him, even
as she had, without real enthusiasm. Even the most
vivid ball of Mardi Gras was not enough to stir the interest of one for whom existence as a whole had ceased
to be a hopeful, vital thing.

The King came up to him.

"Great Scott, man!" he exclaimed impulsively. "You
don't seem to understand. This is a scene of gayety.
I can't see your eyes and there may be no tears in them,
but your mouth droops with a gentle melancholy which
would fit a funeral far better than it fits the carnival.
No matter how and where you've traveled, it's not possible, is it, that Mardi Gras can *bore*——"

The King stopped speaking, almost with a gasp. The
expression which had so astonished him, because of its
indifference in the midst of all this life and merriment,
suddenly quite had ceased to be indifferent; the figure
which had drooped with listless lack of interest had
grown unexpectedly tense with repressed energy.

A woman, dazzling even in that crowd of beauties, was
approaching on the arm of a French cavalier. Gowned
in yellow satin, long trained and embroidered with seed-
pearls, of the fashion of the First Empire, with diamonds
a-sparkle in her coiffure twinkling like far stars, her
splendid neck encircled by a double rope of pearls, she
was, undoubtedly, the loveliest in that throng of lovely
women. In her hands she carried lilies-of-the-valley,
and, as she approached, smiling faintly at some speech

her escort had just made to her, she raised them to her face to get their fragrance.

As she advanced, the man who gazed at her with such tense interest saw that she caught and held all eyes, heard exclamations of astonished admiration following her.

The unwonted life and gayety absorbed her utterly, at last; the old-time rose-leaf color had come back into her cheeks; her eyes were sparkling with a brighter brilliance than that of any of her jewels.

The King's eyes curiously turned, first from his friend's half-hidden face to that of the advancing beauty, then back to watch the tense, slightly-parted lips of his companion.

"Who—is she?" asked the Continental soldier, in a whisper.

"Oh, of course; you've been away, and don't remember her," said the King, casually. "Isn't she a raving beauty? She's a young widow—Mrs. Arthur Armsby. You must have known her. She was once Miss Marquis."

"Almighty God!" his questioner breathed. The depth of his emotion, the force of the great shock, were almost overwhelming.

"What is it? What's the matter, Stoddard?" asked the King with some anxiety.

The Continental soldier pulled himself together with an effort. "I'm more weary, perhaps, than I supposed," he answered. "I've been traveling very steadily, you know—first on the ship, and then by rail down from New York. I think I'll find a seat somewhere—unless —unless you will present me."

The King smiled knowingly. "Of course I will. Come on!"

"And when you do," his friend adjured, "don't give—my name. You, only, know that I am here, you see, and ——"

The King laughed indulgently. "And the great sculptor wishes to remain *incognito*. Well, this is Mardi Gras. All right; I'll mumble it and run."

When, in the midst of much mock ceremony, way was cleared for the advancing King and the strange masker, Doris, weary from long dancing, had just found a seat and was surrounded by a group of courtiers.

"My lady," said the King, with great formality and a low bow, "allow me to present a worthy soldier of the Army of George Washington—a general so great that even Comus bends the knee in reverence to his memory. He craves the honor of a dance."

The Continental soldier humbly bowed above her outstretched hand, but said no word.

The woman to whom the pair did homage found herself athrill with unaccustomed emotions; her heart leaped mysteriously; the color, though she did not guess the reason, rushed to her cheeks, making them even lovelier than before.

She answered somewhat hesitantly, for she was curiously confused, and for a second, inexplicably but not unpleasantly, embarrassed. "To one presented by the King, refusal surely would be ungracious."

The stranger bowed still lower over her extended hand.

Then she realized with a quick pang of disappointment, as hard to understand as any other of the tumultuous emotions which possessed her, that, of course, her card was filled. Her lovely face showed genuine regret as she remembered this.

"But I have not a dance to give," she added. "My card is filled."

"Fair lady," said the King, who, of course, had been certain in advance that this would be the case with one so beautiful and popular, "I foresaw that, and have decided on a royal sacrifice. So high is my regard for this brave stranger that I graciously resign to him my right to the next waltz. Greater proof of my esteem I could not show to any man. Hear! The music even now begins. I confide you to his care."

He bowed, turned, and departed, surrounded by a merry crowd, leaving them together.

Still silently the Continental soldier held out his hand; as silently she took it.

With the firm pressure of his fingers came an accentuation of the puzzling thrill which had possessed her at the very moment when the masker paused before her. Her emotions became turbulent; but the slow, languorous strain of the old Creole waltz immediately caught her in its rhythmic swing. Without the passage of a syllable between them, they swept out upon the crowded floor.

Was there ever such a dance as that? The world and life seemed measured verse which sang itself in tune to the sweet music; the lights were those of fairyland; the undulating, swaying dancers, gay in bright costumes, became fit inhabitants for such a realm—a new world, wondrously compounded of light, laughter, life,—and love.

Her silent partner's arm was strong; his step was sure, and Doris, trusting him completely, abandoned herself to his unwavering guidance, faultless time. With eyes half closed, she watched the swinging throng through an obscuring screen formed by her lovely, drooping lashes. Sweetly, exultantly, throbbed the deep tones of the 'cellos; pure, perfect and inspiring sang the higher notes of violins; deep rich and comforting was the ceaseless murmuring of brass. It was as if they floated on the crest of rhythmic waves; the fragrant air of the great room intoxicated like mild wine. Her soul sang, wonderfully, joyously.

It was not until the dance was over and the still voiceless Continental soldier had bowed his reverent head above her hand and disappeared, that she realized what had occurred. Who was he?

But when she made inquiry, the King, with smiles, refused to gratify her curiosity, and made escape before she could insist.

. . . .

Once more, the rose-garden. A shower had freshened the sweet scented place; like a brilliant arrow a cardinal-bird flashed, just above the level of the highest blossoms, swerving slightly, but unfrightened, to avoid her. Filmy clouds still overcast the sun, and, in the distance, streaming from the sky like trailing veils, the shower passed. The fountain's subdued song was sweet and silvery, the fragrance of a multitude of new-born flowers spiced the air of the young spring; from the earth came wholesome odors of plant-life in creation.

In and out among the winding graveled pathways, quietly enjoying all the beauty of the buds and blooming flowers, listening to the fountain-melody, watching the cloud-drapes with delighted but still dreamy eyes, Doris wandered in a reverie. The music of that wonder waltz still throbbed in her heart; not once had its sweet harmonies and intoxicating lilt been entirely absent from her mind since she had trod the magic measure of that dance.

She scarcely recognized herself, so great a change had Mardi Gras—no; that one dance—made in her heart, her life, her very soul. Just what had come to her she did not know, but everything was new. A sweet, mysterious longing filled her soul. Ah, the marvelous alchemy of that dreamy measure at the ball!

The sound of an approaching footstep caught her ear, but she did not turn her eyes in its direction, for a growing spectacle in the sky arrested them. The sinking sun had caught the distant shower, and arched a brilliant rainbow over the wide east.

The step drew nearer, but the rainbow held her gaze, and still she did not turn.

Then came a voice, and at its tones, her heart leaped joyously—amazed, delighted, marveling. Here, then, was the explanation of her new-found joy.

"Doris!" the voice said, softly, tenderly, caressingly, "The goddess in her garden!"

Now, had she tried, she could not have turned, for the remembered intonations of the voice held her, a prisoner of joy, quite motionless among the roses.

The step approached until, in all humility, in supplication, yet with the gentle dominance of never doubting love, the speaker took his place before her, and with arms outstretched and radiant face spoke tenderly.

"You did not know me; but I knew you, and I have come to tell you that I love, and have loved only you."

"Stoddard Thornton!" she breathed softly, and yielded both her hands to him.

"My goddess of the dawn."

THE END.

NEW *and* POPULAR BOOKS

GODDESS OF THE DAWN
By MARGARET DAVIES SULLIVAN. The spirit of youth and lightsome joy permeates this story of pure, exulting womanhood. The dominant love episode of Doris with a high-minded sculptor, struggling to retrieve his father's sin; her revolt against marriage to Chapman and her brief union with weak, handsome Arthur make a love story par excellence. It depicts love as it really comes and molds and mars. Its happy ending tells how it rewards. 12mo. Cloth. Illustrated. Net $1.25.

FLYING U RANCH
By B. M. BOWER. The best Bower story since "Chip of the Flying U." Here we have the well known characters of Chip; Pink; Andy Green; Irish; Weary; Big Medicine; the Countess; the Little Doctor; the Kid and a newcomer—Miguel Rapponi. How the Flying U was harassed by the sheep herders and how "the bunch" wins out, completes a story without a peer in the realm of Western fiction.
12mo. Cloth. Illustrated. Net $1.25.

THE LURE
By GEORGE SCARBOROUGH. Founded upon his great play that aroused such wide-spread controversy, the book tells of a secret service officer's investigations into the White Slave traffic; of his discovery of the girl he loved in a disreputable employment agency and of her dramatic rescue. A true situation, depicted boldly and frankly but without pruriency.
12mo. Cloth. Illustrated from scenes in the play. Net $1.25.

THE WASP
By THEODORE GOODRIDGE ROBERTS. A picturesque tale of an English pirate whose depredations on the high seas were so ferocious that he was called *The Wasp* because of the keenness of his sting. Glutted with looting, he enlists in the navy and gives up his life defending his country's flag. A love story with the winsome Kitty Trimmer for its heroine lends a fascinating charm to the narrative. 12mo. Cloth. Illustrated. Net $1.25

THE PRICE
By GEORGE BROADHURST and ARTHUR HORNBLOW, authors of "Bought and Paid For." Founded upon the play, this is a powerful story of a woman's desperate struggle to save her reputation and her happiness. How she tries to sink the memory of a foolish entanglement with another woman's husband in her own marriage with the man she really loved and how she paid the subsequent bitter price of her folly forms a dramatic theme of deep human interest.
12mo. Cloth. Illustrated with scenes from play. Net $1.25.

MATTHEW FERGUSON
By MARGARET BLAKE, author of "The Greater Joy;" "The Voice of the Heart." How the hero, by virtue of a self-evolved, infallible system, speedily climbs to the top of his profession in New York; how he saves the woman he loves from a fate worse than death, and then, to save his honor, discards the system that made his success, forms a vividly realistic and powerful story. 12mo. Cloth. Illustrated. Net $1.25.

Breinigsville, PA USA
02 August 2010
242889BV00003B/7/P

9 781142 727567